Halibut Blue, LLC.

LAUREN STAHL began her legal career as an assistant district attorney, prosecuting felonies with a focus on SVU crimes. She is a graduate of Pennsylvania State University's Dickinson School of Law and received her MFA from Wilkes University. Stahl resides in northeastern Pennsylvania with her husband, two children, and a giant but sweet mastiff, Myra Ellen. *The Devil's Song* is her debut novel.

THE DEVIL'S SONG

A NOVEL

LAUREN STAHL

This is a work of fiction. All names, characters, places, and incidents are a product of the author's imagination. Any resemblance to real events or persons, living or dead, is entirely coincidental.

Published by Akashic Books
©2018 Lauren Stahl

ISBN: 978-1-61775-596-5
Library of Congress Control Number: 2017936302

Kaylie Jones Books
www.kayliejonesbooks.com

Akashic Books
Brooklyn, New York, USA
Ballydehob, Co. Cork, Ireland
Twitter: @AkashicBooks
Facebook: AkashicBooks
E-mail: info@akashicbooks.com
Website: www.akashicbooks.com

For Myra Ellen, whose couch support is unwavering

And for BPS—all my love

Acknowledgments

I owe a massive amount of thanks to a lot of people. To Kaylie Jones, mentor, friend, and dream maker: thank you for believing in this book, its characters, and seeing it through every step of the way. To Susan Cartsonis, fellow lover of the strong female protag: thank you for your endless support, hospitality, and friendship throughout the revision process and beyond. To the Akashic team, especially Johnny Temple and Ibrahim Ahmad, who have championed this book since its inception: I'm beyond thankful.

To the first readers—Nicole Bednarek, Joseph Bednarek, Kelly Cesari, Dan MacArthur, Tammy Tokach, Lauren Cardoni, Debbie Timko—thank you. And to Scott "I like your bike" Weiss, who was brutally honest and supportive and asked all the right questions.

I am particularly grateful to those who offered their expertise: Tommy McLaughlin, for your knowledge on caretakers; Frank Kishel, and your behind-the-scenes knowledge of managing a pharmacy; Jenny Roberts, prosecutor extraordinaire; and Jason Cesari, for all things involving a trigger.

To the Stahl Crew, especially John and Dianne—thank you for your interest and lightbulb moments.

To my mom Cindy and dad Mark, who both think everything I do is nothing short of amazing even when it's very clearly not: thank you for always having my back and being my biggest cheerleaders.

Marco Ciavarella and Nicole Ciavarella—I think this book warrants a free pass for all those times I was reading. Marco, the 1997 Subaru WRX is on its way.

Last, but nowhere close to least, to Brian, my toughest reader and critic and my biggest supporter: your humor, pep talks, and love have been beyond words. And Prim and Phee, when I'm not writing about serial killers and crime, you fill my world with unicorns and sparkles. Love you huge.

Finally, thanks to family, friends, and readers, Kate Magda will be back. Just give her a little time.

I was born with the devil in me. I could not help the fact that I was a murderer, no more than the poet can help the inspiration to sing. I was born with the Evil One standing as my sponsor beside the bed where I was ushered into the world, and he has been with me since.
—H.H. Holmes

CHAPTER ONE

KATE MAGDA PACED THE LENGTH of the tiny conference room, the legal intern, Winter-Dawn, on her heels. Kate's directive from the DA was to teach the intern the art of trial—a punishment, she supposed, for having the highest conviction rate in the DA's office.

Kate stopped moving and Winter-Dawn's legal pad rammed into her back for the third time.

"I'm so sorry," the intern rushed to say.

"And for the third time, perhaps it would be best if you sat down to take notes." Kate smiled through gritted teeth.

"I'm trying to embrace the experience. You're pacing. I thought I should pace. You know, like method acting."

"Let's both sit." Kate slid into the cushioned chair across from Winter-Dawn, careful to keep her skirt—the one that was a little too short for court and clung a little too much to her ass—from rising to upper-thigh territory. She massaged her temples, unsure if her current state of exhaustion was a result of the sleepless nights that had accompanied the week-long rape trial she'd just wrapped, or from Winter-Dawn taking the term "shadowing" so literally. The intern had been assigned to Kate for the first four weeks of the rotation, and only a week in, Kate already felt like a conjoined twin.

"Where were we?" she asked, trying to sound pleasant.

Winter-Dawn looked at her notes. "You were discussing the importance of convicting the defendant and then obtaining max jail time." She cleared her throat and began reading verbatim and in the same tone in which Kate had been dictating to the intern, *"Max time leads to bigger cases, better cases. It leads to federal appointments and helps launch platforms for political careers—"* She flipped the page. *"The conviction and sentencing go hand-in-hand. Not getting max jail time after a conviction is like taking Johnny Depp home, getting him in bed, and realizing he has whiskey dick."* Winter-Dawn cleared her throat a second time and looked up.

Kate stifled a laugh. She wondered if Johnny Depp was still considered good-looking among the early-twenty-something crowd.

"What happens when the victim doesn't want to prosecute?" Winter-Dawn asked. "Or wants the defendant punished, but not given max jail time?"

Kate waved a dismissive hand. "Worrying about the victim will get you nowhere in this job, other than burned and out of work. Forget the victim. Prosecutors don't represent victims, we represent the state." It was the same speech that had been given to her when she was starting out in the DA's office—words to stand on when a case left an ADA feeling vulnerable and helpless and when the desensitization techniques failed her.

Andy Barber, the ADA in the novel *Defending Jacob* had said it best. Lure. Trap. Fuck. That was the key, the only key, to being a successful prosecutor.

Kate had been trapped and fucked years ago, before

she even understood the significance, though she admitted it to no one. She ran her fingers through her reddish-blond hair, wondering when she had started taking the advice of fictional characters.

"You can't tell me the victim is completely lost on a prosecutor. That's absurd." Winter-Dawn was finally putting her foot down—method acting session over.

Kate glanced down at her fingers, the skin around her nail beds still tinged orange. The rape trial had cost her four bags of cheese curls and an extra hour in the pool each morning just so her trial suits would still fit. "That's exactly what I'm telling you."

"That won't be how I prosecute my cases," Winter-Dawn said self-righteously.

Kate rose, leaning slightly over the table, palms on the plastic wood. "Then I guess you're going to make a shitty prosecutor. And shitty prosecutors don't help the state . . . or the victims—"

"Kate!" District Attorney Lee Bowers stood in the doorway of the conference room. "We need to talk about Reds."

Reds was the interoffice name being used for what the Pennsylvania media had dubbed, "The Mission County Murders." The women being murdered had red hair. Assigning monikers to cases was yet another way the police and DA's office subconsciously attempted to desensitize themselves from their cases. Kate also knew the Reds case was intensifying. A case she should have been assigned to as first chair. A case that had, instead, been assigned to ADA Winn, who had a horrible conviction rate and less time on the job, but dished out blow jobs the way politicians handed out campaign pens. A case Kate's overprotective father, who also happened to be Mission County's president judge, had most likely demanded the DA assign to someone other than Kate. It frustrated her to no end that at thirty-four years old, she still needed a green light from her father, especially when it came to prosecuting high-profile cases.

Winter-Dawn rose, preparing to excuse herself from the impromptu meeting. Kate's cheeks flushed, hoping the DA hadn't overheard her harsh comments.

"Stay," DA Bowers ordered the intern. He looked at Kate. "I want the Winter-Dawn to continue working with you. She can hear this."

Why Bowers added a "the" each time he referred to the intern, Kate had no idea, but leave it to Bowers to turn what was already a ridiculous name into something that sounded like a feminine douching product.

"Your skirt," he said, pointing at Kate. "Judge Roberts?"

Winter-Dawn's mouth formed an O while Kate simply raised an eyebrow, a half-smile on her face.

As Bowers approved with a nod, Kate contemplated filling Winter-Dawn in on how a short skirt or tight blouse meant a smoother day in court when appearing in front of the defense-oriented Judge Roberts.

"A serial killer. Right before the primary election. Catch-22. Landslide win if we close the case. I'd hate private practice." Bowers swiped his hand in front of his face and squared his shoulders. "Kate!"

She looked up while sipping her cup of cold coffee, accustomed to the DA's discombobulated monologues and hectic thought process.

"Winn's on leave. She blew out her knee. Such a shame . . . too young to already have knee problems."

"She'll have to come up with a new position," quipped Kate.

Bowers coughed into his fist while *the* Winter-Dawn appeared unsure as to whether she should be writing something down in her notebook.

"You're on Reds. First chair." Bowers shoved an accordion-sized folder stuffed with papers in Kate's direction. "Homicide wants you briefed. Call Detective Hart."

Kate had heard nothing past, *You're on Reds.*

CHAPTER TWO

IT HAD TAKEN KATE LESS THAN TEN MINUTES to clear the conference room. Four minutes for Bowers to stop talking about ADA Winn's knees, and three minutes to assign Winter-Dawn a research assignment that required use of the courthouse's law library. With the conference room empty, Kate let out a slow whistle. Reds had the potential to skyrocket her career, maybe even land her in the US attorney's office. There was no way she was going to allow herself to screw this up.

Still, she felt an odd resistance in her gut. She blamed it on her need to micromanage. For the past two weeks, she'd missed out on crime scenes, case files, and working with the homicide team. It was one of the reasons she had wanted the room cleared. Before she contacted Sam Hart, before she reported back to Bowers—she wanted time to look through the file.

Kate needed to be alone with her thoughts, alone with the victims, and alone with the killer.

Ignoring the beads of sweat that pricked at the back of her neck, she examined the photos taken at the first crime scene. The Mission County DA's office mandated that ADAs examine crime scenes to help prevent chain-of-custody issues and aid law enforcement in the procedural aspects of a case, which basically meant ensuring cases weren't lost on technicalities. Whether she had observed the scene firsthand or through a packet of photos, Kate had perfected the ability to recreate the crime for the jury. By the time she'd finish delivering her closing argument, the jury had seen, smelled, tasted, and above all feared the way the victim had feared.

Looking beyond the yellow tape and numbered plastic markers—a sign that the cemetery had been crawling with police, the homicide team, and CSIs—she studied the leafless elms surrounding the immediate scene: the way their limbs seemed to jut and pierce the ash-colored sky. She noticed the tree roots that snaked aboveground and had caused some of the headstones to lean and pitch. A significant pile of loose dirt rested between the open grave and a nearby headstone.

Kicking off her heels, Kate paced the length of the conference room, a stack of photos in hand, imagining she was at the crime scene. Barefoot. Cold. Just like the victims.

Next, she picked up a picture of victim #1—a twenty-something redhead who, like the other victim, had been found naked and dumped in a cemetery. Kate glossed over the matted red hair, clenched facial muscles, and bruised bottom lip. She then took a closer look at the victim's face. Not her face donning a smile like the one that had been used in the newspaper, but her face as she'd taken her last breath. Kate focused on the black trail of tears that stained the victim's cheeks. The woman had known she was going to die. She had stopped fighting. Tears didn't have a place in a fight for survival. Kate knew this from experience.

Thoughts entered Kate's mind, thoughts she didn't

want to admit to thinking. Thoughts that had her now frantically searching the crime scene photographs until she had a clear shot of the victim's hands—more importantly, her nails. Each photo showed her nails still intact—practically clean. The victim hadn't struggled, thought Kate. At least, not in the grave. Had she been alive when she was dumped in the grave, she would have clawed at the dirt walls in an attempt to climb out. To save herself. Her fingers would have been bloody, scratched, ripped open. Like Kate's had been. A long, long time ago.

She closed her eyes and shook her head to clear the cobwebs of her past, knowing it would take much more than a head shake. The dark of Kate's eyelids reminded her of that night. And then like a slide show on an old projection screen, the images appeared, fuzzy and faded, but she saw them nonetheless. A child's hand clawing at the dirt wall. A shovel spearing the rocky earth. His chin-length salt-and-pepper hair stuck to his sweat-stained face. Blackness. Blackness. Blackness.

Kate's eyes flew open, her tongue so dry she couldn't unglue it from the roof of her mouth. Her hands were poised in front of her like claws. She moved her body toward the wall, butting herself against it and then using it to steady herself as she slid to the floor. Her mind was still focused on the past and the blackness of that night. It was in that blackness—when the space between life and death had blurred, when the seconds had felt like hours and she'd realized that life as she once knew it was no longer—that Kate had heard him singing to her, his voice a deep baritone that passed through the earth, streamed through her ears and into her head as the dirt and gravel piled around her, suffocating her.

The conference room door was flung open and Winter-Dawn sailed in, notebook in hand. "I finished the . . . uh . . . Are you okay?"

Kate rose, not bothering to adjust her skirt. "It's how I work my cases," she replied, offering nothing more. "Put these photos back in the envelope. Please."

While Winter-Dawn cleaned up, Kate attempted to still her racing mind. Wasn't the real reason Kate was uneasy about this case more than the attempt to take down a serial killer? Wasn't it more than the career doors it could open or close? The real reason involved night terrors, which had recently returned, and thousands of dollars in therapy, which she should probably start up again. Not to mention how the lack of sleep was now affecting her during the day too—seemingly unable to shake the constant feeling that she was viewing life through a dense fog, and the bouts of dizziness she'd been experiencing. Twenty-seven years later, either her PTSD was acting up or he had returned for her. To finish what he'd failed to do all those years ago. Kate had a feeling—like a twisting fist inside her gut—that he was murdering these women to lure her, trap her, and fuck her. He'd come back singing for her—the devil's song that only he could sing.

"Kate? . . . Kate?"

"For chrissake, what?" Kate finally responded, feeling a twinge of guilt. She knew she was being a total bitch.

"I wanted to talk to you about my research project."

Kate's tone softened. "Listen, we've put in one hell of a week. I'm meeting colleagues at Blondie's Bar. Join us for happy hour." A smile trembled on her lips.

Winter-Dawn's face broke into such a look of happiness, Kate was certain the intern was about to hug her. It was as if the intern had been accepted into the sorority of her dreams—and this time, Kate did not want to break her spirit.

C HAPTER THREE

THROUGH A SMALL CLEARING OF TREES, the downtown lights of Mission Valley sparkled as Kate eased her way into the hot tub, warmth encircling her body, steam rising so that even her face felt the heat. She wondered if the sparkle and blur of lights had less to do with the valley and more to do with her current state. Happy hour at Blondie's had inevitably resulted in an after-hours party at Kate's house. She waved to Bundy, her 200-pound mastiff, who had wisely stayed in the sunroom, cozied up on the couch and looking out the window at her.

"You and that dog. It's weird," Kate's cousin Tess said, handing her a glass of red wine. Tess was already in the hot tub, a bottle of beer at her lips. Kate was admittedly obsessed with her canine giant. Despite Bundy's submissive personality, he looked tough, like a linebacker, and he made Kate feel safe and protected. Especially now that she lived in such a big house with Tess, who didn't always come home at night.

"What are we celebrating?" Tess asked, motioning toward the others in the hot tub having their own conversations and the slew of people inside. "Your millionth trial win?"

"We need a reason to throw a party?" Kate replied,

hearing the slight slur in her words despite having limited her alcohol consumption to "just a few."

"Though I did kick some ass in that rape trial," she added, trying to formulate her words properly, "and DA Bowers assigned me to the Mission County serial killer case."

"Oh, the dead redheads?" Tess said, flipping her long reddish-blond hair as she took a sip of her beer. The cousins looked a lot alike. "We'll be next on the list. You can prosecute your own murder."

"You're ridiculous." A ghostly draft hit Kate in the back. She immediately tried to wash it away with a gulp of wine.

"Does your father know yet?" Tess asked.

"According to Bowers, my father's given his blessing." Kate had called her father numerous times on her way to the bar to discuss being assigned to Reds, but she kept getting his voice mail. He never went anywhere without his phone tucked in his back pocket. It was strange that he hadn't picked up her calls. Even stranger was that he had actually agreed to Kate sitting first chair on Reds.

Tess downed the rest of her beer and hopped out of the tub, quickly wrapping herself in a towel. "I'm heading out. I probably won't be home until morning," she said, already making her way to the glass-enclosed porch.

"You're not staying for the after-party?" It was unlike Tess to miss one of Kate's infamous rippers.

"And hang out with a bunch of lawyers and law enforcement, most of whom try to hit on me before I can even swallow my first sip of alcohol? I'll pass."

"See, I thought that would be your idea of a dream night," laughed Kate, trying to mask her disappointment.

"Maybe I'll stay for one more, but then there's somewhere I need to be." Tess stepped back toward the hot tub and lowered her voice. "Did you have a nightmare last night?"

"Nope. Slept like a baby," Kate answered.

"You're lying. I heard you shouting. We should talk about it."

Shit. Kate didn't feel like getting into this with Tess. Especially right now. "I must have fallen asleep with the television on again."

Tess walked off, letting the door to the house slam behind her.

Kate tried to pinpoint the moment in the past few weeks when she first began to notice the strain on their relationship. There had been no argument, no cross words shared between them. But something had changed the dynamic and now, no matter what Kate did or how she acted, she often managed to piss off Tess.

She should have told her cousin about the nightmare, but she couldn't bring herself to admit it. Admitting meant discussing, and although Tess liked to play therapist, Kate knew, for now, it was best to avoid it. Still, Tess had been there too that night so many years ago. If Kate thought she was in danger, Tess could also be in danger.

Kate rested her head on the lip of the hot tub and looked up at the house, which had been built after she'd left home for college. It had been gifted to her by her father and his much younger wife, Rachel, several months ago, when her father had been up for retention—a yes/no vote at the polls that would determine his fate as judge for another ten-year term. Her father and Rachel then bought a smaller house with the hope that the public and press would focus more on his campaign and what he'd accomplished as judge than on his assets and lifestyle. She had found it strange that her father—not one to shy away from the fact that he'd come from nothing and had made something for himself—was so quick to give up the house. But she wasn't complaining.

Kate attempted to count the number of drinks she'd had at Blondie's and then here at home. Her head felt fuzzy. Too heavy for what she was certain had only been four, maybe five drinks over the course of an entire night. The last thing she heard before passing out was the muted sound of the music blaring inside the house and Bundy's incessant barking, which seemed to fall in line with the thump of the bass.

C HAPTER FOUR

SHE LOOKS UP, THE STARLESS SKY BLACK, *the moon nothing more than a sliver. She claws frantically at the dirt walls, trying to escape. Above her, the sound of the shovel spearing the soil and gravel bleeds in her ears. The rocky earth pelts down on her. She can't breathe. Dirt piles around her face, burning her eyes, filling her nose and then her mouth as she tries to scream.*

Kate lay in bed, her breath heavy, her T-shirt drenched in sweat. She silently repeated the words, *It was just a dream,* until her heart slowed. She had no recollection of leaving the hot tub. Or changing out of her bathing suit. She slowly turned her head, hoping there was no one in bed beside her, embarrassed by her behavior, when the lights above her flicked on. She gasped, squinting her eyes.

Sam Hart stood in her doorway, a mixture of concern and surprise on his face. He also had his gun drawn and pointed in her direction.

"What the fuck?" she blurted.

"You were screaming." He quickly checked behind the doors that led to her closet and bathroom.

"You can put your gun away. There's no one trying to kill me." *Lie,* she thought.

Sam slipped his gun into the back of his pants and began walking toward her.

"Stop," she said, sitting up. "What are you really doing here?" She wondered if it had been Sam who had put her to bed, though she didn't remember seeing him at her house.

"You in any condition to accompany me to Moses Cemetery? Where we found the body of the first Reds victim?"

Kate knew the private cemetery off King Street—it was close to her house. It was also where her mother was buried. "Now? It's four in the morning." She wished she had gotten through more of the case file. She also wished she could silence the hammering in her head. She reached over to her nightstand and rummaged through the drawer for the Excedrin she'd been keeping on hand. She couldn't remember a time in the last few weeks when she'd woken up without a borderline migraine. She'd begun popping pain relievers as frequently as she drank her mugs of coffee.

"If you aren't up for it—"

"I'm up for it." She wasn't up for it. Not even a little bit, but it wasn't as if she'd be falling back to sleep anytime soon.

"Good. There is something I want to check out. Figured I could brief you on the way and have you there for any procedural issues that come up."

"Give me ten minutes." She heard playful shouting coming from downstairs. "And do me a favor, tell anyone still here to go the hell home." She hoped she sounded better than she felt as a cold sweat broke out over her body.

CHAPTER FIVE

SAM SAT OUTSIDE KATE'S HOUSE in his county-supplied Crown Victoria and polished off a double cheeseburger and fries while he waited. He knew her "ten minutes" would really be twenty and had decided to swing by a nearby fast-food drive-through.

Six months. That's how long it had been since Sam Hart had last slept with Kate. And it wasn't for lack of trying. She'd ended their casual on-again-off-again fling for unknown reasons. Rumor was that she had started sleeping with Cameron Cox—a high-powered defense attorney currently running for district attorney. A high-powered defense attorney who was very much married.

Sam had known the minute he'd seen Kate walk into Blondie's last night that the party would end up back at her house. Work hard, play hard. But when Kate played *this* hard, Sam knew something was wrong.

He had only been to her house one other time—their late-night "meetings" invariably taking place back at his apartment. He usually skipped out on her infamous after-parties, though he always got an earful from the other detectives. He wasn't surprised that her house reminded him of the aftermath of a college party, but instead of a trashed fraternity basement, Kate had trashed a McMansion.

She was supposed to have called him after Bowers assigned her to Reds. They had to discuss the case and it wasn't like Kate to duck out on work. Especially such a high-profile case. And she hadn't answered any of his calls or pages. This had nothing to do with their personal relationship; it was work. And Sam was pissed.

He had headed upstairs, figuring he was crossing a line and unsure what he'd encounter behind her bedroom door. He hadn't much cared. He'd been close to the top of the stairs when he heard the shouts. Twenty minutes later, sitting in the car, he could still hear Kate's shrill screams in his ears as he tossed the empty wrappers on the passenger seat in exchange for his case file.

He glanced over what he had compiled on the first murder, which wasn't much. He then began reviewing the map of Moses Cemetery. Again.

Moses Cemetery was privately owned by the Moses family, continuously passed down through the generations. Gunnar Moses, at thirty-four, was the youngest to inherit the property. Sam and Gunnar had both played cornerback in high school football but on rival teams. They always got along, and with a quick call to Gunnar, Sam had been given access to the cemetery without having to secure a search warrant.

He had asked Gunnar not to notify the caretaker that he would be visiting. Rarely did a cemetery still house a caretaker on the premises, but the Moses family had been carrying on the tradition since the mid-1800s. Six months prior to Gunnar taking over the family property, the longtime caretaker of the cemetery had passed away. The position remained unfilled until Gunnar, who, like the other Moseses, didn't seem to embrace change, hired Nick Granteed. According to the newspaper article, Nick Granteed had moved to Mission County from New Jersey, leaving a comfortable grounds-crew job at a golf course.

Sam had questioned Nick Granteed the night the first victim was found. That night, Gina, Nick's wife, had been visiting her mother and father in Upstate New York, allowing Nick the perfect opportunity for a night out with the boys. According to Granteed's signed statement, a night out consisted of a few beers and two rounds of pool at Pockets. He left the bar around one a.m. and claimed he hadn't seen or heard anything unusual on his way through the cemetery and back to the caretaker's house, an important fact considering he had to pass the gravesite where the first victim was found. He maintained he'd heard nothing from the time he came home until the time the police pulled up at three a.m., lights flashing and sirens blaring. His wife had a hard time sleeping amidst the dead and insisted the television always remain on through the night. Nick had grown so accustomed to the white noise that he kept it on even when his wife was away.

Sam had visited Pockets the next night. He spoke to the bartender, who corroborated Granteed's timeline. The bartender said Nick threw forty bucks on the bar, mumbled something about having to be up in only a few hours, and left. With two hours unaccounted for and Gina unable to confirm that Nick had come straight home and gone right to bed, Sam thought it was time he paid Nick Granteed another visit. And he'd like to do it before daybreak. He was about to text Kate and tell her to pick up the pace when she rushed out the front door, her coat draped over her arm and a thermos in her hand.

Sam reached over to the passenger-side door and swung it open, sweeping the fast-food wrappers from the seat to the floor.

Kate immediately reached for the heat button, as if the car was hers, and turned it on full blast. "How do you stay so fit?" she mumbled, shaking her head, as she stuffed the wrappers on the floor into the empty fast-food bag.

Sam rolled the car up to the cemetery gate's access control pad. He punched in the code and waited for the gate to slide open. They drove through the cemetery, the only car on the newly paved road.

"Why revisit the scene? And why with me?" Kate asked, then took a long drink from her thermos.

Good question, thought Sam. Normally the on-call ADA accompanied the detectives to crime scenes to determine if search warrants were necessary. He could have asked another detective to accompany him and preserve the scene in the event he discovered new evidence. Instead, he had asked Kate. When he'd found out earlier today that she was taking over the case, he'd felt relieved and annoyed at once. Kate was an excellent prosecutor, no question. She worked harder than anyone in the office—often going beyond what her duties required. He imagined her hard work ethic, in part, had something to do with her wanting to prove to everyone that she was more than a political hire, and while he admired her ambition, working with her meant answering to her father, and it irritated the hell out of him. A few years back, before

Sam had made the homicide team, President Judge Magda used to call him into his chambers and request a full report on his daughter. How was she handling the crime scenes? If they were working late, could Sam follow her home? Hell, he'd even been given a case file on her. It's how their relationship had started—classic case of a job turning into something more. Sam was certain Kate had no idea about any of it; still, he knew he was walking a fine line between Kate and her father. He shouldn't have been surprised when he was contacted yesterday by the PJ to yet again keep an eye on Kate throughout her prosecution of Reds. In fact, Sam was the reason Bowers had been permitted to assign the case to Kate in the first place. *No pressure or anything,* he thought.

"As you know, Red #1 was found here, by police, in an open grave, two weeks ago at approximately three a.m. The victim was naked and shaved."

"Shaved?" Kate said.

"Both victims were shaved. The only hair left on their bodies was the red hair on their heads. Didn't you read the file?"

She rubbed her hands along her arms and shuddered. "I reviewed some of the crime scene photos." How the hell had she missed that the victims had been shaved? She was so busy worrying about her own past that she'd missed an important piece to the puzzle. If she was going to help find and prosecute the killer, she needed to focus.

"Based on what we have to work with, which isn't much, I think we're dealing with a pedophile."

I know we're dealing with a pedophile, Kate wanted to say, but instead asked, "How did the police get word of the first murder?"

"Anonymous 911 call," he said. "The caller told the operator there was a dead body in Moses Cemetery and hung up. Our trace showed the caller used a prepaid disposable phone but we didn't get anything beyond that."

"Was the caller male or female?"

"Not sure. Voice was digitally altered and the disposable phone had no name on record."

"What about the second victim?"

He shook his head. "Red #2 was found in the county cemetery by a bunch of drunk high school kids. The victim's body was slumped against a headstone. Red #1 was last seen alive on January 12. The 911 call came in on the fifteenth. We're unsure if the body was warm or cold when it was dumped. Although I'm heavily leaning toward cold."

Kate knew that if the body was cold, it could be assumed the killer had murdered Red #1 elsewhere and then brought her to the cemetery to be staged. It could also mean the victim was staged prior to the fifteenth and just hadn't been discovered right away. "Do you have direct evidence that points to the death occurring before January 15?"

Sam slurped the last drops of his milkshake while Kate held out her hand. She took the cup and stuffed it in the bag on the floor and then went back to drinking from her thermos.

"The autopsy reports the death occurred on January 12," he said.

"That's three days before we know the victim is in the open grave."

"Right. We know the killer didn't dig out the grave.

The grounds crew dug it out two days before Red #1 was found. Several burials were scheduled for the upcoming weekend—"

"Did you question the crew?"

"I did. Personally. No one had anything to offer."

"I noticed in the photos there was dirt covering most of the body of the first victim," Kate said. "I think it's material to the crime."

"Why is that important?" Sam asked, frowning. "The victim wasn't buried alive; and I already told you the second victim was found slumped against a headstone and not in an open grave covered in dirt."

"How do you know Red #1 wasn't buried alive? You just got done telling me you're unsure if the body was warm or cold."

"Because both #1 and #2 were killed by toxic asphyxia, cyanide poisoning, not suffocation from dirt and lack of air."

Kate opened her mouth, closed it, and then opened it again. "I figured they hadn't struggled in the grave," she murmured, and shifted in her seat. "Was rigor mortis present?"

"No."

Kate sipped from her thermos—the coffee warming her throat. She knew cold preserved the body, slowing down rigor mortis, which meant if the first victim had been killed and dumped in the open grave right from the start, rigor mortis would've still been present. But that wasn't the case. If the victim was killed elsewhere, then rigor mortis would have set in within hours of death and then dissipated after seventy-two hours. Right about the time #1 was dumped in the open grave.

"I'd say the killer took the victim, killed her almost immediately, and then waited. Once rigor mortis left the body, he transported her to the cemetery and staged her in the open grave."

"I think your theory is accurate, but we have nothing to go on. No evidence. What we do know is that a five-foot wrought-iron fence encloses the entire cemetery. I personally walked the perimeter the morning we discovered #1. I found no tampering, nothing broken, bent, or otherwise messed with. If the killer didn't have access to the gate, he would've had to carry the victim quite a distance, which includes hopping a fence with the body. That's a big *if*."

Kate sighed. "Any leads?"

"The autopsy and crime scene investigation provided no usable DNA, fibers, markings, or footprints around the crime scene. We really can't get a handle on any of it."

"Do you think the second killing didn't go according to plan? Maybe that was meant for an open grave too. The second victim was found in Mission Hill, a county-owned cemetery with a poorly paid crew. There's no planning ahead—those guys probably dig a grave and it's filled with a coffin that same day."

"No way," said Sam. "The grave isn't the killer's message. A cemetery? Maybe. But not the open grave." He believed the seemingly random spot in the county cemetery used to display the killer's work had actually been calculated.

"How can you be sure?"

"Serial killers are known to be methodical in their thinking. Control freaks, OCD, narcissistic. If the open grave was important to the killer's message, or important for him to get his fix, then #2 would have been in an open grave. Period."

"*Control freak, OCD, narcissistic*—you just described the personality of every attorney in the DA's office." Her tone was flat, making it unclear to Sam whether she was joking or not. She seemed on edge and harder to read than usual. "And why are the police reporting this as serial? You need three similar deaths to establish a serial. Why put the community in such a state of fear so early?"

"You're dumbing down what we know. Two red-headed women in their mid-twenties, naked, rid of body hair, both found in cemeteries, and poisoned to death by cyanide. That's more than mere coincidence." Of all the things he had anticipated her fighting him on, the killings being serial wasn't one of them. "Lay off the research. Save it for when we catch this asshole and you prosecute him. And you can thank the media for the current state of fear instilled in the community. We're doing everything we can to keep this under wraps." Which was why his team hadn't released to the media or even to the DA's office what was potentially the most important clue in the case: the killer was leaving a signature mark—a small cloth, no bigger than the size of Sam's palm, with the letters *RJW* written in black marker—stuffed inside the victims' throats after they'd been killed. Movies and crime television depicted serial killers as leaving a signature or psychological marker on, in, or near the victim. In reality, not only were signature marks left by serial killers rare, inserting an object in a body after death was even more rare. His team thought it was important to keep this quiet, to not give the killer more airtime on something he most likely wanted the public to know. And yet Sam was beginning to have second thoughts. Maybe releasing the news would lead to new evidence, or a potential suspect. At least he could clue in the DA's office. But now wasn't the right time.

Kate said nothing in response, her lips closed in a tight line, her eyes focused on the road. They pulled up to the yellow tape lining the perimeter of the scene.

"We'll have to walk from here," said Sam, putting the car in park. "The gravesite is forty yards away—over that hill." He pointed off to the right and then reached over and opened the glove box, grabbing a flashlight. He stepped out of the vehicle, walked around to the trunk, popped it open, and removed a shovel. He held out the flashlight for Kate but she stood at the side of the car, frozen in place.

"Take the flashlight. I'll carry the shovel," he said.

She took the light but kept her eyes on his shovel.

"What's with that?"

"I want to conduct a little experiment. C'mon, let's go, it's freezing out here."

They moved along in silence. Sam tried to concentrate on the scene, the surrounding area, the different paths that led to the grave, but Kate was distracting him. She seemed shaky. A graveyard at night was creepy, sure, but he'd seen her unfazed in worse situations. She walked alongside him, maybe half a step ahead.

"So, how about dinner tonight? Unless you already have big plans. I heard Cox's wife is out of town this weekend," he said, immediately regretting both the invitation and the mention of Cox.

Kate stopped walking and pointed the light directly

in Sam's eyes. "Hasn't my father already briefed you on my weekend?"

So she knew her father had called Sam into his chambers—he wondered if she knew about all of it. "How did you—"

"I figured the moment Bowers left my father's chambers, my father was dialing your number. How else would I have been 'allowed' to prosecute Reds?"

"Kate—"

"Please, I know how the game is played."

"It has nothing to do with 'the game.' I—"

"I'm curious, was it just too hard to say no to the PJ or is there a benefit to you acting as my father's spy? Another promotion?"

Sam remained silent. When they reached the site, he stopped abruptly.

"What's the plan?" she asked.

"See that house right there?" He pointed to the caretaker's place a hundred feet away. It was a simple ranch built on top of a small hill. The back of the house faced the crime scene.

"Go stand underneath that window." He pointed to what he knew was Nick and Gina's bedroom. There was no light coming from it and the curtains were drawn. "That's the caretaker's bedroom. I believe he and his wife are sleeping. Don't make a lot of noise. I'm going to dig up some dirt and toss it in the open grave. I want you to tell me what you hear, if anything."

"Don't mess up my crime scene, Hart." There was a lighter tone to her voice now, as if all had been forgiven. Though he knew better.

"The scene was combed, reports written, and evi-

dence submitted. You won't lose this case on a technicality. At least not on my end."

Kate walked to the house and stood under the bedroom window. She turned off the flashlight and gulped
down what was left of her coffee.

Back at the grave, Sam raised his shovel in the air
and drove it into the mound of dirt. In a fluid motion
he speared and dumped, speared and dumped, until he'd
matched the amount of dirt piled into the grave by the
killer. He looked back to Kate but was unable to see her
in the dark. What he did see was a light flick on in the
Granteeds' bedroom, a yellow glow streaming through
the small separation in the curtains. He spotted Kate's
silhouette and watched as she turned and looked up toward the light. Nick Granteed's head appeared in the
window, glaring out into the cemetery. Sam dropped the
shovel and jogged toward Kate. Maybe he would need
that search warrant after all.

C HAPTER SIX

SAM AND KATE WALKED TOWARD the front door of the caretaker's house.

"Describe the noise for me," Sam said.

"Somewhat muted, almost rhythmic, but audible from where I stood."

"Would you be able to hear it over a television?"

"The sound of the dirt falling into the hole was loud enough to hear inside the house but you'd never hear it over the sound of a television. Regardless, if the caretaker and his wife were in the bedroom during our experiment, they weren't watching TV. No light came from that window until just now."

"Exactly."

Kate's heart rate quickened, pulsing against her chest. "You don't think that Nick Granteed had something to do with—"

"His alibi checked out, but he has a few hours unaccounted for. What I think is that he heard something or noticed something suspicious and chose not to tell us. I also think he flat-out lied to me about sleeping with his television on. And that makes me question everything."

"Did he have an alibi for the night Red #2 was found in the Mission Hill Cemetery?"

"I called Granteed's house on my way to Mission Hill. I clearly woke him up. He mumbled something about his alarm going off in only an hour. I questioned him on where he had been the night before. He told me he and Gina had gone out for a quiet dinner at Pasquale's Ristorante, came home, and went to bed early because he had three funerals the next morning. Later, I stopped by the restaurant and the maître d' furnished me with a copy of the restaurant bill, which Gina Granteed paid for with her Visa and signed. So, we know he isn't lying about dinner. Again, Nick has a few hours unaccounted for the night we believe Red #2 was taken to Mission Hill Cemetery, but his story checked out and he was home, in bed, when I phoned."

Kate hung back while Sam walked onto the porch just as Nick Granteed swung open his front door.

Granteed was a thin man, the kind of thin that show-cased every muscle in his body. More reedy than lean. He looked to be in his mid-thirties—close in age to Kate. He scowled as he stepped through the doorway. Sam took a few steps back so that he wasn't pushed out of the way. The two men stood face-to-face, but Nick stared past Sam and straight at Kate. She stared in return while casually tapping the empty thermos against her leg. She wanted to assess him as much as he apparently wanted to assess her.

"What the hell is going on here?" Nick barked, finally directing his attention toward Sam.

"I'm sorry, Nick, were you sleeping? We didn't wake you, did we?" Sam sounded to her like a cat playing with a mouse.

"It's close to midnight. Of course you woke me."

Nick hesitated. "And my wife. Do you mind telling me why you're here, detective?"

"I have a problem with you, Granteed. I think you're a liar." He took a step toward Nick, who in turn stepped back. "I hate liars." Another step toward Nick. Another step by Nick away from Sam. "So, let's try this again." Step. Step. "We're going to revisit a few of your answers to my questions, starting with what the hell you were doing on January 15 at three a.m. Only this time you're going to skip the bullshit story." Step. This time Nick stepped forward.

"I already told you. Sleeping. I'm not answering any more questions without a lawyer present."

"You want a lawyer? You see her?" He pointed to Kate, who was still standing off the porch listening to the heated exchange. "She's a lawyer. It must be your lucky night."

Kate was caught off guard by this, but she recovered quickly. "Let's be clear, boys, I'm not Granteed's lawyer. It's my understanding you lied to Detective Hart when he questioned you about the murder, isn't that right, Sam?"

"I believe that's right," Sam replied.

"Mr. Granteed, not only am I *not* your lawyer but I'm about ready to have you arrested for obstruction of justice and then I'm going to personally see to it that I'm assigned to prosecute your case." She took her eyes off Nick and focused on Sam. "He said he wanted a lawyer. Let's go. We can draw up the charges tomorrow morning." She began to walk away, surprised at her acting skills, considering she felt anything but tough. Sam was close behind. They got as far as the side of the house when Nick came panting around the corner.

"Wait! I'll tell you the truth. Come clean."

Kate raised her hand in the air, palm out. "Mr. Grant-eed. You made it clear that you want representation. I don't feel comfortable discussing anything without the presence of counsel."

"I'll waive my rights. Once you hear what I have to say, I'm sure you won't prosecute me with anything. I lied, but it wasn't to obstruct justice. Honest, it wasn't. I was embarrassed, mortified. I panicked when Detective Hart questioned me."

Kate wanted to leave and not engage with Nick Granteed until he had an attorney and she was in a safe setting, but Sam felt otherwise. "We're listening."

"Please, come inside. I'll make some coffee."

Kate looked at Sam and shook her head, but he ignored her and followed Nick. She stood by herself and glanced around at the cemetery, eyeing the leafless trees that reflected darkly on the pale headstones. The moment she was alone, she felt his presence—someone watching her from the darkness. She swallowed, her spit catching in her throat. She decided a technicality rather than a casualty was a much better option and quickly caught up to the men.

Inside the house, little plaques with phrases such as *Live well* and *Laugh often* decorated the walls along with black-and-white framed photographs of flowers and trees. They stepped into the kitchen. Spotless. So clean you could eat off the counters and floor. In fact, Kate wasn't sure the Granteeds had ever used the space. Nothing, not a toaster, coffee maker, or paper towel roll, was set on the L-shaped countertop. But the wall décor made up for the lack of appliances and clutter. More black-and-white photos—this time of puppies, kittens, and barn-yard animals—covered every inch of the yellow walls. Nick saw Kate staring at the photos.

"My wife. She's trying her hand at photography. She took a few classes back in New Jersey before we moved here."

The pictures were masterful. A little sweet for Kate's taste, but if she had to live in a cemetery, she'd probably want pictures of cute kittens tangled in yarn too.

Nick rummaged around the kitchen, removing the coffee maker from a large cabinet full of small appliances, opening and closing drawers stuffed with junk, and taking the cream from a refrigerator so stocked you'd have thought Nick and Gina had ten kids to feed.

Sam and Kate sat down at the kitchen table, their seats facing Nick. He turned toward them, leaning his back against the counter while the coffee brewed. In the fluorescent light Kate realized Nick was older than she'd first thought. He had lines on his face and deep creases around his eyes from too much sun.

Sam looked at his watch. "Mr. Granteed, you said you had something to tell us. Something other than what you told me on January 15 when I originally questioned you."

"I'm not sure if either of you can imagine what it feels like to come home on your lunch break and find your wife and her lover in your house."

Kate watched Sam absently rub his thumb against his bare ring finger. Though both he and his ex had enjoyed playing the field while their marriage was slowly collapsing, Sam claimed he drew the line when it involved other married women. And friends. His ex hadn't had the same scruples. Kate knew it had been a matter of contention and was also why he kept fishing about Cameron Cox. Neither Kate nor Sam said anything, and Nick continued.

"They never saw me. Too wrapped up in each other to realize I had walked in the front door. I didn't say anything. Never even got a good look at his face. I walked back out the way I'd come in and went about my workday as if nothing ever happened.

"When I came home she had dinner on the table and she was humming some stupid song. She never hums. To tell you the truth, I hadn't seen her that happy in a long time and, well, the humming, it pissed me off."

He walked over to Sam and Kate with two cups of coffee, then retreated back to the coffee pot. "I confronted her. I'd be lying if I told you things didn't escalate. We argued, first in our chairs and then inches away from each other in the middle of the kitchen. She's screaming at me—her voice so high-pitched it sounds like nails on a chalkboard, telling me how much she hates me, how I disgust her, how she deserves better. All the while, she's hitting and scratching me."

He unbuttoned four buttons on his shirt and pulled it open, showing Sam and Kate remnants of scratches and bruises on his neck and torso. "Then she started pounding my chest, banging on it, fists closed tight, demanding that I tell her what I'd seen at lunch. Asked me what I was going to do about it as if I didn't have the balls to do anything at all. She had me backed up against the wall, I couldn't move, I couldn't breathe, my chest felt so tight I couldn't think straight, and then I hit her. I actually hit her, right in the face. I don't know what came over me. I've never hit anyone in my entire life.

"She went down like a shot and I couldn't even bring myself to make sure she was all right." Nick put his hands over his face. "Do you want to know what she did after I hit her? She begs me to forgive her. Tells me I need space from her and that she's going away for a few days—to her parents'—to give me time to cool off. And what did I do? I pleaded with her not to go.

"I stood alone in the kitchen for a minute and then I grabbed my keys and headed straight to Pockets. After a few beers, I felt myself getting upset again. I didn't want to make an ass out of myself in public so I got in my car and went home. Sat in the kitchen with a bottle of vodka and a shot glass. I drank until I passed out. The sirens woke me up. I stumbled to the bathroom, stuck my finger down my throat and made myself get sick, took a hot shower, and tried to sober up.

"You," he casually pointed at Sam, "showed up at the house moments later."

Nick walked over to Sam and Kate, pulled out a chair, and joined them at the table. His voice grew quiet, as if he didn't want anyone else to hear what he had to say. "Gina wasn't even home so you wouldn't have seen her face. I panicked. I didn't want Gunnar to know anything was wrong—last thing he needs to be dealing with is a domestic dispute on his property. I can't afford to lose my job so I told you I'd been sleeping, not drinking, with the television on in my bedroom. Truth was, I was right here, drooling all over the kitchen table."

"You're sure it was the sirens that woke you up and nothing else?" Sam asked.

"Yes. That much was true."

"What about tonight? What woke you up?"

"Well, you did. And your lawyer friend." Nick focused once again on Kate. She looked down at her coffee, swishing it around in the mug, this time avoiding his stare.

"Describe what you heard that made you turn on the light in your bedroom," Sam said.

"I know exactly what I heard. The sound of dirt and rocks hitting the bottom of a dug-out grave. I hear that sound almost every day. Only difference is that it's usually louder. Much louder, because the soil and pebbles echo off the coffin."

"Where's your wife now?"

"She's home. She's been sleeping in the spare bedroom."

"Why weren't you sleeping with the television on tonight?"

"I don't sleep with the television on. Only my wife sleeps with it on. With her out of the bedroom, I've slept better in the past two weeks than I have in six months. Tonight, I had just fallen asleep when I heard something outside, thought maybe it was kids screwing around with the crime scene—wouldn't be the first time. They keep climbing the gate and I've been chasing them away over the last two weeks. Turns out it was you two."

"Is your wife still sleeping?"

"I woke her up when I saw you outside. She's probably wondering what's going on, but she won't come out of the bedroom because of her eye. She doesn't want to press charges." He looked at Sam. "If you have to arrest me, I understand."

Now it was Kate's turn to peer at Sam. She gave him the *It's your call* look and he nodded.

"Listen, Nick," he said, patting the man's shoulder

like they were old buddies, "I'm not happy that you lied the first time I questioned you. But we all do stupid shit, right? Just to make sure you're not lying to me again, any chance you can get your wife and have her come into the kitchen? I want to see her eye."

Nick walked away, wiping his eyes with the back of his hand.

"When I gave you that look," Kate said, "I thought you understood it to mean charge him with abuse. Those were crocodile tears."

"Nah. I'd say the only thing our boy abuses is alcohol."

"What makes you think he has a drinking problem?"

"Just a gut feeling. When I checked up on his alibi at Pockets, the bartender told me he's been stopping in three or four days a week. Usually only has a couple of beers but he shows up already tuned. Never gets out of hand, never causes any trouble. Bullshits with the other patrons, plays pool, drinks his beers, and heads home."

"Okay, so he has a drinking problem *and* abuses his wife." *He also has a staring problem,* Kate thought. "You're charging him if Gina's bruised, right?"

"Not unless you insist. I hate domestics, I hate babysitting adults who know better and don't want to help themselves. My concern is the Reds case, not a drunk who socked his cheating wife."

"Wow, remind me not to nominate you for the Domestic Violence Advocate Award this year. No man should touch a woman like that."

"And no woman should lay her hands on anyone either. Did you see the bruises and scratches all over his chest and neck? C'mon, Kate. You heard Nick. Gina doesn't want to press charges. And it would be bad publicity for Gunnar Moses."

"The victims never want to press charges. Doesn't mean you should turn a blind eye." She mumbled the words "Bad publicity" and rolled her eyes toward the ceiling.

"Let's compromise," said Sam. "I'll keep my eye on Nick and Gina's domestic bliss and make Gunnar aware of the situation. In return, the district attorney's office doesn't press charges against Nick." Then he added, "Or Gina."

They stopped talking as Gina Granteed entered the kitchen. She stood before them in flannel pajamas with messy hair and a bruised but healing cheekbone. She was pretty, with raven-colored eyes and matching hair. Petite but solid, built like a gymnast. The complete opposite of her husband.

Sam got up from the table. "Mrs. Granteed," he said, sticking out his hand for her to shake, "I'm Detective Sam Hart and this is Assistant District Attorney Kate Magda. We're real sorry to have bothered you tonight."

"I was up anyway. Haven't been sleeping much," Gina replied.

"Well, it's time we left." Sam turned to Nick. "I'll be in touch, and if you remember anything or notice anything unusual, you have my cell phone number."

Kate started to follow behind Sam, then stopped. She turned around and walked toward Gina with purpose. She reached out and took hold of the woman's hand. "If you ever need to talk to someone about what's going on, here's my card. My work and cell phone number are on it." She handed Gina the card, noticing what looked to be the start of a fresh bruise on her neck. "I work closely with the local women's shelter and the Domestic Violence Advocacy Center." She smiled reassuringly. When she noticed Nick rolling up his shirtsleeves, her blood ran cold and her knees almost gave out. Nick Granteed had no hair on his arms. She stumbled back, away from the couple.

"Whoa! You okay?" Sam caught her as she reached out and gripped his arm. When she didn't answer, he inched closer to her, his shoulder holster pressing against her ribs.

Kate took a deep breath and slowly exhaled. As her fear dissipated, it was replaced with anger. She was angry that men like Nick reminded her of him—of Ron Wells and what he had done to her and Tess. Tess pretended it had never happened. For Kate, the trauma reminded her to always look over her shoulder, to mistrust before trusting. Ron Wells had come in and out of her family's life twenty-five years ago, but within the blink of an eye she could see him as if it were yesterday, smell him as if he'd never left. And over the past two weeks he'd been invading her sleep and her thoughts. She felt her world spinning out of control; the constant fuzziness in her brain was driving her insane.

Collecting herself, she took another deep breath. What she planned to say out loud was, *I'm fine. Let's go.* Instead, keeping her eyes on Nick, she asked, "Gina, did you enjoy your dinner at Pasquale's a few nights ago?"

Without missing a beat, Gina replied, "I did, thank you."

"Weren't you worried someone would notice your bruise?" Kate asked, but again directed the words at Nick.

This time Gina wavered and glanced at Nick before

answering. "I was worried but I covered it up the best I could with makeup. It was Nick's birthday last Friday and Pasquale's is his favorite restaurant. It's dimly lit, especially the booths in the back . . ." Her voice trailed off.

"And you," Kate pointed at Nick, "you actually wanted to go to dinner with her, sit there at a romantic restaurant, just the two of you? C'mon! You can't even look at her."

Sam's arm encircled Kate's waist and he began escorting her toward the front door.

"Wait! I want to hear his answer," she said, pushing herself away from Sam.

"ADA Magda," Nick spoke calmly, "I know you don't like me. I can tell by what you said to my wife that you think this isn't the first time I've struck her. I'm having a hard time with all of this, but like I told you before, I'm trying."

"Let's go, Sam." Kate stormed out the door with Sam on her heels.

"What the hell was that display in there?" Sam asked as they walked back toward the car.

"He's lying and she's covering for him."

"I already told you his dinner alibi checked out. Are you really *this* upset over the idea of Nick and Gina eating dinner together?"

"No. I, well, maybe."

Kate was sure of something but she wasn't about to share it with Sam. After her display in the Granteeds' hallway, telling him what was bothering her would probably have him running to DA Bowers on Monday morning, begging to have her taken off the case. If he wasn't already planning a visit.

"Listen, Kate. If something is bothering you about the case, or the Granteeds, you need to tell me. I've never seen you handle yourself like that. What the hell happened?"

She embraced the cold air that swirled around her body and rushed at her face, chilling her anger until she felt only a dull ache in her heart. She gave herself a moment before answering Sam's question.

"You're the one who dragged me out here after a night of drinking. What do you think happened? I should have never agreed to come here with you." She knew blaming the alcohol was silly—she no longer felt its effects, though she was exhausted. "Lack of food, the wine, and running around the cemetery must have gotten to me."

It was the middle of the night, they were standing in a graveyard, and the skeptical look on Sam's face showed that her lie hadn't gone undetected.

C HAPTER SEVEN

KATE SAT AT THE HIGH-TOP TABLE in the back of Cali's Coffeehouse, sipping her black coffee and reading through the Reds case file, looking for something she may have missed the first dozen times she'd poured over the documents.

Friday night's trip to the cemetery felt like a distant memory, although the way she'd acted at the Granteeds', in front of Sam, still made her wince with embarrassment. She wondered how long before he reported her behavior to her father, which would surely result in him making a phone call to take her off the case.

Sam and Kate had used each other in the past, occasionally sleeping with each other in part to benefit themselves—Sam to stay in the president judge's good graces, though she was certain it wasn't what her father had in mind when he had summoned Sam for the job; and Kate because sleeping with the top homicide detective, who also happened to be good-looking, guaranteed her access to better cases. At least that's what she told herself. But that had all ended when Kate realized just how deep in her father's pocket Sam actually was. A little protection was one thing, but running full-blown intel on her—well, that was something else entirely.

"Kate?"

She looked up. *The* Winter-Dawn stood in front of her with a laptop case slung over her shoulder and a large drink in hand.

"Do you come here often?" Winter-Dawn asked with nervous excitement.

The little coffee shop was open twenty-four hours and was only a few miles from her house. It offered free Wi-Fi and a safe haven for Kate when she couldn't sleep and didn't feel like traveling the extra distance to the courthouse. "Rarely," she replied.

Winter-Dawn sighed. "You always look so put together. I'm a complete mess lately. You've been assigning me so much work, I had to cancel my hair appointment this week." She tilted her head so Kate could see her half-inch dark roots among her blond-highlighted locks. Kate watched as Winter-Dawn's slender fingers slid a ruby stone back and forth along a thin gold chain around her neck. The young woman wore the necklace to work every day, regardless of whether it matched her suits.

"I mean, it's a Sunday and you're in heels. Designer heels, no less." Winter-Dawn pointed at Kate's nude patent-leather heels with red soles as she adjusted her bag on her shoulder.

Kate smiled and shook her head. "I'll let you in on a secret. My personal life is a total shit-show. The clothes and shoes are my beard. The heels are my therapy."

Winter-Dawn smiled as if she'd finally broken through a barrier. She looked down at what Kate was reading and Kate immediately began stuffing the papers back in the file. The last thing she wanted was to open the door for Winter-Dawn to join her. Maybe reviewing the file undisturbed at home would be best. Tess hadn't been around much over the weekend, popping in and out for the last two days, but she had come home earlier with all the fixings to cook Kate's favorite meal—chicken parmigiana over angel hair. Add a glass of red and Kate's mouth was already watering in anticipation. She could read through the file while Tess prepped the meal and then they could catch up over dinner.

She plucked her bag off the back of the chair. "I have to run," she told Winter-Dawn.

"Thanks again for the invite. I had a great time hanging out with everyone." Winter-Dawn had mingled easily with the other ADAs and cops during Friday night's happy hour, but Kate had been careful not to invite her back to her house for the after-party. She didn't want any issues of blurred lines or having Winter-Dawn privy to the not-so-legal behaviors of some of Mission County's finest.

"Maybe we can go over the Reds case tomorrow. You know, since DA Bowers assigned me to it with you."

"Not much to report, but sure," Kate replied.

"I just hope the police crack the case soon. Before anyone else suffers."

"Ah, still choosing not to think like a prosecutor," Kate said, smiling, as she brushed past the intern and headed for the door.

CHAPTER EIGHT

WITH HER BELLY FULL, KATE LAY IN BED fighting to keep her eyes open while she read through the file one more time. Winn's case notes were meticulous, with bulleted lists, and even a chart comparing the crime scenes and the victims' statistics. Kate was convinced that something would pop out at her or she would make a connection, catch a clue that Sam and the homicide team had missed, and make sense of it.

Sam had told her back at Moses Cemetery that he suspected it was the differences between Red #1 and Red #2 that, in the end, would lead the police to the killer. Kate had this eerie feeling that *she* was the connection. And unfortunately, her instincts were usually proved right.

Feeling brave, she reached over to the bedside lamp and flicked it off. From the floor Bundy whined and Kate knew she'd find the dog on the bed with her in a few minutes. She turned onto her side, sliding her hand underneath her pillow until she felt the screwdriver she'd begun sleeping with a few nights ago. *So much for brave,* she thought as her hand wrapped around the base of the tool and she drifted into unconsciousness.

The shadowy figure walks toward her bed. Without

*yet seeing his face, she knows it's him. He reaches for her,
slowly scraping the blade of his knife across her throat.
She shuts her eyes, unable to watch.*

*Against her will, her lids flutter open. She is no longer
in her bed, but in the backseat of a moving car. A young
girl with long red hair sits beside her, her face turned
away. The car slows to a stop and she hears the crunch
of gravel under the tires. The door opens and she expects
to see him, but it's the little girl. She motions for Kate to
follow her.*

*Kate runs through the wooded lot after the girl. She's
afraid to turn around. Afraid he's right behind her. She
stumbles, scraping her knee and the palms of her hands
on the rocky earth. Wheezing, she knows she can't run
much farther. She sees the girl in the distance and forces
herself to keep going. If she can reach the girl, she will be
safe. Soon, she stands within inches of her. Relief floods
her body until she watches in horror as the girl begins to
claw and rip at her own skin, shrieking in pain, until her
little face is nothing more than a mask. And under the
mask is something hideous and grotesque. Underneath
the mask is him—*

She woke to the shrill ringing of her phone, her heart
pounding. The clock read 3:54 a.m. Kate, wet with sweat,
just lay there in bed, making no attempt to answer the
phone. Finally the ringing stopped. She ran her fingers
over her shoulders, remembering how Ron Wells's arms
had felt against her skin. Shaved arms. Just like Nick
Granteed's. The phone began to ring again. She recognized the number—it was the communication center. She
sat up and cleared her throat. "ADA Magda."

"Hello, this is the COM center calling. The homicide

division needs someone from the DA's office at the General Hospital morgue."

"Thank you. I'm on my way." Kate was already out of bed and pulling on her suit pants. She buttoned her dress shirt and picked up the gold locket from her nightstand. With trembling fingers, she clasped it around her neck.

She passed through the living room on her way out and was surprised to see Tess sitting on the couch painting her toenails.

"What are you doing up?" Kate asked.

"Can't sleep." Tess's mascara was smudged around her eyes, giving her a goth look.

"The communication center called me. There's been a murder. I'm on my way to the morgue."

"I figured as much," Tess said, eyeing Kate's suit and then directing her attention back to her purple toes. "Oh, I had to borrow your car last night. I didn't pull it back into the garage. Didn't want to wake you. You may want to run out and start it, so it has a chance to warm up."

Kate silently cursed her cousin as she put on her coat and gloves. There was no time to allow the car to heat up since everyone was already at the morgue waiting on her. Kate hoped she had enough gas to get to the hospital. Her teeth were chattering as she turned over the engine of her Audi Q5, the SUV her father had bought her for her thirtieth birthday, and she headed down the driveway.

She dialed Sam Hart's number on her cell phone, connecting it to the car's Bluetooth.

"Kate, are you on your way?" Sam asked without a hello.

"I am. Does the victim have red hair?"

"Yes." He sounded distracted.

"Shit. Fill me in."

"Not over the phone. We'll talk when you get here."

She pressed the *END* button on the steering wheel. That was weird. And a first. Driving toward the hospital in desperate need of caffeine and a shower, she stared out at the snow-covered mountain peaks, the barren land, and the leafless trees surrounding Interstate 81.

She noticed a few reporters standing in front of the hospital and wondered if they had already caught wind of the homicide. She jogged to the side entrance, glancing over her shoulder, and used the key fob to lock the doors to her car.

Uneasiness crept up her spine as she lingered in the dim hallway of the morgue. The fresh images of her nightmare returned and she glanced over her shoulder one last time. Not a soul, yet she felt someone's presence. With a quick breath, she pushed open the double doors. Sam was there in the room, waiting for her along with Dr. John Friar, the medical examiner.

Kate plucked a face mask from the stack on the shelf and placed it over her nose and mouth as Sam briefed her.

"We think it's connected to the Reds case. Won't know for sure until we open her up. But we're looking at a female Jane Doe, reddish hair and a recently shaved body."

She wasn't following him. "Why do we need to open her up to figure out if she's connected to the case?"

"A few things have been kept off the books. Keeping it up here." He tapped his pointer finger on the side of his head. "I planned on discussing everything with you this morning at work, after you had a chance to properly review the file."

First, the evasiveness on the phone when she had asked Sam about the murder; and now he was keeping facts about the killings from the DA's office. Everyone was being secretive and on edge with this case. "Now would be a good time for you to fill me in," she said.

Sam told her, his voice morose, how a piece of terry cloth with three initials on it had been found in each victim's trachea. He'd been wrestling with whether to bring it to the public's attention. She wanted to ask Sam what the initials were but he continued talking about what he'd been keeping from everyone, not giving her the chance.

"Remember when I told you I thought it was the differences and not the similarities that we should be focusing on? Well, during Red #2's autopsy, a strand of animal hair was found on the cloth inside her throat."

"What kind of animal hair?"

"I'm not sure. We sent the strand to a crime lab in Allegheny County that specializes in animal forensics. If the hair has the root still attached, which isn't likely according to the technician, then DNA testing can be performed. We'll know what kind of animal it came from. It's worth a shot."

"Did #2 have any pets?" asked Kate.

"A fish."

"Maybe she'd been visiting with a friend who had a cat or a dog right before she was killed."

"A single strand found on a cloth inside the throat of a body that's been completely shaved? It means *something*. It's a difference. A clue."

"What are you going to do if you find out the breed? Knock on the door of every Siamese cat or golden retriever owner in town?"

"If it puts me a step closer to finding the killer? You're damn right I will."

"Where was the body found? Another cemetery?"

Sam's mouth formed a circle. "You didn't hear? It's all over the news. Even the Associated Press is reporting it. DA Bowers found her on the steps outside the courthouse."

"DA Bowers!" Kate gripped the steel table.

"He'd been working late. He walked out the employee entrance and found the body lying on the courthouse steps. He called me personally. I directed him to immediately dial 911, but the heads-up from Bowers allowed us to move the body before the press showed up at the scene. We have forensics over there now."

"I'm sorry, but I can't get past DA Bowers finding the body." She moved closer to Sam and whispered, "We all know he doesn't do much work around the office, let alone at that hour."

"Bowers tells me he used his employee badge at three a.m. to gain entry into the courthouse, went to his office, and remained there for about thirty minutes. Walked out of the building, again using his badge to exit. Security will have his entry and exit on record and we'll be able to confirm the time frame. He told me he couldn't sleep and went to the office to research an issue related to the upcoming election. I didn't question him on it. You need your employee badge to swipe into the law library after hours and if he used the computer to do his research we'll have his history. I have my guys checking it out now."

"We may have caught a break."

"I don't want to get too excited about it, but if Bowers's time frame is correct, I'm dealing with a thirty-minute window. The cameras that surround the courthouse were spray-painted last night, except for the camera that hangs above the employee entrance. So we don't have much to go on there. However, we have traffic cameras set up on Main Street and Chestnut Street. Not many cars will be on those roads at that hour. I can figure out which cars passed the courthouse, run their plates, and take it from there.

"The killer knew what he was doing and knew the building. Not spraying the camera that hung above the employee entrance—where the body was staged—was deliberate. But the camera was turned toward the door, no longer pointing out at the landing and steps."

"The killer wanted to record the look on whoever's face it was that ended up walking out the door to find a dead body sprawled out in front of them," Kate replied.

"I don't think the killer could've anticipated anyone being in the building," said Sam. "Usually, everyone is out of there by midnight, including the cleaning crew. If the killer wanted to record the look on whoever's face that found the body, then the camera lens should have been pointing toward the steps and landscape to capture the face of an arriving employee."

Not necessarily, thought Kate. If Sam pulled the logs, he'd see she had signed in after hours for the past four Sundays. Whenever she was in trial mode she spent almost all her waking time at the courthouse. She worked better at her desk than at home, often pulling all-nighters, pacing the office floors barefoot, working on her closing argument, cross-examinations, jotting down possible defense theories. She would then rush home, shower, and come back to work.

"The victim's face was badly beaten," warned Sam as

Dr. Friar removed the white sheet to begin the external examination of Jane Doe. "I think, unlike the other victims, this one put up a decent fight."

Friar spoke loudly so that his voice could be recorded on the Dictaphone set up on the table as he ran his hands over Jane Doe's body, poking and prodding at her limbs and appendages. "Large contusion on forehead. Busted left eye socket. Broken nose. Large contusion on right cheekbone. Subject is missing a front tooth."

Kate averted her eyes from the victim. In just a few short hours, the victim's broken face had swollen so much, her features were unrecognizable. Her hair was matted, its color a deep, unnatural red.

Friar moved along the victim's body. "Red-painted fingernails. I'm now clipping the subject's fingernails and placing said clippings into an evidence bag for forensics. Small bruise on hip bone, size of a blueberry, almost healed. Scar, right leg, above the kneecap." Jane Doe was a thin woman, and from the looks of her muscular legs, arm definition, and flat stomach, she most definitely worked out. Maybe a runner. She had tan lines from where she'd worn a bikini and Kate wondered if she had recently been away on vacation. As she took in the freshly shaved body, goose bumps appeared on her arms and a shiver pricked at her neck.

"The murders are too close together in time for the killer to have an established relationship with the victims," Kate said. "I think he's taking these women randomly and killing them."

Sam shook his head. "Or the killer might have known the victims for a long time and just started to act on his desires. We can't rule anything out."

"Well, it's safe to say brunettes aren't in any danger," Kate said, and absentmindedly combing her fingers through her ponytail.

She grew quiet as Dr. Friar made a scalpel incision in the shape of a Y from the shoulders down the center of Jane Doe's sternum to her pubic bone. He pinned the sections of skin away from the incision, revealing the rib cage and abdominal cavity. Dr. Friar reached under the ribs, cutting away the lungs from the heart and trachea with a pair of scissors. "The smell of bitter almonds is present in the lungs, leading me to believe the cause of death is cyanide poisoning."

"Bitter almonds?" said Kate, interrupting Friar's dictation. "I don't smell anything."

"Yes, the smell of bitter almonds during an autopsy is a sure sign that cyanide is present. The ability to smell it is genetically determined. Only about 50 percent of the population can detect its odor. Luckily, I'm of the people who can, which is how we initially figured out the killer's method of death was by toxic asphyxia—specifically potassium cyanide. The toxicology report confirmed our suspicions in the first two cases."

Kate looked at Sam, who shook his head. "I can't smell it either," he said.

Friar removed the heart and made crosscuts in it with a scalpel, exposing the coronary arteries. His delicate precision could be described as beautiful, had he not been dissecting a human body that was most certainly killed by a homicidal maniac.

"No clogged arteries," he said, speaking toward the recorder.

Kate took notes alongside Sam, jotting down anything

that popped into her head, while Dr. Friar continued to remove and weigh Jane Doe's organs on the round scale that hung above the table. As each organ was removed, the stench of death became more pronounced, and by the time Friar made his way to Jane Doe's stomach, the gastric acid was so rancid that not even her face mask protected her from the smell.

"Jane Doe ate dinner last night. Looks like spaghetti and meatballs. I'd estimate that 30 percent of the meal remains in her stomach. With the food consisting mainly of carbohydrates, you're looking at Jane Doe's last meal occurring approximately ten to twelve hours ago."

Kate glanced at the contents in Jane Doe's stomach and almost gagged. *Add that to my list of foods I can no longer eat thanks to autopsies,* she thought. She was always amazed at how medical examiners were able to figure out the time of death based on meals, body temperature, or the environmental surroundings of where the body was found.

"Once we receive an ID tag on Jane Doe, I will contact her family to find out if she was home having spaghetti or if she was reported missing prior to last night, which might mean the killer fed his victim."

"If she ate at home then we're looking at the killer taking Jane Doe, killing her, and staging her body all within as little as ten hours," Kate said.

"I can help you out with the time frame. Rigor mortis has yet to fully set in. I believe we're looking at the death occurring only four to five hours ago."

"I'm going to call the office, see if anyone's reported a missing person," said Sam.

Kate glanced at the clock as Sam stepped out of the

room and saw it was nearly six a.m. She was due to appear in front of Judge Roberts in three hours. Her mind drifted to this week's calendar and the endless sentencings and guilty pleas she'd be handling along with Friday's Call of the Trial List. She had yet to drudge through the four trial boxes she'd been assigned.

She watched as Dr. Friar opened Jane Doe's trachea, revealing the square piece of terry cloth. She took off her face mask, now oblivious to the pungent smells in the small room. "This solidifies the connection between the other victims in the Reds case," she said to Friar. "It doesn't matter what the toxicology shows. No one knew about the cloth, not even the DA's office, so it's not a copycat. Can you tell me what the initials are on the cloth?"

Friar quickly hit the stop button on his Dictaphone and rewound the tape, erasing Kate's voice.

"Sam gave me strict instructions to leave the cloth and the initials out of my autopsy report. I don't even feel comfortable including it in my personal dictation," he said as he removed the cloth with a small pair of forceps and sealed it in a baggy. He pushed down the record button with his thumb, the tiny bulb once again lit in red as he spoke into the machine and placed the undocumented evidence next to the other bags he'd collected during the external portion of the autopsy. Fibers found on Jane Doe's body, nail clippings, and jewelry.

Kate wanted to see the cloth. The initials had to mean something. As her hands moved toward the plastic bag that contained the cloth, the evidence bag with Jane Doe's jewelry caught her eye. Inside was a necklace. She fingered the bag so that the necklace's ruby stone winked at her. A ruby necklace on a thin gold chain. She looked over at Jane Doe and then back at the evidence.

"Sam!" she shouted, and he came running into the room.

"What's going on?" he asked.

Kate dropped the bag of jewelry as if the plastic had scalded her. She hurried over to Jane Doe's body, touching her hair, separating the strands. "But her hair was blond. Really blond."

Sam grabbed Kate by the shoulders and looked hard into her eyes. "What's the matter with you?"

"I know who this is—I know this person," she said. "She doesn't have red hair. She has blond hair."

"Kate, slow down."

"Winter-Dawn Harris, our intern—don't you know her?" Kate couldn't stop the room from spinning, her head reeling. "Winter-Dawn," she repeated, and then she did something she hadn't done in her four years of viewing autopsies as an assistant district attorney. She lunged at the garbage can, barely reaching it before she got sick.

Chapter Nine

SAM INSISTED ON DRIVING KATE HOME. He'd never seen her throw up during an autopsy. Come to think of it, he had never seen her anything but tough. She'd been jumpy on Friday night in the cemetery and all but lost it in the Granteeds' home, and then this morning. There was something going on with her.

"I hate this frigid weather," he said, trying to keep the conversation light. He glanced over and was relieved to see the color had begun to return to her cheeks.

"Let's talk about Reds and Winter-Dawn," she said.

"Are you sure you want to talk about the case?"

She adjusted herself in the seat, sitting up taller and turning her head toward him. "Yes, I'm sure. I want to tell you what I remember. Every little bit helps, right? Winter-Dawn was a law student and an intern in the DA's office. She just started last week and was assigned to me for the first four-week rotation. I could have sworn you met her Friday night, but I must have been mistaken." Kate's voice cracked. "Oh, Sam, I was horrible toward her. I treated her like she was a flea."

Sam reached out his hand and squeezed hers. "I'm sure that's not true."

Kate sighed and attempted to regain her composure.

"She had dyed-blond hair, not a strand out of place." Kate omitted the part about her roots. "She never would have dyed her hair that awful red. The killer did that. Which means we have something concrete to work with. Red hair is obviously important to the case. He's sending us a message. I'm sure of it."

"Can I interrupt you for a moment?" Sam made a right and headed down the gravel road surrounded by trees that led to Kate's house. "So, Winter-Dawn interns for your office, you work with her for about a week, and she hits up a happy hour with you. Is that the extent of your relationship?"

"I also ran into her at Cali's Coffeehouse last night. She spotted me and we ended up chatting for a bit. Mostly about fashion."

Sam raised an eyebrow and Kate clasped a hand over her mouth. He thought she might get sick again and considered pulling over.

"We talked about Reds. Bowers put her on the Reds case with me though she hadn't seen the case file and we hadn't discussed the case. The last thing she said to me was that she hoped no one else had to suffer at the hands of the killer."

"Did anyone overhear the exchange between the two of you?"

"I'm not sure. I wasn't paying much attention. I was focused on leaving the coffeehouse. Why?"

"Like you said, every little bit helps. Tell me what happened back in the morgue. When you made the realization that the victim on the table was your intern."

Kate leaned forward in her seat, looking at Sam. "I think I became so overwhelmed with the fact that I knew the victim, who also happened to be killed at the hands of this maniac, that it put me very close to the situation."

Sam felt there was more to the story and he was determined to get it out of her, but now was not the time. The gravel road eventually gave way to a paved driveway and Kate's McMansion set at the top of the hill.

When he stopped the car, Kate said, "Thank you for the ride. I really appreciate it."

"I'm walking you in."

"Sam, I'm fine."

"Glad to hear it, but I'm still walking you inside."

Kate opened the car door. Her knees buckled under her as she tried to step out. Within seconds, Sam was by her side.

"Kate, I'm worried about you. Maybe we should've had a doctor check you out back at the hospital."

She didn't need a doctor; she needed sleep, a shower, and maybe a loaded gun to protect herself from the Reds killer.

After morgue visits, she usually stripped in her garage before entering the house, an attempt to erase the smell that clung to the fibers of her clothes, but this time she climbed the stairs to the front porch fully clothed and reeking of death, her arm held in Sam's grip. She thought about Winter-Dawn and the odd feeling of speaking with someone and then watching an autopsy being performed on them hours later. And then her mind revisited her nightmare and Ron Wells. *Damnit, just stay out of my head until I have a minute to think.* She was desperate to get in the house and talk to her cousin about her fears regarding the Reds case. Without Sam. She was determined not to allow him past the front door.

"Sam, I threw up. I didn't have a stroke."

He stopped, turned her so that she faced him, and took hold of both her hands. "And you're shaking like crazy."

She quickly released her hands from his, her cheeks flushed. They stood in awkward silence as Kate reached into her coat pocket and took out her keys. She noticed her hands were still trembling as she attempted to fit the key into the lock and hoped Sam wasn't able to see. The door flung open as she was fumbling to unlock it.

Sam stood, mouth agape at the sight of Tess. She wore nothing but a tight tank top, lacy undershorts, and a gold locket around her neck.

"Oh! I didn't realize you were bringing company home." Tess bolted out of view, leaving Kate and Sam standing in the doorway.

"Your sister, right?"

Kate gave an uncomfortable smile. "Cousin."

They walked into the foyer and Bundy came padding in to see them.

Sam took a step back. "I never get used to the sheer size of that dog. He's a horse."

Kate let out a genuine laugh as Bundy leaned into Sam for a scratch.

He crouched down to pet Bundy, although he could have easily reached the dog's head standing up. After Bundy had sniffed almost every inch of Sam's body, he gave Sam's face a sloppy kiss, almost knocking him over.

Tess reappeared, this time wearing a hoodie and yoga pants. "Bundy, a kiss on the first date? You dog, you!" She laughed. "I'm sorry about before," she said to Sam. "I got a call from Kate's boss that she wasn't feeling well and was on her way home."

Sam stood up, wiping the slobber off his cheek with the back of his hand, and extended his clean hand in Tess's direction. "Detective Sam Hart. I work with Kate."

"Nice to meet you, Detective Hart. I'm Tess Conway. I think we've seen each other once or twice at Kate's after-hours parties, which I try to avoid, but we've never officially met. Please come in. I just made a pot of coffee."

Kate watched her cousin evaluate Sam, her eyes roaming over his body. Evidently she liked what she saw because when he wasn't looking, she turned to Kate and mouthed, *Oh. My. God.*

Kate didn't like Tess eyeing Sam. Nor did she like that Tess had invited him in for a cup of coffee. Torn between staying put and heading upstairs to erase the stench of the morgue, she looked at her watch. If she didn't get in the shower now, she would never make it to court on time.

Kate trudged up the steps and stood on the second-floor landing, listening to Sam and Tess converse below. Feeling paranoid, she took out her cell phone and quickly texted Tess: *Keep me out of your conversation please.* She didn't want her cousin blabbing stories about her to Sam. She heard Tess's phone ring and within seconds she received a text back: *Relax. Hopefully in a few minutes we won't be talking. Joking! But, hello, he's hot!* This was just like Tess, Kate thought. Never serious about anything. She left the landing and headed to the bathroom.

After a couple minutes of awkward small talk, Tess filled two mugs with coffee. "Cream and sugar?"

"Black," said Sam. "Thank you."

Tess sauntered over to the couch and handed him his coffee.

"Not a coffee drinker?" He nodded in the direction of her barely filled mug.

"I'm trying to cut down on my caffeine." She rubbed her forehead with the tips of her fingers. "Migraine sufferer. I used to get a migraine every six months but recently I've been experiencing them daily. The doctor said to reduce my caffeine intake and see how I'm feeling."

Sam stared at the way Tess's mouth moved while she spoke, the same slightly crooked smile as Kate's giving way to perfectly aligned teeth. Tess cleared her throat.

"Sorry. I'm staring. I can't get over how much you and Kate look alike."

"We get it all the time. Even more so growing up. Everyone thought we were twins."

"Did you spend a lot of time together as children?" Sam knew that had he been talking to Kate, the lines of communication would have already been shut down, but Tess seemed more willing to engage in personal conversation.

"I moved in with Kate's family when I was five. We're only four months apart. She's older and never lets me forget it. Anyway, we were totally inseparable. We even roomed together in college. The only time we were apart was when she went to law school. I had to draw the line. No way in hell was I going to law school. Undergrad was bad enough. Had it not been for all the fraternity parties and pub crawls, I would have dropped out three months into freshman year!" She paused. "I'm rambling. Sorry."

Sam wondered why Tess had moved in with Kate's family when she was only five years old, but felt it was out of line for him to inquire.

"What happened to Kate at the morgue?" Tess asked.

"Her boss said she has been pretty worked up over the case."

Sam set his mug of coffee down on the table and evaluated Tess, but this time he wasn't comparing her to Kate. For the second time in less than thirty minutes, she had mentioned Kate's "boss," and he knew there was no way that DA Bowers had notified Tess or even knew of the incident at the morgue. And for a girl who rushed to the door half-naked to see if her cousin was okay—she didn't even ask Kate how she was feeling or offer to walk her upstairs. Instead, she sat on the couch rambling, or perhaps cleverly offering him information. As he wrestled with whether or not to question her on DA Bowers, Kate appeared at the top of the steps.

Sam stood. "Are you feeling better?"

"Much better," Kate replied.

Tess fingered the locket around her neck and gazed up at her cousin. "Sam and I were just talking about you," she said in a wheedling tone. "Kate, did you get upset because of the shaved body? I know that's always a weird issue for you."

Kate stared hard at her cousin but ignored her question. "I'm going to have Tess drop me off at work," she said abruptly to Sam. "Thank you for driving me home. Let's meet up after my nine o'clock court hearing and go over a few things related to the Reds case."

"Sounds good." He turned to Tess. "Thanks for the coffee. It was a pleasure officially meeting you."

Tess smiled, batting her eyelashes.

"Kate, do you mind walking me to the door?" he asked.

When the two of them were alone in the foyer, he

said, "I'll keep you posted on Winter-Dawn. I'm sure there's been a family ID by now."

"Yes. I'd like to attend the service if they're having one. Let me know what you hear, okay?" Tears pooled in Kate's eyes and she gave a self-deprecating laugh. "You'd think we were the best of friends the way I'm acting. I didn't even know her for a full seven days."

"Hey, it's okay to not be okay." He placed a comforting hand on her shoulder.

She inhaled, letting her breath out slowly while carefully wiping away a tear so as not to smudge her mascara.

"I'm concerned about what your cousin said about DA Bowers telling her you got sick," he said in a low murmur. "As far as I know, Bowers isn't aware of what happened to you in the morgue."

"I know. I was thinking the same thing while I was in the shower." She bit her lip. "I'm sure there's a logical explanation. I'll talk to Tess about it on our drive to the courthouse."

"Okay. One more thing . . . I'm not trying to make you upset, but the victims' bodies being shaved hasn't been reported in the press. Even you didn't know about that fact until I briefed you on it Friday night in the cemetery. Right?"

"That's right. And speaking of shaved bodies," said Kate, "I noticed the other night that Nick Granteed shaves his arms. His chest too."

CHAPTER TEN

KATE TRAMPED BACK INTO THE LIVING ROOM where Tess was reading the morning paper. She sank down on the oversized leather chair and put her feet up on the matching ottoman. "I thought he'd never leave," she said.

"I was hoping he wouldn't. I could have stared at him all day." Tess sighed, closing the newspaper and slipping it behind her. "It's nice to finally put a face with a name."

Kate had openly discussed Sam Hart with Tess—from a professional point of view. She had left the sleeping-together part out, though she wasn't sure why.

"After four years of working with that specimen, why aren't you sleeping with him? Talk about a perfect butt!"

Kate admitted to Tess that she thought Sam was good-looking. He had a rugged thing going on—like he'd been under the hand of a woman for too long and was now rebelling. What she didn't say to Tess, and hesitated even admitting to herself, was that she felt a jealous twinge at the thought of her cousin eyeing him.

"He's interested in you," Tess said.

Kate waved her off. Sam's interest was in her father and moving up the political ladder.

"Oh good. So you don't mind if I ask him out?"

"Don't let me stop you," Kate said, absentmindedly pulling on her lip.

"Hah! You *are* interested. It's about time, if you ask me."

Kate dropped both hands onto her lap. "And what's that supposed to mean?"

"It means you haven't been out on a date since you-know-who."

Kate's most recent boyfriend, the one Sam thought Kate was still dating, had proved to be a cheating jerk. A married, cheating jerk. Kate had been totally blindsided by him. "It's only been three months!"

"Three months is an eternity when you're our age. And you haven't been on a date since."

Kate quickly changed the subject: "Tess, how did you know about the shaved bodies? That aspect of the case hasn't been reported by the press."

"I read it in the file you had on the Mission County Killer case."

Kate thought she'd misheard. Tess couldn't possibly have just told Kate that she had read through her files. "My files are highly confidential, Tess. Especially the Mission County Killer file. I'd be fired if anyone knew you read it."

"I'm sorry. It's hideous, I know. I saw the file lying open on the table and my curiosity got the better of me." Tess fidgeted, drew her legs up onto the couch, and rested her chin on her knees like a child.

"Well, since you read through the file, care to tell me whether or not you think there's a link between us and the murders?" Her tone came out much harsher than she'd intended.

Tess gasped. "Is that why you got sick in the morgue?

You think we're connected to this?" She pushed the newspaper behind her back even farther under the couch cushion.

"I know it—the facts point to it and my gut tells me so." Kate paused. "The nightmares are back." Saying the words out loud didn't make her feel any sort of relief. Instead, she felt as if she were unshackling the demons that, until now, had remained only in her mind and her memory. And when it came to the nightmares, she always had to be careful with what she said to Tess. She worried that something she'd say would send Tess back into a catatonic state.

Tess let out a sigh. "I haven't been sleeping well either. Images of him have been creeping into my mind. It's so similar to the Mission County Killer case. The way the police found the first victim's body—in the open grave. Even though I can't remember that night, it sounds just like what you remember." Tess paused. "Maybe you're right. Maybe the murders are linked to us." She shuddered, then moved off the couch and over to Kate, throwing her arm around her cousin.

For the first time in weeks, Kate didn't feel crazy. She felt vindicated and determined to find the answers she was searching for. She wished she could stay all day in the house with Tess. They could lay everything out, their own theories—work the case until they could make sense of it. She was sure, now more than ever, that the murders had to be connected to their past. The two of them rarely spoke about what had brought Tess to live with Kate's family when she was five years old. Back when Tess only mumbled while sleeping, never uttering an actual word. The events of Tess's childhood leaving her literally speechless. It was a little over a year before Tess began speaking. The joke being that once she started talking again, she never stopped. But she never spoke of what had happened to her as a young child and her stepfather's name was never mentioned. Because of that, Kate avoided the topic too. She'd tried once, at the suggestion of her therapist, to "talk about it" and it hadn't gone well. Maybe she should have tried harder. Maybe she should have been having this conversation with Tess weeks ago, when the nightmares first started again.

Tess released Kate from her embrace.

"You're crying," said Kate.

"I'm fine." Tess wiped away the tears that were sliding down her cheeks. "You need to know something," she said, looking to the newspaper and then at the clock. She jumped up. "Oh crap! We need to get moving if you're going to make it to court on time. C'mon, we can talk in the car."

Kate rested her hand on Tess's shoulder. "Court can wait. Talk to me."

"No, let's go. The car's as good a place as any for a conversation." She rose.

While Kate threw on her coat, Tess poured the remaining coffee into a to-go mug for her cousin. She crushed up the pills she had in her pocket and mixed the powder into the liquid. Just like she'd been doing over the past few weeks. She sealed the lid and headed for the front door.

Kate wrapped her ungloved hands around the coffee cup and they walked outside together, back into the bitter cold.

"Tell me what's bothering you," Kate said, wiggling her toes under the heat vents as they drove to the courthouse.

"I've been sleeping with John Friar," Tess blurted.

"The medical examiner?"

"Yes."

"But he's so . . . old. And he has two kids. Our age!"

Tess ignored Kate's comment and continued: "We met at the Child Advocacy Center. I'm actually headed there after I drop you off. I'm going to put in a few hours and then John's meeting me for lunch. I really like him."

"You like him so much that you were ready to take Sam up to your bedroom for a quickie," Kate said.

"I said I *like* him, not that I'm *in love* with him."

Ahh, Kate thought. "So that's how you knew I got sick at the morgue."

"Yes. John called me after you left the hospital. Told me you'd been acting funny during the autopsy and that you got sick. He was worried about you and wanted to make sure I was awake when you got home. I heard the car pull up, and without thinking I rushed to the door. I never expected to see Sam standing with you. And then I didn't want him knowing my personal business with John so I lied and said your boss called the house."

Tess pulled up to the crosswalk in front of the courthouse and put on her flashers. She reached over across the console and for the second time that morning gave Kate a hug. "I love you. No matter what, please know I love you."

Kate smoothed her hair and unbuckled her seat belt. "I love you too." They both took their lockets from around their necks and rubbed their thumbs on them as if rubbing genie bottles, something they hadn't done in years. They both smiled and Tess winked, acknowledging the cheesiness of the moment.

"Don't forget your coffee."

CHAPTER ELEVEN

KATE CLIMBED THE WHITE MARBLE STAIRCASE to the third floor, her coffee cup glued to her lips. She ignored the bitterness, figuring Tess had bought a new brand, and practically gulped the liquid now that it had reached the perfect temperature. Judge Roberts was hearing cases in courtroom #3 today—Kate's favorite. It had been her father's courtroom when he first took the bench. As a teenager, Kate would sit there and fantasize about appearing in front of a judge, arguing a motion, cross-examining a witness, or addressing the jury. She watched how the lawyers conducted themselves in court, posed questions to the judge, and interacted with one another. After court was adjourned, her father would call her into his chambers, where she would report to him on the cases and the attorneys.

Now, here she was, walking into the same courtroom as a prosecutor. Kate strode past the empty pews to where Jenn Finn, the commonwealth's victim, sat in the first row.

"Is it really necessary for me to be in the front like this?" Jenn asked, her eyes darting toward the line of shackled prisoners sitting only feet away.

"Yes. The judge may want to hear from you and it's best for you to stay up front."

Jenn's black-and-blue eyes, still purple and swollen from the beating her husband had given her over a week ago, would be hard for the judge to miss. Her broken nose was stuffed with packing and bandaged, and a set of crutches rested against the pew. Kate wanted Judge Roberts to take it all in and then deny the defendant's bail modification request.

She spent the next few minutes telling Jenn what to expect when the judge called her case. When she saw Jenn's shoulders relax a bit, she knew she could make her way to her seat.

She passed through the swinging doors that separated the gallery from the counsel tables, jury box, and judge's bench, and walked toward the prosecutor's table ignoring the faint whistles and catcalls from the male inmates. She put her briefcase down on the table and looked up when Cameron Cox strolled through the doors as if he was on a beach with all the time in the world.

Cameron Cox worked part-time in the public defender's office, had a successful private criminal defense practice, and was currently running for district attorney. He was so put-together you almost wanted to walk up to him and ruffle his hair, untuck his shirt. And she had, on more than one occasion. Kate noticed the wedding band on his ring finger as he set his files down on the table. She wondered if his newly restored love for his wife, who happened to be four months pregnant, was helping him in the polls.

"All rise," the bailiff announced as Judge Roberts walked out from his chambers and onto the bench.

"Be seated, be seated," Judge Roberts said, adjusting his black robe and taking his seat.

"*Commonwealth v. Finn!*" the bailiff bellowed.

Judge Roberts motioned for both Kate and Cameron to come forward. They waited while the defendant was unchained from the row of prisoners and ushered to the judge's bench by the sheriff.

"Your Honor, we're here today for a bail modification hearing of—"

"Your Honor, the bail modification is for *my* client, Peter Finn," Cameron said. "Mr. Finn is asking this honorable court to modify his bail to $50,000 unsecured."

"ADA Magda, what are the charges?" the judge asked.

"Your Honor, as I was going to say before I was interrupted by the defense, the defendant has been charged with . . . um . . . ." She was suddenly overtaken by a bout of dizziness and couldn't remember the specific counts the defendant had been charged with.

"Ms. Magda, is there a problem?" Roberts asked.

"I'm sorry, Your Honor. It seems I have left my notes at the prosecutor's table. Excuse me for a moment." She took a few steps back, reaching for her notes, careful not to turn her back on the judge. "The defendant has been charged with one count of simple assault, one count of aggravated assault, and one count of reckless endangerment. His current bail is set at $50,000 straight. The prosecution vehemently opposes the proposed bail modification. While bail is not meant to punish the defendant, it is meant to protect the public. One such member of the public is the victim who is present today in court." Kate looked toward Jenn Finn, hoping the judge would do the same. Kate blinked. Before her eyes were two Jenn Finns. Kate closed her eyes, swallowed, and quickly turned her attention back to the judge. Her double vision had corrected itself. "As I stated a moment ago, the district attorney's office opposes the defendant's request for a bail reduction in the hopes of protecting the public from a violent man."

Cameron Cox snickered, whispered something to his client, then said, "While we appreciate Ms. Magda's explanation of the term *bail*, my client is not a danger to the public. On the contrary, Mr. Finn works two jobs to support his children. He coaches his son's Little League team and is a member of the Lion's Club."

"When did supporting a child give someone the right to abuse the mother?"

"Your Honor, I think the prosecution meant to say *allegedly* before the word *abuse*," Cameron said.

"I meant exactly what I said. There's nothing alleged about the defendant throwing his wife against a dining room breakfront and then taking a closed fist to her face." Kate felt her face flush with anger.

Judge Roberts banged his gavel. "Let's leave the backbiting outside the courtroom, shall we? ADA Magda and Mr. Cox, consider yourselves warned." He looked over to where Jenn sat. "Ma'am, would you like to come up and add anything to the record?"

Jenn shook her head back and forth, eyes wide.

"Fine, then. I've heard enough. I am modifying Mr. Finn's bail to $50,000 at 10 percent, with the condition that he's not to set foot within thirty feet of the victim, her home, or her place of employment." He turned to the defendant. "Do you understand what I'm telling you, Mr. Finn? I want you to have absolutely no contact with your wife until the resolution of these charges."

"Your Honor," said Kate, "the commonwealth asks

this honorable court to order the no-contact to include phone calls, text messages, and any third-party communications. In addition, the commonwealth would like the defendant to verbally acknowledge the order of the court."

Cameron exhaled and shifted his body to let Kate and Judge Roberts know his time was being wasted.

"Mr. Finn, I agree with ADA Magda. You need to make a verbal acknowledgment of my order for purposes of the record, more than a mere nod of your head."

"I understand, Your Honor."

"Let the record and disposition sheet so reflect. Dismissed." Judge Roberts banged his gavel.

The sheriff stepped forward and placed his hands on the defendant's lower back, leading him back toward the other chained prisoners.

Roberts looked over at Cameron and smiled. "I hear your campaign for district attorney is going well. Up five points in the polls."

As Kate watched the interaction, she could have sworn she saw Cameron wink at the judge. Frustrated at her own behavior and with the outcome of the hearing, she took a few deep breaths before briefing Jenn. Beads of sweat had formed at her temples and on the back of her neck but she didn't feel hot. She sat in the pew next to the fragile woman and explained that her soon-to-be-ex-husband's bail was reduced but that he still needed to come up with $5,000 to be released from prison.

"He'll come up with the money." Tears slipped down Jenn's face and she hiccupped. "He's going to kill me."

The look of defeat in Jenn's eyes crushed Kate. She wanted to keep the young woman safe, worried the justice system had failed her, but Kate didn't know what else to do. She could hear her father's voice in her head giving her his usual speech. *You're not viewing this through the eyes of an attorney, Kate. You can't change the events that impact a person's life. That's not your role. If you lose in court, lives are no different than they would be had you won. You're giving them closure at best. So do your job and move on. And stop biting your nails.* Unlike her father, she had a hard time believing everything was so black and white.

"Jenn, have you recently dyed your hair?" Kate asked, standing and touching her client's reddish-brown strands. "I don't remember you having red in your hair."

"My girlfriend did it. She said it would make my eyes look greener. Although I doubt anyone's looking into my eyes." She motioned toward her broken nose and the bruises on her face.

"Dye it back to brown."

"Huh?"

"Haven't you been reading the papers? There is a serial killer on the loose. Killing women with reddish hair. You need to get the red out of your hair. Immediately."

Jenn looked over at the chain of shackled prisoners that included her husband. "I don't think the Mission County Killer is my biggest problem right now," she said. "Are you okay? You don't seem right. You're . . . skittish. Acting more like me than you. Maybe you should sit down." Jenn patted the pew.

Kate was horrified. Words lately seemed to fly from her mouth before she had a chance to register them. She felt fine one minute and totally paranoid and on edge the next. She smoothed her skirt and tucked her hair behind her ears. "I think it's a good idea to stay at the women's shelter once your husband is released from jail. I agree with you that he might not adhere to the judge's order."

Kate finished advising Jenn, gathered her things, and walked out of the courtroom. She rounded the corner and pushed the elevator button, too tired to take the stairs.

As the elevator door closed, Cameron Cox's arm reached in and shot it back open. He stepped inside with a grin. "Kate, such a pleasure."

"I'm sure. How's your wife doing, Cam?" Kate swallowed the lump in her throat. She had known he was married. Cameron and his wife had been separated for close to a year; she was making a career for herself in New York City while Cameron was happy practicing law in Mission County. Kate and he just had to keep their relationship quiet until his marriage was officially dissolved. And Kate had believed him. It wasn't until she went over to his apartment one night, unannounced, that she found a very married Cameron enjoying his wife's company.

She didn't take his calls after that night, ignoring the voice mails he left on her phone, and eventually he stopped calling. Shortly after, he announced his candidacy for district attorney, with his wife, recently relocated to Pennsylvania for good, by his side.

"My wife would be doing a lot better if you'd stop calling and hanging up at all hours of the night."

"Come off it. I have better things to do than ring your house."

"I have a friend at the police station. She traced the calls back to you."

"Sleeping with her too?" Kate hadn't dialed his number once since that night.

Cameron reached over to the elevator buttons and pulled out the red stopper. The car lurched and then hung suspended between floors. He leaned over so that he was not more than an inch from Kate, his hot breath on her face. "Speaking of friends at the police station, it seems your father has a few cops on his personal payroll."

Kate wasn't following.

"For your sake and your father's, you best leave me and my wife alone. You meant nothing to me, Kate. So do me a favor and walk away. No more phone calls, no more anything. If you don't listen to what I'm telling you, you'll be sorry." He backed away from her, pushing in the red stopper, and the elevator jolted into motion.

Kate's cheeks flushed with rage as she imagined slapping him across the face. Who the hell did he think he was, threatening her like this? What had happened to the confident, kind person she'd fallen for? She had little time to recover before the door opened. Cameron Cox stepped out of the elevator as if nothing had happened, his political smile painted back on his face as he said his hellos to the courthouse employees.

Kate made a beeline for the detectives' office located in the basement of the courthouse. She punched in the code and let herself in.

Sam Hart stood on the other side of the door. "Looks like we're still giving suits access to our digs," he joked to the other detectives standing around the office as he ushered her into one of the meeting rooms.

CHAPTER TWELVE

"HOW ARE YOU HOLDING UP?" Sam asked. "Bad morning in court?"

"You could say that. The day can't end fast enough." Kate sank into one of the chairs that surrounded the oak conference table and guzzled down a bottle of water.

"Your father called me. He heard about your episode in the morgue this morning and knows that you were mentoring our third victim."

"Looks like my day isn't getting any better."

"He planned on calling Bowers this afternoon to have you taken off the case," said Sam.

She rocked back on her chair, her eyes focused on the ceiling. She slowly counted to ten, not wanting another freak-out moment in front of Sam.

He sat down next to her at the table, swiveling his chair so that he faced her profile. "Your dad has good reason. I'm not saying he should involve himself in your professional life, or determine if you should be on or off a case, but I can appreciate his concern." He bent forward, resting his hands on the arm of her chair. "You're good, Kate. I'd rather work Reds with you than anyone else in your office, but the case has gotten to you. Maybe you're meant to sit this one out. But it should be your call. Not mine and not your father's."

"Yes, it should be my call. It *is* my call." But even she knew that if her father wanted her off the case, a phone call was all it would take. She had anticipated this moment but it didn't stop the sting she felt over Sam discussing her with her father, or Sam not wanting her on the case. She wanted to be straightforward with him, let him know why the case was affecting her. But until she had concrete information to give him, she couldn't jeopardize her career. She settled for a half-truth. "I'm not sure what has been going on with me the last few days. The new developments in the case have me rattled. But that doesn't mean I want to take myself off. I've never wanted to prosecute a case more. I won't let the ball drop and I certainly won't let the district attorney's office down. That's a promise, Sam."

"I know," he said with a heavy sigh. "I asked your father not to make the call to Bowers."

Kate was stunned. "What did he say?" She held her breath.

"He agreed with me."

She exhaled. "What's the catch?" She knew with her father it was never that easy.

"I'm going to be honest with you. I've agreed to run detail on you, with the condition that while I report back to your father, you are also aware of what I'm doing and you'll work with me in keeping you safe."

Kate had a feeling this went beyond her father's typical overprotectiveness. This was her father's way of ensuring she remained safe from this particular killer. After all, he had to be making the connection to Ron Wells too. And if he and Kate were on the same page, keeping her assigned to the case was a better option than being left in the dark. "So it's either I take myself off the case or you babysit me until the case is closed?"

"Pretty much."

"Tell me why you agree to his every request. Tell me why you're willing to follow me around."

"Believe it or not, Kate, I don't have a problem saying no to him. I'll admit that years ago, as I was making my way up the ranks, I was willing to do whatever I was asked. I respect your father. But more than that, I've come to respect *you*. You're a rare breed of prosecutor. You believe in the justice and honor that comes along with the job, but you question the system. You become so consumed with right versus wrong that you're willing to do anything to prove your point—even if it means sacrificing—"

"If you're suggesting I unethically cross lines—"

"I was going to say that you sometimes sacrifice your well-being in order to beat the system."

"I've learned to follow my gut when it comes to my cases because the system has cracks in it."

"But that's not what you're trained to do. You're like a rogue prosecutor, going off on your own, following your own rules. Sometimes you have to embrace the cracks."

Kate scrunched her face in disagreement. Sam sounded like her father. She also thought his basic assessment of her was unfair. She wasn't rogue; she was a zealous advocate for the victims of crime. There were so many advocates for the wrongly accused and incarcerated, and as a victim herself, she knew there was far too little attention paid to victims' rights. Many would say she needed better boundaries, but Kate believed, wholeheartedly, that when you are on the side of right, the ends justify the means. Period. A sadness fell over her as she wished more than anything that *this* was what she had told Winter-Dawn about prosecuting cases, and not the bullshit story about not giving a damn about the victims.

"So you're vouching for someone who's gone rogue?" she asked with a raised eyebrow.

"I know how much prosecuting Reds means to you. For you, and unlike some of your colleagues, this case isn't just another notch in your prosecutor's belt. That's why I'm willing to answer to your father. That's why I'm willing to vouch for you and keep you on the case. Now, agree with me that we'll work *together* on this and that you'll tell me if anything is bothering you."

She took a moment before speaking. Like in a high-stakes poker game, this was the instant she could either hold or fold. Folding meant she'd have to take herself off the case, tell Sam what was bothering her, and lose control of the situation. She'd be an outsider looking in, no longer privy to the information that she desperately needed—the information that would prove the killings were tied to what had happened to her and Tess as children.

Sam was right. This case had never been about her career—she'd used that notion to steel herself. When DA Bowers assigned her to the case, it gave her an "in," a way to remain in control, and she couldn't let it go. Giving her and Tess up to the system—a system Kate knew didn't always deliver justice—terrified her.

"Agreed," she said, because when it came down to it, there really wasn't an alternative.

"Good. Now, let's discuss Reds," he said. "Remember at the morgue when I told you I was keeping the killer's signature mark out of my notes and away from the press? Well, there's no need to do that anymore. The information was leaked. It's all over the news."

"Who leaked it?"

"Maybe someone in forensics? I have no idea. Bowers is pissed that his office was unaware of the signature mark. And even more pissed that he didn't have a heads-up before being swarmed by the press."

"Do you think it's going to hurt the case?"

"You tell me," he said, tossing the newspaper on the table.

Kate didn't read the article. She saw nothing beyond the bolded initials, *RJW*, at the top of the page.

Kate sat at her desk sucking down a bottle of water, foregoing her usual endless coffee refills. It had been torture listening to Sam while he finished filling her in on the leak, but she made herself sit through it, not wanting to run out of the detective's office appearing bat-shit crazy, which was how she felt.

She glanced around the DA's office, trying to play it cool. When she was sure no one was paying attention, she quickly pulled up the New York State Department of Corrections website on her computer. She clicked on the *inmate look-up* icon. She knew Ron Wells's inmate number by heart and typed in the six digits and letter. In less than a second his name flashed at the top of the screen along with information about him, his arrest, and his time in prison. His name was listed last name first: *Wells, Ronald.* No middle name or initial. Could the killer's signature mark possibly be a coincidence?

She scrolled down until she saw the words *custody*

status, and followed her eyes across the screen. *In custody*.

Banging away on the keyboard, she next entered the words *Hettrich County, New York Prison, escape* into a search engine and waited for the results. She scanned the hits. Nothing.

She returned to the inmate database and scrolled past the crimes for which Ron had been convicted, past his aggregate minimum and maximum sentence, to where it displayed his earliest possible parole release date. Only one year until he became eligible. She'd been lucky it had been this long. Thanks to his prior record and the sentencing judge running his convictions consecutive, what could have been as little as eight to ten years in prison ended up closer to thirty.

She decided that after her hellish weekend and recent morgue episode, she was done playing the scared victim. There would be no more throwing up or sleeping with a screwdriver under her pillow. She'd made a promise to Sam that she could handle the case, which meant she needed to handle herself and her own demons too. Hopefully, her new outlook would clear the static that still clouded her thoughts. Taking another swig of her water, she began rummaging through the trial boxes covering her desk. She needed to make some headway before Friday's Call of the Trial List.

One of the ADAs came over to her cubicle. "Bowers wants to see you in his office."

She stood, grabbing a pen and notepad, ready to discuss Reds with Bowers.

"A bunch of us are headed to the Drunken Dog after work," said the ADA. "Swing by if you can."

She looked at the mess on her desk and almost declined, but maybe hanging out and having a few drinks would help give her that fresh perspective she was hoping for. "I'll see you there."

CHAPTER THIRTEEN

Tess was nowhere near the volunteer center. She also wasn't meeting John Friar for lunch. She pulled her car into an empty parking space in Cunningham Valley Psychiatric Hospital's lot and cut the engine. She rubbed her fingers around her temples, trying to relieve the pain slicing across the middle of her forehead. Today was the fourth hospital visit she'd made over the past two weeks to see her drug-addicted, pill-popping drunk of a mother, who had checked into Cunningham Valley for addiction treatment. Again.

The locket around her neck felt like a hundred-pound weight and as she reached around to unclasp it, her mind drifted back to the day she and Kate had received the necklaces.

On her sixth birthday, Uncle Tommy and Aunt Cathy had thrown her a big party. She had only been living with them for a few months but they were pulling out all the stops to make her feel a welcome part of the family.

She hadn't gone to kindergarten with Kate. Instead, her aunt and uncle had employed a tutor to homeschool her because she still wasn't speaking. She'd overheard her therapist tell Aunt Cathy that her lack of speech was from the trauma she'd suffered and that with continued therapy sessions and social experiences, she would probably speak again. She had wanted to tell her aunt that her therapist had been wrong. That she wanted to talk, but Ron had always warned her that if she uttered one word about anything to anyone, she wouldn't live to see her next birthday. That she'd never see her mom again. Or Kate.

Because she was not in school, she didn't have any classmates to invite to her party, so her aunt and uncle had invited all the kids from Kate's kindergarten class, none of whom she knew. Everyone ran around the backyard in bathing suits, cotton candy and snow cones in hand, while Tess stood off by herself, watching the action. The kids' parents had gathered on the back patio, the women sipping fruity drinks, the men drinking beer and advising her uncle on how to grill the burgers just right, when she saw her mother Judy stroll through the screen door and into the backyard.

Judy had just been released from the county jail after serving a sixty-day stint for driving under the influence of drugs. Tess remembered people staring at the way her mother was dressed, in cutoff shorts that gave a clear view of her butt and the cut-up thin cotton of her T-shirt that exposed her belly button and the outline of her braless breasts. She looked nothing like the other moms in their sundresses, the summer humidity and warm breeze unable to affect their perfect hair and makeup.

"Baby, come over here and give your mama a hug!" she had shouted in Tess's direction, her teeth looking too big for her mouth and her cheekbones jutting out so far they seemed to hide her eyes. By the time Tess reached her mother, Uncle Tommy was standing next to her.

"Tess, honey, why don't you show your mom how you can swim a whole lap of the pool underwater?" Uncle Tommy suggested, giving her a light tap on her bottom. Tess didn't move. Her uncle lowered his voice and turned his back toward his guests so no one could hear what he was saying to Judy, but Tess caught every word.

"What the hell are you doing?" he asked. "You have some nerve showing up here after everything you've done to destroy this family."

"Nice to see you too, big brother."

"You have no place here anymore."

"If my daughter is here, then I have a place here. Speaking of here—nice house. Looks like Pennsylvania is treating you better than New York."

"You're lucky you're not in jail for what you did to your daughter. Or more like what you failed to do."

Judy kept a smile painted on her face. "I found an apartment. Not even ten minutes from your house."

"We made a deal, Judy. No more contact with Tess. No more contact with this family. Please don't make me get lawyers involved. I mean, look at yourself, showing up to her birthday party dressed like—"

"Hi, everyone, I'm Tommy's sister Judy," she announced to the crowd of onlookers. "Bet he never talks to you about his favorite sister." She gave a crooked smile, one of the only traits Judy and Tommy had in common—a trait passed down to both of their daughters—and then she curtsied. As she dipped down, she lost her balance and stumbled forward, her shirt falling open and exposing her breasts. Tess could hear a few of the women gasp.

In an attempt to take the focus off her mom, Tess ran toward the pool. She leaped into the air, pulled her legs up toward her chest, and wrapped her arms around her shins. She hit the water with as much force as she could, splashing some of the kids standing by the edge of the pool. When she emerged from underwater, a big smile on her face, she searched for her mother's eyes, but Judy was already off talking to the bartender, facing the opposite direction. Blinking back tears, she swam to the pool steps, thankful to see Kate heading toward her.

Kate approached with two wrapped boxes in her hand. "Tess! Let's open these! They're from Mommy and Daddy. They're for both of us." The girls removed their necklaces from the boxes. Gold lockets with their initials engraved on the back.

"Here, you take mine," Kate said to Tess, "and I'll take yours. Wear it forever, okay? We can never take them off."

Tess said nothing, but gave her cousin a big hug as they exchanged lockets. Tess ran, locket in hand, to Aunt Cathy and Uncle Tommy, with Kate close behind. Again, Tess didn't speak, but she wrapped her arms around her uncle first and then her aunt.

"We traded," said Kate. "Is that okay?"

Aunt Cathy took the locket from Tess, bent down, and clasped it around her neck. "Of course it's okay. Happy birthday, Tess. We love you so much."

As Tess ran her fingers over the etched letters engraved on the locket, Judy made her way toward the four of them, drink in hand. The alcohol sloshed around her glass, spilling over the rim as she reached into her back pocket and took out a necklace made of macaroni pieces, some broken, and put it in Tess's hand. "I made this for you while I was away. Happy birthday, baby." Her breath stank and her eyes were glassy.

Kate spoke before Tommy or Cathy could say anything. "Tess made a necklace like that with her tutor. The one Tess made is prettier than that one. It's painted and everything. Plus, my mom and dad already got her a necklace. A locket. We can put our pictures in them!"

Judy's half-filled glass smashed on the concrete patio. She gasped. "Oh God! Kate, look what you made me do! I'm so sorry. Here, let me clean it up." She bent down, picking up the shards of glass and placing them in her cupped hand. She seemed distraught, but Tess knew she'd done it on purpose.

"Daddy, I didn't make her do that! I swear!" Kate protested.

Uncle Tommy grabbed Judy's arm, gripping it so hard that a pained look washed over her face. He spoke to her through clenched teeth. "Get the hell out of my house."

Judy turned toward Tess. "C'mon, baby, we're leaving." She extended her hand toward her daughter, but Tess didn't grab hold of it. She stood motionless, as if paralyzed. She waited for her aunt or uncle to speak up and tell Judy she wasn't allowed to take Tess. "Tess Patricia Conway, I said we're leaving. Now."

Images flashed through Tess's mind. Images of her old house in New York. The way the couch smelled like stale cigarettes and how her mother slept on it for hours, sometimes days. Dirty ashtrays with cigarette butts, empty bottles of liquor strung around as if it was her mother's decorating theme. Garbage littered throughout the TV room, bathroom, and kitchen—the aftermath of her mother's nightly parties. She thought about Ron, her stepfather, and his thick cologne that made her gag and how when he smiled she could see his missing tooth. How she was certain he was going to break out of jail, come home to her mother's house, and kill her.

A sound emerged from Tess's throat. The first sound in months. A scream filled with panic, hate, and, above all, fear.

The car alarm in the vehicle parked next to Tess's went off, jolting her back to the present. She didn't see her mother for twelve years after that. She had told herself it was because her uncle refused to let Judy visit, even, at times, resenting him for keeping her mother away. But deep down she knew the truth: Her mother loved a lot of things. Men, drugs, alcohol. But her mother didn't love *her*.

The Magdas became her only family. They gave her everything. Sometimes Tess felt guilty for how her life had turned out and how her mother continued to suffer, haunted by inner demons that couldn't be exorcised.

Her mother was a user. She used Tess when it benefited her. She used Uncle Tommy, dropping his name every chance she could in the hopes of special treatment when she was pulled over for yet another DUI. And despite her better judgment, Tess couldn't help but hope for a changed woman. After all these years, after all Judy's failed attempts at rehab and being a mother, Tess still longed for her love.

She climbed the stairs that led to the automatic sliding glass doors, whispering to herself, "*Om Shri Ganeshaya Namah.*" A few years ago, at the suggestion of her therapist, she began practicing yoga, and this particular phrase, chanted in class, was meant to remove obstacles that stood in the way of new beginnings. She teetered between feeling ridiculous for even wanting a new beginning with her mother and her deep belief in the mantra. Still wrestling with her thoughts, she made her way to the desk where the receptionist sat paging through a tabloid magazine.

"She's in the sunroom," the receptionist said without looking up. "You have forty minutes before she goes to class. Don't forget to sign in."

Tess's mother sat in a rocking chair facing the window, her black hair hanging over the back of the chair. She wore acid-washed jeans and an old pullover sweatshirt with a tie-dyed peace sign on the front.

"Mama," Tess said, her voice echoing off the walls.

Judy leaped out of the chair and wrapped her arms around Tess. "Baby! I'm so glad you're here."

Tess listened while her mother told her how healthy she felt. She couldn't help but think of all the other drug and alcohol classes that her mother had successfully completed, only to end up back in rehab within months, sometimes weeks. She stared at Judy's arms as she pulled up the sleeves of her sweatshirt, revealing a line of faded track marks.

Her mother caught her looking and smiled. "Baby, I'm better this time. I feel different. Things are finally working out for me. I promise." Her mom had a glimmer in her eyes. A look Tess couldn't remember if she had ever seen before. "Maybe when I leave here you and I can find a place and move in together?"

"I'm almost thirty. I'm supposed to be leaving the nest, not creating it."

Her mother smiled again. "What's the difference between living with Kate and living with your mama? I'm cool." Judy looked down at her jeans as if to say, *I'm*

wearing acid-washed jeans to prove it. "Kate's so uptight.
I'm not sure how you two live together. Although the digs
are nice. Real nice. That would be hard to give up. But the
two of us living together would be so much fun. We could
have movie marathon nights and I'll make you those ice
cream sundaes you love. Just like old times."

Tess had been five the last time they'd had movie
night and ice cream sundaes. Ten minutes into the movie,
her mother had passed out on the couch with a cigarette
dangling from her lips.

"I bet Uncle Tommy would even buy you a small
house or a condo if you asked him. You know, have him
put it in your name so you have equity in something."

Ahh, there it is, thought Tess. Judy didn't want to live
with her to catch up on the years she'd played hookie
from being a mother. Tess sat trying to rekindle some sort
of relationship while all her mother cared about was a
free ride, willing to use her brother and daughter to secure one. Tess wasn't sure what she'd expected after all
this time. Her mother had battled her entire life with an
addiction to drugs and alcohol and Tess had battled her
entire life with an addiction to her mother.

"Baby, go tell the nurse we want some hot tea. Decaf-
feinated."

Tess walked to the doorway of the sunroom, located
a nurse down the hall, and went to fulfill her mother's
request. She returned and sat down in a rocking chair
across from her mother, feeling completely deflated.

"How about that serial killer on the loose here in
Mission County?" Judy said. "Some lunatic is killing
women with red hair."

"How do you know about that?" Tess asked. Her

mother never read the newspaper unless Tess brought it with her to the hospital, and if the television happened to be on it was permanently fixed on reality programs, not the nightly news.

"Everyone in the hospital is talking about it. You should hear some of the theories going around." Judy tipped her head back and gave a deep chuckle, the rocking chair swaying back and forth. She didn't bother to let Tess in on the joke. "I heard the last victim was found outside the courthouse. Could you imagine if Uncle Tommy or Kate would've been the ones to find the body?"

"Then you've heard that the killer is leaving a signature mark inside the victims' throats?"

"Just like on TV."

"What do you make of the initials?"

"Those aren't his initials," Judy offered. "Your stepfather doesn't have a middle name."

"Kate thinks we're connected to the killings."

"You better tell Kate to be careful when she goes to sleep tonight," Judy quipped. She opened her eyes wide and wiggled her fingers at Tess.

Tess mustered all the calm she had in her. "What is wrong with you? Why would you say that?"

"Lighten up."

"Lighten up? In all your years of drug abuse, did you forget what actually happened to me? To Kate?"

"I remember your cousin sleepwalking when she was younger, making up stories, and being a pain in the ass. That's what I remember." Judy rolled her eyes.

"I was there too. You can't tell me it didn't happen."

"You've confused the situation. Too much of Kate whispering nonsense in your ear."

Tess couldn't remember anything of that night, only a vague picture of sitting in the backseat of Ron's car, and then nothing. Even after years of therapy, she had no recollection of the event; only images based on what Kate had told her.

"You're delusional!" Tess heard her own voice escalating. "Just because you claim you were wasted and so high that you had no idea what was happening doesn't give you the right to make jokes or excuses for the pathetic piece of shit you called a husband. Maybe if you'd been more present, more of a mother, none of this would have happened. I wouldn't have to read something in the newspaper and connect it back to a horrible man that I know you still keep in contact with."

Judy snatched the newspaper from the table and threw it across the room. "I know what you're trying to do, bringing in this paper, showing me those stupid initials."

"I'm not *trying* to do anything." Tess lifted her hands to her head; her mother's words filled her brain, pulsing and thumping violently against her temples. The pain was so great she tasted bile rising in the back of her throat. She lowered her voice. "Why? Why can't you love me even a fraction of how much you love him?"

As Tess stormed out of the building toward her car, Nick Granteed waited in the shadows around the corner and watched her. He saw her hands shake as she reached into her purse for her keys, dropping the bag on the macadam and scrambling to pick it up again. Unlike her cousin, she never looked over her shoulder or seemed aware of her surroundings. Following her was so much easier.

He rose slightly from his crouch so he could remove

the picture from his back pocket. Tess as a small girl. There were others in the photograph but his focus was only on her. He traced his thumb over her face. Beads of sweat formed along his hairline and his upper lip was moist despite the icy air. He watched Tess as she climbed into her car.

He stared at her through the glass window, watching the way her body shook, her hair falling forward over her shoulders, covering her face. He knew she was crying. He held his breath, certain he could hear the sobs emanating from her, through the car, piercing his heart. He swallowed, tasting the salt of her tears.

C HAPTER FOURTEEN

KATE GLANCED AROUND DA BOWERS'S OFFICE. His desk was a scattered mess, much like the district attorney himself. She fixed her eyes on the pictures above his head while he finished his phone conversation. Four mahogany frames hung on the wall, displaying key evidence held by the prosecution in the George Carlow trial. The prosecution had charged Carlow, a local prison guard, with criminal homicide, alleging that he shot a bullet through his wife's head after he found out she was having an affair. The defense team maintained the gunshot wound was self-inflicted, as evidenced by Carlow's frantic 911 call that his wife had committed suicide. Bowers, an assistant district attorney at the time, had been assigned to the trial.

Kate cast her eyes over the pictures of a 9mm pistol, Carlow's right hand (which contained more gunpowder residue than what was found on his wife's hands), the location of the spent shell, and a photo taken by forensics of the blood spatter. She remembered being in the courtroom during the trial, home on holiday break from college.

While he'd been on the stand and under oath, Carlow had an answer for everything. Whatever the prosecution threw at him he handled with ease. Why was there gun-powder residue found on his hands? Because he reached for his wife as she pulled the trigger and his hand was close enough to the gun for bits of residue to cling to it. The prosecution's own gunpowder expert had testified to the plausibility of Carlow's version of events. When asked why, if Carlow was close enough to pick up the residue, there was no blood found on his hands, he said he had washed them in the kitchen sink, leaving traces of the gunpowder residue but removing the blood. The fact that he'd openly admitted this detail hurt the prose-cution's chance of making it look like the hand washing was a sign of guilt. He was so good at playing the part of the innocent widower that Kate had started to question the prosecution's case.

Next up for the defense had been George Carlow's mother Sylvia. After Sylvia's direct examination, which Kate felt hadn't done much to help or hurt the defense, Bowers rose to begin his cross-examination. Bowers didn't grandstand, make over-the-top gestures, or ask argumentative questions. Throughout most of the ques-tioning, Kate wondered if someone had slipped Bowers a quaalude.

"Your son called you, upset. He was so upset that you couldn't make out what he was saying, right?" Bowers had asked.

"Yes, that's right."

"So you decided to go over to your son's house, which is only four houses away from yours?"

"Right."

"And how long did it take you to leave your house and get to your son's?"

"I'd say it took me a minute, maybe less, from the time I got off the phone with George to the time I was over at his house. I ran the whole way. I didn't even put my shoes on or lock the door on my way out."

"Less than a minute." Bowers took a long pause as if trying to work something out in his head before he spoke again. "Okay, so we know from the 911 tapes that George called 911 at 12:09 a.m. The call lasted a minute and forty seconds. And according to phone records he called your home number at 12:11 a.m., so it's a fair assumption that your son called you immediately after hanging up from the 911 call." Bowers didn't wait for an answer. "And then you ran over to his house in less than a minute from the time your phone call ended. Is that a fair statement?"

"Yes sir. That's fair."

"When you were on the phone with George, did you hear anything in the background?"

"No, I couldn't hear anything other than George sobbing into the phone."

"Okay. Let's move on. Let's talk about when you actually arrived at the house. You said you entered through the back door?"

"That's right. I have a key to the back door, which leads right into the kitchen."

"And tell me again, where was your son when you entered the kitchen through the back door?"

"He was still upstairs. He came down when he heard me yell his name."

"Was he out of breath?"

"Out of breath?"

"Yes, like he'd been running around the house?"

"I can't remember for sure, but—"

"That's okay, ma'am," said Bowers. "If you're not sure, don't answer."

Kate remembered almost falling out of her chair. Had Bowers really just counseled the defense's client? She thought he might get pulled off the case.

"What about his hands? Did you see blood on his hands?"

"No, there wasn't any blood on his hands."

"And just so we're clear, was there blood on *your* hands?"

"Goodness no. There was no blood on me."

"You're certain?"

"I think that's something I would remember, sir."

"Yes, I agree. So, my question for you is when you saw George enter the kitchen, walk over to the sink, turn on the faucet, and begin washing his hands with the dish soap, did you ask him what he was doing?"

"No, I didn't—"

"Why would he be washing his hands if you don't remember seeing any blood on them?"

"Objection!" yelled the defense counsel while at the same time Sylvia responded to Bowers's question.

"My son already told you he washed his hands before I got to the house!" she shouted, clearly exasperated.

Kate realized the discrepancy that Bowers had discovered. The jury hadn't seen it. Defense counsel didn't even realize it. But they would soon. Bowers had kept Sylvia focused on her son washing his hands, which had been openly admitted by the defendant. And because it had been admitted, the action itself held little significance to the prosecution's case. But Bowers didn't care about the action, he cared about the timing of when Carlow had washed his hands. Bowers had the inconsistency tucked up his sleeve, ready to pull it out any second. Kate held her breath.

"Yes, Sylvia," said Bowers, "that's the story. That your son washed his hands in the kitchen sink before you came over to the house, which would mean that you're right. There would've been no blood on his hands, or yours for that matter. But that didn't happen, did it? Because how could George wash his hands in the kitchen sink *before* you came over to the house, scrubbing his wrists and hands, underneath his nails, erasing all signs of Kelly's blood, and then sprint back upstairs in less than a minute, only to come back *downstairs* to greet you in the very room he'd just left?"

"He washed them upstairs. He washed them—" Sylvia was losing it. Not fully understanding what was going on but aware that Bowers was no longer her friend.

"No, Sylvia. He didn't wash his hands upstairs. Your son testified that he washed his hands in the kitchen sink. Which means either you're lying or he's lying."

"There was too much blood!"

"Nothing further, Your Honor," said Bowers.

Sylvia had stepped out of the witness box with her head bowed.

Bowers had been smart to cut off his cross-examination at that point. He didn't want to focus on Sylvia's lie, but instead on the defendant's. Why would Carlow lie about *when* he washed his hands, if he was openly admitting to it? Kate swore she'd heard the defense attorney whimper in defeat.

The cross-examination had been reported by the local

media and when the jury returned a guilty verdict, Bowers was put not only in the spotlight, but also on the political map. After the trial, he was appointed first deputy attorney in the DA's office and successfully ran for district attorney the following year.

Bowers was now hoping to win the election for another four-year term. Thanks to the press and small-town politics, the public was all too aware that the one-time hard-working, take-no-prisoners district attorney hadn't tried a case in almost eight months. He made himself appear busy, popping in and out of the ADA's office and barking orders, but Kate wondered as of late if the DA had ever finished what he set out to do. To make matters worse, Cameron seemed to be running a successful campaign against DA Bowers, no longer making him a shoo-in for the election. Kate had her fingers crossed that a small fire would ignite under the DA's ass in the remaining months before the primary. She would love for him to sweep the Democratic ticket, leaving Cameron Cox crying like a little kid.

DA Bowers hung up the phone. He slid a thick file across the desk in Kate's direction and licked his dry, cracked lips before speaking. "ADA Winn had her knee operation. Her husband told me she should make a full recovery. We'll have her back in no time. We need her. I'm short. Too many cases. Too many trials." He waved his hand back and forth in front of his face as if swatting a fly—a signature trait of his and one the ADAs never missed an opportunity to mock.

"How are you doing?" Kate politely cut in. "I mean, you must have been rattled this morning when you found Winter-Dawn's body." She remembered seeing Bowers's reaction on the video Sam had showed her. Truthfully, she was shocked he had showed up at work.

"I was. I was. But to be honest, my thoughts are elsewhere. That's horrible to say out loud, isn't it? That poor intern. Hard worker. It's just . . . I need to stay busy. I don't want my mind wandering, you know. Plus, this election is what really has me rattled."

Rattled? The primary was still four months away.

"I'm thinking of dropping out of the race."

"WHAT?"

"My opponent is playing dirty and it's gotten to be too much."

"It's always dirty. Regardless of your opponent. You know that." She thought about her own experiences with what her father called "the game." The endless fundraisers, the rallies, and the commercial spots. The handshakes with people you didn't know, the cheek kisses with people you were supposed to know, the ones who kissed you and then pulled the lever for the opponent on election day. Anyone involved in politics accepted the game. They accepted it because the rush of winning outweighed the mud that had been slung during the campaign.

"I know," said Bowers. "I knew you would understand this more than anyone in our office. Which is why I've called you in here. I need you to research the crimes code. Specifically the section on threatening a public official."

"Cameron is threatening you?" Kate blurted out. She knew she shouldn't be surprised, not after everything she'd come to know about him. But threatening the incumbent district attorney? That was a new low, even for Cameron.

"Yes."

"Go to the authorities. Report him. Don't drop out of the race." She couldn't fathom working under Cameron, and if Bowers dropped out of the race, Cameron would run unopposed.

"I can't."

"Of course you can. When the scandal goes public it will probably help you in the polls."

"It's a sensitive subject. You grew up surrounded by politicians. You know the bullshit that's involved. What I'm about to tell you can't go any farther than this room. I trust that you will honor my request." He paused and when she said nothing in return, he took it to mean she was in agreement. "I have a son." Bowers smoothed his hand over the thinning tuft of gray hair on top of his head.

Kate peered past him at the three photographs on his console table. One showed him and his wife standing in front of a Christmas tree, the other two were school portraits of his daughter. She didn't see any pictures on the table of a boy. She kept quiet, wanting Bowers to continue with his story so she could get a handle on where this was headed.

"I got a girl pregnant when I was in high school. I'd been at a bar, underage. I spent the night flirting and drinking with a college girl and lied to her about how old I was. One tequila shot after the next and she ends up sleeping with me. I go home the luckiest teenager around and so hungover I couldn't recall her name. I don't hear from her for months and then she somehow manages to get in touch with me to tell me she's eight months pregnant with my child." He glanced at Kate, who remained tight-lipped. "I had no choice but to come clean and tell her I was barely seventeen, a junior in high school and in no position to have a baby. She never told anyone it was mine. And I never heard from her again until two years ago. Turns out I have a son—Luke Byrne." He opened the top drawer of his desk and took out a photograph. "This was taken years ago but it's the only one I've got." Kate looked at the photo. DA Bowers and Luke had the same round eyes and slightly hooked nose. "My son's an addict. In and out of the system most of his juvenile and young adult life. When his mother called me, she told me he'd been arrested on felony drug charges, and because of his priors, he was facing major time in state prison." Bowers shifted in his seat. "What was I supposed to do?"

Kate looked down at the file Bowers had given her when she'd first walked into his office. The label on it read, *Commonwealth v. Byrne.*

"Cameron Cox handled the case as my son's public defender. Cox advised Luke that the DA's office had zero tolerance for drug abuse, especially selling and distributing, and that he was facing a considerable amount of jail time. You could imagine Cox's surprise when the district attorney himself, and not an ADA, appeared in court to prosecute an open-and-shut drug case.

"To make matters even more suspicious to Cox, the arresting officer shows up on the day of the hearing and claims the selling and distribution charges don't hold up, can't be proven. The officer requests, in open court, that the charges be dismissed. Normally, the DA's office would've hemmed and hawed, claiming they had a prima facie case, but I made no objection to the officer's request. Of course, I'd cut a deal with the cop ahead of time. I guess it's funny what you'll do for family." He swatted the air and muttered something that Kate couldn't hear. "Your father presided over the case. He grants the request, no questions asked, and orders Luke to be placed in a rehab facility. Cox is beside himself with the outcome, tells Luke he got so lucky he should go play the lottery. Luke responds by telling Cameron that it wasn't luck. That I'm his old man."

"I take it your wife doesn't know about your son. You can't have it get out, right?"

"No. My wife knows."

"Okay. So you helped your son. It will hurt you if it comes out to the public because you claim to have a zero-tolerance policy for drug charges, but you have the arresting officer as your out. The cop claimed the more serious charges against your son wouldn't stick. I'm sure the officer stated as much on the record. You didn't ask for the charges to be dismissed, the cop did. There was nothing you could do about that."

Bowers put his head in his hands and rubbed his eyes. "But I did ask for the charges to be dismissed."

"We make deals with cops every day. It's what we do. There's even a name for it—prosecutorial discretion. So you cut a deal. Happens all the time. It's not like you made a promise in exchange for—" Kate stopped talking as she began to put two and two together.

"Cameron comes to me six months ago and tells me he knows that Luke's my son. He said the cop I cut a deal with is not only willing to make a public statement that I paid him to drop the charges, but that I also threatened his career should he decide not to follow through with the deal. I—"

Kate raised her hands. "Don't tell me if you threatened the cop. I don't . . . *can't* know."

"Well, I didn't. But it won't matter because if the cop steps forward with that story, the public perception will be that I did. My campaign for DA will be sunk."

Kate knew a way to sink Cameron's campaign and have him dead in the water too: allow Bowers to go public with Cameron's affair with her. The community wouldn't think too highly of a married man with a baby on the way sleeping with his future assistant DA. She wasn't quite ready to put her reputation on the line in order for Bowers to combat Cameron's threats, but surely if Cameron was the type of guy to have an affair with one woman, she'd guess he had a bagful of other indiscretions in his closet.

"I'm still not seeing why you can't report Cameron," she said. "I will do the research for you but I'm almost certain you could charge him with threats and improper influence in a political matter. It's clearly tied to the election because if you weren't running, none of this would be an issue. And the fact that he is running against you—I think the charges would stick. He's looking at a Felony 3."

Bowers stared at her. His eyes were sunken, bags rimmed his lower lids. He looked like he hadn't slept in days, maybe weeks. "Let me finish," he said. "Cox also tells me he'll report your father. He'll claim I went to the judge ahead of time, had an ex parte communication with him, and cut a deal. That's case fixing."

"Did you have ex parte communications with my father?" Was this what Cameron had been alluding to in the elevator?

"Of course not. I dealt with the arresting officer. Period."

Kate kept quiet, worried she might say the wrong thing.

"I need you to research the consequences to what I've done, if any," said Bowers. "I can't use my work computer and the library requires a sign-in name so it's a dead give-away. I also need to know what I'm up against with Cameron and what, if anything, we can charge him with."

"I will handle the research for you. No problem. I'll draft a memorandum and sample brief in support and have it on your desk in the next few days."

"Thank you." He paused. "But there's more."

More? Any more and she'd be wishing she kept a flask of vodka in her desk drawer.

"I think Cameron has an 'in' at the police department. Maybe it's with the arresting officer from my son's case; maybe it's someone else. But I think my cell phone is tapped, the office phones, maybe even my home phone. Cameron seems to know information before I do, before police can brief me on an arrest. Before I can set forth my election platform, he's speaking to the press and under-cutting it."

Kate was thrilled with Bowers's "more." She could easily build a case on what he had told her about the possible phone tap. That must be why Sam had shut her up on the phone today. Bowers must have alerted Sam to the situation. She thought about how Cameron had accused her of calling his phone and had admitted in the elevator that he had a friend in the police department checking his calls. If Bowers's assumptions were true, Cameron could be disqualified from running. He'd also be ripped apart by the media to the point that his political career would be over. *This will be easy,* she thought. It was everything else Bowers had told her that left her head spinning.

"I will research and draft memoranda on both issues for you."

"I knew I could count on you."

"If Cameron is threatening to use my father's name to extort you, my father needs to know about it. I think you should be the one to tell him." She rose from the leather chair, straightening her skirt. "I like you, boss. I respect you. I want you to win the election and sit in this office for another four years. But it's not going to happen if you don't deal with this situation head-on. Any information leaked to the public or information that comes from anyone else's mouth but yours and you're sunk."

The color drained from Bowers's face. "Thank you. That will be all."

CHAPTER FIFTEEN

SAM MET THE SECURITY GUARD in the basement of the annex building where the surveillance monitors and digital recordings were housed. He couldn't believe it was already five thirty. His day had been filled with meetings and crazies flooding the phones to report all the people they knew with the initials RJW, along with a slew of others who thought they knew what the three letters might stand for.

He scanned the digital tapes, paying closer attention to the footage when it was within the relevant time frame. At 2:49 a.m. the first camera on the perimeter of the courthouse was spray-painted, the nozzle of the paint can visible before the screen turned black. The killer had managed to tilt the camera upward so that the lens recorded the sky and not the courthouse perimeter before being sprayed. The tilt could've been accomplished using anything from a long stick to the handle of an umbrella, depending on the height of the killer. Again, all speculation. Nothing that aided him in formulating a suspect list or helped corroborate the small amount of evidence they had compiled in the case. What he did know was that the tilting of the cameras ensured that no part of the killer's body was captured. By 2:56 a.m. all cameras except the one located at the employee entrance had been sprayed, making the footage on six of the seven monitors appear as if the power had been shut off.

Sam switched to the camera that focused on the employee entrance and watched as it rose toward the sky and then rotated until it faced the door to the entrance rather than the steps. The back of Bowers's head came into view at 3:01 a.m. Sam watched him swipe his card, pull open the door, and enter the main courthouse.

He fast-forwarded through the tape until he saw Bowers exit the employee entrance at 3:34 a.m. Bowers stared in the direction in which the intern's body lay, his facial expression frozen, then he clutched his chest, stumbling backward. *Poor guy,* Sam thought, as he continued to review the recording.

Next, he pulled the footage from the traffic light cameras between 2:20 and 3:34 a.m., backing up the tape by almost fifteen minutes to allow whoever spray-painted the cameras time to drive and park outside the courthouse. Here Sam ran into some luck. The courthouse stood on the corner of Chestnut and Main, with vehicle access off Chestnut. However, Chestnut was a one-way street and not heavily traveled. Sam skipped the footage on Main and went right to Chestnut. He watched the tape and by the time he got to 3:34 a.m., he had counted only nine vehicles that had been on the road during that time, one of them, an Audi SUV, having traveled down the street twice within ten minutes. Why would someone drive their vehicle down a one-way street twice in a matter of ten minutes at three o'clock in the morning?

He had only a few minutes before he needed to meet Kate and give her a ride to the morgue so she could pick up her car. He entered the license plate numbers on the nine cars and ran them through the database. Within seconds he was viewing the list of names registered to their respective vehicles. He gasped.

Kate's name there on the screen had to be a mistake. The Audi SUV was registered in her name, but she wasn't on the logbooks for being in the courthouse last night. He ran the plates again, with no change in the results. Kate didn't live anywhere near the courthouse, so why had she traveled down Chestnut at three a.m.? Twice?

He stuffed the list in his back pocket, grabbed his coat off the chair, thanked the security guard, and made his way to the employee parking lot. There was only one bit of information that concerned him more than Kate's car showing up on the surveillance footage. Preceding both of Kate's runs down Chestnut, there had been a second vehicle. The license plate linked to another familiar name: Nick Granteed.

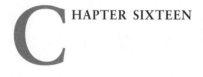

CHAPTER SIXTEEN

KATE CLOSED THE BOOK she had been using to research Bowers's situation and placed it back on the shelf in the law library. She hadn't been able to concentrate after her meeting with him and decided that delving into the legal issues was the only way to quell her current bout of attention deficiency.

She had one more order of business to take care of back at her desk before she met Sam in the parking garage. Her father had called her earlier and left a message, and she had yet to return the call. Now that the office had cleared out and she was alone, she dialed his cell phone number but her call went directly to voice mail. Weird. She dialed the extension to his chambers instead, and Tommy Magda answered on the fourth ring.

"Since when do you play secretary as well as president judge?" Kate asked. "Has the county cut funding? I'd love to watch you try your hand at typing."

Her father laughed. It was a hearty laugh from deep in his belly. "You're just the person I was hoping to hear from."

Kate could picture him sitting behind his monstrosity of a desk, feet up, leaning back in his chair.

"Dad, there's something wrong with your cell phone.

I called it just a minute ago and it went right to voice mail. Actually, it's been happening more often than not."

"I . . . I . . . just got out of a meeting here in chambers. I turned it off so as not to interrupt."

"Since when do you care about interrupting the parties?" Kate replied with a chuckle.

"We need to talk about Tess."

Kate wasn't expecting her cousin to be the topic of conversation. She'd figured her father wanted to address the incident in the morgue and his concerns about her working the Mission County Killer case. Surely he would have read the paper by now and made the possible connection between the initials and Ron Wells.

"What's going on with Tess?" she asked.

"Well, that was my question to you. Why didn't you call me about this? Your stepmom is a complete mess. I think it would be best to cancel family dinner tonight. I'm going to take Tess out for Italian. Talk some sense into her, you know?"

Kate all but slapped her forehead. She'd completely forgotten about her family dinner. But what was going on? "Tess will be thrilled to have dinner with you, but I have no idea what you're talking about."

"Your cousin went to Cunningham Valley Hospital this morning. The visit went horribly, which doesn't surprise me. She called Rachel in hysterics. Your stepmom couldn't even make out what she was saying through the sobs and sniffles. We wish you'd told us. There's no sense in protecting Tess when it comes to Judy."

"*Judy*? Tess has been visiting Judy? For how long?"

"From what Rachel could gather, Judy's back in rehab at Cunningham Valley and Tess has been visiting her over the last few weeks. I thought you knew and were keeping it from us."

Kate tried to dismiss the feeling of betrayal before formulating her next sentence. "Do you remember what happened the last time Tess decided to visit Judy?" She thought back to a little over ten years ago—Tess had been a teenager when Judy had reentered her life. Kate remembered the unnecessary lies Tess had conjured about where she was spending her time; and then the headaches that kept her confined to her bed, no light allowed to filter into the room, no one permitted to speak to her above a whisper; the abuse of pills; and worse than all that, the self-inflicted cuts that covered Tess's body.

"That's why I want to take her to dinner. Get her in a controlled setting. Hopefully I can get her to stop communicating with Judy."

"That woman has pure venom running through her blood," Kate said angrily.

"Should we also discuss what happened to you in the morgue this morning? I'm concerned, Kate."

"Dad, I'm fine. The victim was an intern here in the DA's office—I think having known her, it was a rather common reaction." *And I'm going to be late,* she thought, looking at the clock. "Go meet Tess. We'll talk more later."

"This doesn't mean you're off the hook. I'm quite certain there's more to your getting sick in the morgue than you've let on. I'd like to talk to you in person about a few things."

There it was—the comment she'd been waiting for. She chose to ignore him for now, and attempted to keep him focused on Tess. "Dad, do whatever it takes to stop Tess from seeing Judy." She thought back to the last few weeks. She had been working nonstop, too busy to realize what was happening with her cousin. Clearing her throat, she spoke through the phone with the kind of decisiveness she delivered during a closing argument: "Tess has been lying to me. I've caught her at it numerous times over the past few days. And I overheard her telling Sam Hart that she's not drinking caffeine in the hopes that her daily migraines will subside. She's never home anymore, often staying out all night, and while I haven't noticed any cuts on her body, I—"

"I understand everything you're telling me. We will get to the bottom of this. I love you." Her father's end of the line clicked in her ear.

Kate stuffed her keys and phone in her bag, and all but ran out of the office. She planned on skipping the Drunken Dog and heading home—to be there when Tess returned from dinner. She made her way toward the underground tunnel that connected the main courthouse to the annex building and the employee parking garage. The tunnel made it easy to transport prisoners to and from the courthouse buildings, but it was also an efficient way for the attorneys to travel between the two buildings without having to cross the busy highway.

Nightfall had already spread over the valley. Her eyes darted left and right as she eyed the shadows cast by the sconce lighting affixed to the stone-cut cruciform building. As she entered the tunnel, a blast of wind ripped through the passageway and stung her face. The single light that hung from the ceiling of the concrete tunnel flickered and then went black.

She heard a noise over the wind and instinctively turned her head back in the direction she'd just come.

She saw a figure standing in the middle of the entrance to the tunnel. The person seemed to be wearing a jacket, with a hood obscuring the face. She couldn't tell if it was a man or a woman, barely able to make out the person's shadow. How long had he or she been standing there? And why wasn't the person moving? She focused, waiting for her eyes to adjust to the darkness. She could see something hanging from the person's hand. It looked like a scarf or maybe a towel.

Kate turned back around and kept moving. She heard footsteps behind her and considered running. She thought about the four-inch heels she had on and if she'd have time to kick them off and sprint toward the annex building. More footsteps. Louder. Closer. She reached into her bag and fumbled around for her pepper spray. Closer. And then another figure stood blocking the exit ahead of her. She stopped, trapped.

"Hey!" the voice in front of her yelled.

She hesitated, not sure whom to spray first.

"Kate!" Sam's voice echoed.

She dashed toward his voice and was out of breath when she reached him.

"You're late and didn't answer your cell. I was worried."

She turned back to where she'd seen the figure hurrying toward her. No one was there. She took a few steps away from Sam and back into the tunnel. Not a soul. Was her mind playing tricks? She felt foolish and remembered her promise to herself about not allowing Sam to see her worked up. "The overhead light burned out. I was looking for my mini flashlight in my purse."

"You look like you've seen a ghost."

She wondered if seeing a ghost would be better than

thinking someone was possibly trying to kill her. She decided the Drunken Dog was a much better option than going home to a dark, empty house. Who knew when Tess would roll in anyway?

"I was going to stop by the Drunken Dog on my way home. A bunch of the ADAs are there for a late happy hour. Instead of taking me to my car, do you want to head to the pub?"

"A beer sounds good right about now," Sam replied.

As they walked to the parking garage together, she willed herself to break tradition and do something she hadn't done in years. She kept her head forward, her mind on the present, and refused to look back over her shoulder.

C HAPTER SEVENTEEN

THE PUB WAS PACKED with courthouse employees huddled around high-top tables, blowing off steam and cracking jokes. It felt good to be hitting up happy hours again and hanging out with colleagues. Kate had taken a hiatus from the scene while she was seeing Cameron. They had often retreated to her house or to a restaurant on the outskirts of town, one that wasn't frequented by county employees.

Feeling much better than she had in court this morning, she guffawed along with the rest of the crew when one of the guys did an impression of DA Bowers. Sam stood at the bar waiting for the bartender, who was more concerned with the good-looking waitress than getting him a drink. He had driven Kate over as part of their deal. His back was to her, his broad shoulders slightly rounded—one of his tattoos peeked out from his shirt-sleeve. She watched two women approach on either side of him. He turned, oblivious to the women, and caught her looking at him. He gave a smile and a nod of his head. She ambled over and squeezed her way in front of him.

"What's the hold-up here?" she asked Sam, leaning over the bar and giving the bartender a whistle. The bartender gave her the "one minute" sign with his finger. He finished placing a slew of cocktails and beer bottles on the waitress's serving tray and then made his way over.

"What can I get you, sweetie?" he asked.

"Two Miller Lite drafts and an order of nachos," Sam called over her shoulder, and then spoke close to her ear: "I bet if the bartender knew he was coming down here to wait on me and not you, he wouldn't have succumbed to your whistle." He cleared his throat. "Sweetie."

Kate cocked her head to the side and gave him a look that said she wasn't in the mood.

"Did you take lessons in how *not* to let loose or does it just come naturally to you?" he said.

"For your information, I'm very loose—"

Sam burst out laughing. It took Kate a second to realize what she'd said and then she couldn't help but laugh too. "I'd watch it or I'll leave you to fend off the blonde and brunette on your own."

"Who said I planned on fending them off?"

Kate rolled her eyes playfully.

"Why Kate Magda, I hope you're not . . . jealous."

"Oh, please!" she snorted as the bartender set down the two frothy pint glasses of beer. Kate reached for one, sidestepped Sam, and headed toward the jukebox, leaving him at the bar.

She scrolled through the music selections, sipping on her beer. She made her picks and paid the extra fee to have her songs skip the queue. "You Can't Always Get What You Want" began pumping through the speakers.

"Do you mean to tell me I brought a girl to a bar who drinks beer, knows how to finger whistle, and listens to the Rolling Stones?" Sam said over her shoulder with a laugh. "We'll be sleeping together in no time."

* * *

Kate wasn't sure if it was the alcohol or the memory of the older woman in the bar who had grabbed Sam's butt while everyone sang and danced to the Stones song, but as she and Sam drove home, she got a case of the giggles.

"You should have seen the look on your face!"

"Real funny! You weren't the one violated by a woman who looks like my grandmother!"

It was hard to believe that just this morning he had been driving her home from the morgue. She had just been sick, her mind scattered in a million directions. She remembered how he'd taken hold of her hands and how she'd pulled away from him. Now, less than twenty-four hours later, he was making the trip to her house for the second time, still obligatory, and under the direction of her father. As they traveled the dirt road that led to her driveway, she realized it had been weeks since she'd felt so uninhibited and unafraid.

"Why don't you come in for a little bit? Maybe have one more drink?" The words were out of her mouth before she realized what she was suggesting.

"No more drinks for me tonight," he replied. "C'mon, I'll walk you inside."

"The alarm," she said as she opened the front door and heard the familiar beeps. She went over to the keypad and punched in the code, disarming the house. "Tess must be out." She knew her father was no longer dining with her cousin at this hour, which meant the conversation probably hadn't gone as planned, resulting in Tess spending yet another night out partying.

As she began to unbutton her coat, she felt Sam's fingers covering hers and undoing the buttons for her. Kate's hands dropped down to her sides as he slid the coat off her shoulders. "Are you sure I can't get you anything? A coffee for the ride home?"

"I'm not thirsty," he said, moving in toward her.

She took a step backward, her body pressed up against the door, and then his body was pressed up against her. Her heart beat faster in her chest, hammering on her ribs as he brought his mouth down onto hers.

"I'm sorry. This is a bad idea. I think—"

"Do me a favor, Kate. For once, don't think."

Sam should have been exhausted, but as he lay in Kate's bed, he couldn't sleep. He could tick off fifteen reasons why being in bed next to her again was a horrible idea. One of the top five being her father. What the hell would he tell the president judge? That not only did he ensure his daughter got home safely, but he stayed the night too? He tried counting to one hundred, tried clearing his mind in an effort to fall asleep, but nothing was working. He had questioned Kate earlier in the night about driving down Chestnut Street at three a.m. and found out Tess had borrowed her car that night. Kate had no idea where her cousin had been. When he asked her if Tess often borrowed her car, she'd told him only on rare occasions, or if Tess's car was in the shop, which it hadn't been. Now the question was what Tess was doing driving past the courthouse twice, in Kate's car, at the same time the intern's body had been staged on the courthouse steps.

He slid out of the bed, careful not to wake Kate, and slipped on his jeans. In the past, their flings had never resulted in Kate actually spending the night at his apartment. What he wanted to do was take off, head home, and not deal with the awkwardness the morning was sure to bring. But if he left, there was a good possibility he'd risk making the situation even more awkward. With the two still working together, he wasn't sure which would be worse. This felt different than their past encounters. He padded downstairs to the kitchen for a glass of water, passing his and Kate's strewn clothing along the way.

He gulped the water down, then refilled his glass from the tap and drank again. Leaning against the counter, he noticed a jacket crumpled in a ball on the granite countertop. Next to the jacket was a large drawstring purse turned on its side, some of its contents spilling out onto the counter. *Tess must have come home,* he thought.

He knew he should just finish his glass of water and head back to Kate's bedroom. But the detective in him knew that wasn't going to happen. While he didn't peg Tess to be a crazed killer, he certainly had his doubts about her.

He moved so that he could more easily view the spilled items—a set of keys, a cell phone, a tube of lipstick, a pack of gum—and then he began to sift through the purse. He removed an unclasped wallet, opening it and revealing a single credit card, a few dollar bills, and a driver's license that read, *Tess Patricia Conway.* Now that he had confirmation of whose purse he was rummaging through, he should've stopped, walked out of the kitchen, and ended his unlawful search. He could question Tess in the morning on her whereabouts the night the intern was found dead, when he wasn't half-naked, having just left Kate's bed. Instead, he placed Tess's wallet on the counter and continued digging through her bag.

He found an empty box of hair dye, two condoms, another lipstick, a small memo notebook, and a bunch of uncapped pens, their ink staining the bag's silk lining.

He thumbed through the notebook. Each page was dated at the top, with words following underneath. The words didn't make sense to him. They weren't in sentence form, more like a bulleted list without the bullets. He flipped through the book until he saw *01.30*—the night Red #3 was found. The words *migraine, black,* and *Audi* were inked on the page. He figured that *Audi* referred to Kate's SUV, which he now knew Tess had borrowed that night. Could *black* refer to the spray-painted cameras?

He dug around the bottom of the purse, unsure what he was looking for but not yet ready to quit. He picked up a few loose receipts. One from the dry cleaners, another from an ATM transaction, and another from a drugstore. He studied the receipt from the drugstore dated January 30, wondering if the prescriptions would be on it. Instead, the receipt listed a purchase of L'Oreal hair dye at $9.99.

The hair dye. He grabbed the empty box of dye from the counter and looked for a price tag. *$9.99.* He studied the box, noting that the dye color was Medium Red and the model's hair on the front was a much darker shade of red than Tess's own hair color. The model's hair color more accurately resembled the intern's dyed hair. He read the back of the box. *Lasts 28 shampoos.* As he picked up the receipt again, he felt two hands slip around his waist, jolting him from his thoughts.

"My my, you're jumpy! Shouldn't I be the one frightened that there's a detective going through my purse?"

The color drained from his face as he turned around to face Tess. He discreetly stuffed the drugstore receipt into his back pocket and removed her hands from his waist.

"I needed some water." He pointed toward the empty glass on the counter next to Tess's things. "I accidentally spilled it and didn't want to get your stuff wet. I'm sorry," he said sheepishly. He noted her hair was still the same reddish-blond it had been this morning.

"I doubt you spilled anything, but I can play along if you'd like." She winked. "By the way, you look even better half-naked than I imagined." She traced her finger down his chest toward his belly button. "Looks like Kate's traded up from her days with Cameron."

"That's enough, Tess," he said, moving past her and out of the kitchen. He jogged up the stairs, this time collecting the clothes that had created a trail to Kate's bedroom.

So it was true: she'd had an affair with the very married Cameron Cox. Jealousy ripped at his belly, followed by disappointment. What had Kate been thinking, getting involved with him? Sam couldn't help but think of his ex-wife Kristen and the affair she'd had with his then-married best friend and partner, Detective David Stark.

Kate stirred, opening her eyes. "Everything okay?" she asked, sitting up when she realized he was getting dressed. "Was there another murder?"

"There wasn't another murder."

"Oh." She paused. "I see."

He started to walk out the door but turned back around and faced her. "This whole time I really thought the rumors were just that. I didn't figure you for the type of woman that sleeps with married men."

"What?" Confusion spread over Kate's face.

"Cameron Cox." Even without a raised voice he knew

he sounded like a jealous boyfriend, but he couldn't help himself.

She sat on the edge of the bed. Her face flushed, confusion now mixed with embarrassment. She steadied her voice. "Cameron was a mistake. He told me that he and his wife were separated, divorce papers already filed. I was blindsided when I found out he'd lied to me, stringing me along for months while he had no intention of divorcing her. But you're right. No matter what my impression was of his situation, I was sleeping with a married man." She turned away from the door, ready for him to walk out on her.

"I was out of line," he said after a long moment of silence. "Your past is none of my business. I'm sorry. I think we both know this is, and always has been, a bad idea, but we can't change what's happened. I'm going to head home. Call me in the morning if you need a ride to work and I'll swing by."

She shifted her weight underneath the covers. Despite what they'd admitted to one another, Kate didn't want him to leave. She knew she was being selfish but for just one night she wanted normalcy, and if that meant Sam Hart in bed next to her, she wasn't too ashamed to admit it. Her eyes roamed over his body, his clothes still balled up in his hand. "A very bad idea," she said as she reached up, the covers falling around her waist, and pulled him down toward her.

C HAPTER EIGHTEEN

KATE'S FINGERS FUMBLED TO SHUT OFF the ringing alarm clock. She propped herself up on her elbows, feeling refreshed for the first time in weeks.

"What time is it?" Sam asked, his voice thick with sleep.

"Five," she said, throwing the covers off to the side.

"In the morning?" He tugged at her, forcing her to lie back down. "We don't have to be at work for three and a half hours."

"I like to walk Bundy, make coffee, review my files, shower for work . . ." *Alone,* she thought, but didn't say out loud since it was her actions last night that had him still in her bed this morning. As she continued ticking off the items on her to-do list, Sam covered his ears with a pillow.

She succumbed to his distress, lying back down, knowing full well she wouldn't fall back asleep. She waited until she heard his breathing slow before creeping out of bed and heading to her desk.

She sat down, rubbing the sleep from her eyes, and opened the Mission County Killer case file.

Sam and Kate strolled along the park's pathway in an uncomfortable silence while Bundy plowed through the wet snow with his nose, creating mini snowballs on which he'd then chomp down.

Earlier this morning, while Sam slept, she had discovered another chilling connection in the Reds case. A clue she hadn't picked up on before. In most of the pictures taken by forensics at the second crime scene, the victim's body had been slumped against a gravestone, blocking the name and date engraved there. Only one picture had been taken of the headstone without the body covering it. The dates read, *October 1985–June 2010*. October 1985 was the month Kate had been snatched from her bed in the middle of the night by Ron Wells. Any doubt in her mind that she was somehow connected to the Reds case had now been erased. She knew it was time to tell Sam exactly what was going on. She also knew that after Sam heard her story, she'd most likely be taken off the case.

Kate cleared her throat. "I need to talk to you about something."

"Uh-oh. Are we having the postsex talk already? Can we save that for *after* breakfast?"

Kate cringed. "No, it's about the case." She reminded herself to keep the conversation professional regarding Ron Wells and the Mission County Killer. "You've worked with me for four years. I'd like to think I'm clearheaded and rational when it comes to a case. And I'm not easily rattled. Until now." *Here goes nothing,* she thought. "I reviewed the case file again this morning while you were sleeping and I'm certain whoever is killing these women and staging their bodies all over Mission County is not a serial killer. I think it's someone linked to something that happened to us—Tess and me—almost twenty-five years ago. The killer is plotting a carefully laid-out plan of revenge." She willed herself to look over at him, telling herself that if he laughed or even had as much as a smile on his face, she'd shut her mouth and say nothing further. But what she saw was concern and confusion.

"What in the Reds case links you and Tess to the killer?" he asked.

"My father's family is from Hettrich County, New York. I lived there until I was five years old. Tess and her mom Judy, my father's sister, lived ten minutes from our house." She took a breath, allowing the cold air to fill her lungs. "Judy's an addict. In and out of rehab her whole life. I don't communicate with her, and until yesterday I was under the impression Tess didn't either. Judy's all bad. My parents were completely oblivious to her drug habit, and they let me play at Tess's house and even sleep over on occasion. They thought she was a nonthreatening wild child and nothing more." She shook her head. "So, I slept over at Tess's house for her fifth birthday. October 26, 1985." She paused and looked at Sam to see if he realized the significance of the date, but she couldn't read his blank stare.

"Judy passed out on the couch before the birthday candles were even lit, leaving Tess without so much as a happy birthday serenade. Tess bawled, shouting her mother's name between sobs and trying to wake her from her drug slumber.

"Where was Tess's father?"

"Her biological father was already out of the picture. I don't know much about him. Probably married Judy before he realized she was a train wreck. They were divorced within a few months of Tess's birth. I once overheard my father say it was a shame her father hadn't taken her with him when he left."

"So, the birthday sleepover consisted of you and Tess, alone in a house with Tess's doped-up mother?"

"Tess's stepfather was there too. He tried cheering Tess up, singing happy birthday to her and letting her smush her face in the cake. She had cake everywhere—in her hair, up her nose, covering her eyelashes. And then her stepfather, Ron, began chasing her around the house, mounds of cake in his hands.

"He took Tess into the bathroom to wash the cake off her. I stayed on the couch, stuffing my face with more pizza. He was singing in the bathroom, a funny song about a boy who ate soapsuds. But then it got quiet. And I got bored. So, I went into the bathroom, without knocking, without announcing myself, and I saw something I wasn't meant to see. Ron was in the bathtub with Tess. He wasn't wearing any clothes."

"Jesus Christ," said Sam.

"He was always playing games with us, allowing us to dress him up, put Judy's makeup on his face, paint his nails. Everything about him screamed *fun,* but for as fun as he seemed, I always thought he was just as creepy. Seeing him in the bathroom with Tess confirmed my suspicions. His mouth was pushed against hers, kissing her with his eyes closed. And his hand was rubbing her privates."

Sam stopped walking and held Kate tight in his arms. "What a horrible experience. For you. For Tess."

Kate didn't answer him, gently shrugging herself out from under his arms, afraid that if her emotions took over her body, she'd lose it, and there was still so much story to get through. She kept walking. "I went to bed never questioning Ron or talking to Tess about what I'd seen.

I woke in the middle of the night to Ron's hand covering my mouth and the blade of a knife inches from my face." She could still recall the anger in his eyes. The hatred he'd developed for her in just a few hours. "He hauled me out of the bed and I can still remember how his shaved arms, nothing more than day-old stubble, pricked at my skin." She absently rubbed her hands along the arms of her coat. "I didn't fight him as he carried me to his car and threw me onto the backseat, next to Tess."

"Tess was in the car?"

Kate nodded. "She was sitting there like everything was normal. I, on the other hand, was hysterical. I had no idea where he was taking us, but even at five, I knew he was going to kill us."

"He took you to a cemetery," Sam guessed, his voice low.

"He sure did. When we got there he yanked me out of the car. Tess got out on her own."

"Why was Tess so compliant?"

"I think she was in shock. He ordered us to start walking. I didn't dare turn around but I heard him open and close the trunk. Eventually we came upon an open grave. To this day, I don't know if he knew ahead of time that the grave had been dug or if he just got lucky. He told us to climb down into the hole. Tess did what he said, but I was frozen with fear. When I wouldn't, he pushed me, and I fell forward into the hole. At first I tried to escape—clawing at the grave's walls—but I couldn't compete with the shovels of dirt."

"What was Tess doing?"

"She was catatonic, totally unresponsive. The dirt from Ron's shoveling climbed up past our necks. It got in my mouth, up my nose, and burned my eyes. I was suffocating and at some point I blacked out."

"Shit," Sam murmured. "How did you manage to survive? And Tess?"

Kate wrung her hands, her breathing shallow as if she was back in the grave, smothered by dirt. "The houses in Tess's neighborhood were practically built on top of one another. That night Tess's bedroom window shade had been left open and the nosy next-door neighbor happened to be looking out his own window. He watched Ron carry me out of the room, knife in hand."

"Did he follow Ron?"

"He did. But first he phoned the police. When he rushed outside to wait for the cops, he saw Ron pushing his car down the street in neutral and decided to follow him."

"Thank God he had the intuition to trail the car to the cemetery."

"I know. No one had cell phones back then, so the cops showed up at Judy's house with no idea what was going on or where we were headed."

"But the neighbor knew."

"Yes. Two things happened that night that Ron never anticipated. First, Officer Dunleavy. Dunleavy was the cop who stayed at Tess's house while his partner took the squad car to search for us after it was confirmed that we weren't there. Without a squad car out front to alert Ron, he came home from the cemetery never thinking the cops were on to him, let alone inside the house."

"Ron walked into a trap," Sam said.

"Dunleavy was at Ron's side as he stepped out of the car. Dunleavy questioned him about where he'd been, but Ron refused to answer. He asked Ron whether Tess or I had been with him and that's when Ron took off, sprinting down the street. Dunleavy tackled him, frisked him, and found a knife strapped around his calf, corroborating what the neighbor had told the intake officer. The cops later found the shovel, still covered in fresh dirt, in the back of Ron's car.

"The second thing Ron never anticipated was that we'd survive. The nosy neighbor watched us walking through the cemetery until we were out of sight. When he saw Ron come back with the shovel, but no little girls, he began searching for us." She tugged on Bundy's leash, knowing the dog was tired of walking. "He later told my family that he figured he was looking for two corpses, never imagining Ron had buried us alive. I don't know how much time passed between Ron leaving Tess and me for dead and the neighbor finding us, but obviously he found us in time."

Sam took hold of Kate's hand.

"There's more." She stopped walking and faced Sam. The dog happily plunked himself down on the cold sidewalk, panting. "Ron refused to plead guilty and demanded a trial."

"On what grounds? He was caught red-handed." Sam's eyes flared with anger.

"When has that ever stopped a guilty defendant? The problem was that the prosecution wanted Tess to testify at trial, but she was unable to remember anything—her mind created a black hole around her fifth birthday. On top of that, a few weeks before the trial, she stopped speaking. With Tess incompetent to testify, I was the government's only other witness. After being interviewed by the prosecution and a counselor, I was found competent to testify."

"Kate Magda. Born tough."

She smiled at Sam's attempt to lighten the mood. "Are you kidding? I was scared to death."

"What about the nosy neighbor? He could've testified."

"He did testify. But I was the only one who knew what had actually happened beginning to end. I was six years old by the time the trial began. I took the stand and told the jury everything. They found Ron guilty on all charges and the trial judge sentenced him to thirty years in prison. He comes up for parole next year."

"I understand the connection you're seeing, but how does this actually link you to the case? Tell me what makes it more than a bad coincidence, one that's forcing you to relive a horrific event?"

"The red hair," she said, pointing to her own hair, which was now more blond than red. "My hair was more red growing up. And the shaved bodies. Ron hated body hair. I don't recall ever seeing a hair on him, except the hair on his head. He used to make Judy shave too." Kate looked up into Sam's eyes. He didn't seem convinced and she began to panic, talking more rapidly.

"This morning I reviewed the case file. I looked through the pictures of the second crime scene. The gravestone marker, the one the body had been propped up against, had the dates October 1985 to June 2010 engraved on it. October 1985, the same month and year we were taken by Ron and left for dead. Winter-Dawn was not only assigned to me for a four-week rotation, but she was also found outside the employee entrance. I'm always at the courthouse working late, often pulling all-nighters. Especially on Sundays. Check the logs. The last four Sundays, I was at the courthouse during the time frame in which the killer left the body. I think the killer knew that and wanted *me* to find the body, not DA Bowers. I'm also positive someone was following me in the tunnel last night when I was on my way to meet you in the employee parking garage. And, of course, the initials. The initials—"

"This Ron guy, Tess's stepfather, what's his last name?"

"Well, that's just it. That's what I'm trying to explain to you. When I saw the initials, I thought for sure he was killing these women. But I looked up his inmate status on the database yesterday and he's still in custody. Unless he has someone acting for him?"

"Give me a name, Kate."

"There wasn't a middle name or even a middle initial listed on the database. But somehow he's doing this." Her bottom lip quivered and she lowered her eyes to the snow-covered grass. Her initial bravery in retelling her story had dissipated now that her secret was out in the open.

"Kate, please. Give me his name. Give me something to go on here."

She looked up, but stared past Sam into the distance of the gray sky and bare tree limbs surrounding the park. Tears streamed down her cheeks and she didn't bother brushing them away. "Do you believe me?" she asked him, her voice barely audible. "It has to be him, right?"

"I believe you," Sam said. "Now tell me Ron's last name." He held her tightly in his arms and she allowed herself a moment. "A name," he whispered into her hair.

"Ronald Wells."

CHAPTER NINETEEN

SAM'S PHONE RANG AS THEY APPROACHED the parking lot near the park's entrance, Bundy pausing to take a rest every few feet. Kate's face was still red and puffy as she tried to drag the tired dog toward the car.

"What do you have for me?" Sam asked Detective Stevens on the other end of the line.

"Ronald Wells, sentenced to prison in '85 in Upstate New York. Child molestation and attempted murder, among other lesser charges."

"Yes, that's him. Is he still in jail? Did you speak to the warden directly?"

"I spoke to the warden directly. Ron Wells is no longer in prison."

"You've got to be shitting me." He mouthed *Not in jail* to Kate, who gripped Bundy's leash tighter, her knuckles turning white.

"I want a full search. I want every officer and detective out looking for this guy. Call the New York police and alert them to the situation. I'm sure they're already looking for him, but let them know about what's going on in Mission County. We can also assume he's crossed state lines since he escaped from a New York prison. Contact the feds. Let them take over the case, they have more manpower, better resources. Anything to find this guy."

"That's not going to be necessary," said Detective Stevens.

"Excuse me?"

"Searching for Ronald Wells won't be necessary. The warden tells me that Wells died two weeks ago while in jail. Heart attack. No foul play, although the state ordered an autopsy to be performed by the local coroner. I'm sure just to cover their asses. Wells isn't our killer, boss."

"Just for the hell of it, were you able to find out his middle name?"

"He was born Ronald Wells. No middle name."

"Let me call you back," Sam said, then ended the call and turned to Kate. "Ronald Wells is no longer in prison because he's dead."

"Dead?"

"Yes. Are you all right?"

She didn't speak for a moment, opening the car door to let the dog into the backseat. "You'd think I'd feel relieved, even happy. But I'm not. I feel . . . disappointed."

They got in the car and Sam turned over the engine. "Because you believed he was the Reds killer?"

"I think I wanted him to be the Reds killer to confirm I hadn't lost my mind, to stop the killings, and to make me feel safe again. Now we have to search for someone connected to Ron, someone acting for him or maybe acting in his honor. I think you should look back into Nick Granteed. I told you about his shaved arms and chest. You said he was on the list of people who had driven past the courthouse the night the third victim was found on the building's steps, right?"

Sam felt disappointed too. Moments ago, as the adrenaline had pumped through his body, he thought they had caught a break. A big break. Especially after Kate had told him Ron's last name.

"You still believe this is about you and Tess? That it's not a serial killer?"

"I'm 100 percent certain. There are too many coincidences for it *not* to be about Tess and me." She looked over at Sam while placing her hands in front of the car's heat vents. "Aren't you?"

He didn't know what to think. One minute he was on board with her and the next he believed Mission County was still dealing with a serial killer. But he knew if he voiced an opinion that was anything other than confidence in her theory, his doubt would hurt her. And she'd been through enough. This case had completely thrown her off balance. Her behavior over the past week now made perfect sense. Sam's phone rang again before he could answer her.

"Detective Hart," he said into the phone.

"Hello, detective. This is the Allegheny County forensics lab calling. We have the results from the animal hair sample you supplied us with last week."

Sam glanced at the digital clock on the dashboard. It was just shy of seven o'clock. "You guys start your day early."

"We're a twenty-four-hour lab and we knew you needed the results ASAP. There was a partial root bulb on the strand of hair you gave us. The hair is confirmed to be dog hair. We were able to detect the sex and general breed of dog."

Maybe he'd catch a break yet. He threw the car into

drive. They weren't in a huge rush to get home, but he felt an urge to race to her house. He looked over at her and whispered, "I'm sorry," as he gestured to the phone pressed against his ear.

The lab technician continued, "The partial root bulb on the hair was that of a mastiff. A male mastiff."

Sam glanced back at Bundy lying on his side and snoring.

"We'll be sending you the official report via overnight mail, but we wanted to personally call you with the results."

"What was that about?" asked Kate when he set the phone down.

Sam hesitated. He knew she would make the connection to Bundy, and maybe right now, given her current frame of mind, that wasn't such a good idea.

"Another case I'm working on," he lied. "A drug-related homicide." Like a drunk driver, Sam swerved his car in and out of the painted lines, maneuvering around the potholes that dotted the streets. "I'm not sure about your suspicions regarding Nick Granteed, but I'll look into it. I'm willing to look into anything if it means finding and jailing the killer."

After that last phone call, Sam was back on board with Kate's theory. And Nick Granteed had nothing to do with it. "Did Tess end up remembering what happened to you two?" he asked.

"She tried like hell. The theory was that if she could recall it, she could properly deal with the intense emotions associated with it. She'd often ask me questions about that night or she'd ask me to walk her through what I knew. The problem was that as time went on, she wasn't sure if she was imagining my narrative of that night or if she was recalling the events on her own. Her frustration grew and she asked me to stop talking to her about it. It's still a touchy subject."

As they pulled up to the house, Sam said, "You head in with Bundy. I need to make a quick phone call. Then I plan on taking over your kitchen and cooking you breakfast."

He stayed silent when she mumbled something about not being hungry, recognizing her subtle hint for him to go home but knowing he couldn't. He waited until Kate was inside the house with the door closed before dialing Dr. Friar's cell.

"John, it's Sam Hart. I need you to do me a favor. Any chance you're at the morgue right now?"

"No, but I can be there in about ten minutes."

"Can you pull our latest Reds victim from the cold chamber? I need you to wash her hair. Use any type of shampoo. Doesn't matter."

"What am I looking for?"

"We know for certain that the victim's hair was dyed a permanent blond, not red, prior to the killer dying it again. I'm looking to see if the red hair dye was permanent or temporary."

"I'm on it. I'll plug the sink to catch the change in water color, if any. I'll be in touch."

Sam hung up and dialed Detective Stevens. "Stevens, can you get me Ronald Wells's date of death?"

After a few seconds, Detective Stevens said, "January 12."

Sam stepped out of the car. January 12 was the day the first murder had occurred. For once, Sam hoped his instincts were off.

CHAPTER TWENTY

THE BACON SIZZLED, GREASE POPPING OUT of the fry pan and onto the cooktop. Sam diced potatoes, throwing them into a bowl, then added all of the other ingredients for his famous home fries.

The girls sat at the kitchen island, Kate sipping her third cup of coffee from the fresh pot Sam had made, trying to make small talk with Tess while she flipped through a magazine.

"How was dinner with my father last night?" Kate asked.

"Fine."

"What did you guys order?"

"Food."

"Did you end up going out with the yoga girls after dinner?"

Tess looked up from her magazine and stared directly at Sam while she answered, "Something like that."

Sam could feel the tension from his encounter last night with Tess. He broke from her stare, concentrating on breakfast and Kate, who, despite having showered and dressed in her work clothes, looked tired. She had dark circles around her eyes.

He put the girls' eggs, home fries, and bacon on

their plates and handed them across the island.

"Aren't you going to eat anything?" Kate asked.

"I'm not hungry." True, since every time he looked at the dog he lost his appetite.

He wondered why Tess had kept the empty box of hair dye rather than throwing it away, especially if she was guilty. Then again, if Tess had something to do with the Mission County killings, he wasn't dealing with a rational person. Maybe she was keeping it as a memento or souvenir. His phone vibrated, wrestling him away from his thoughts. He glanced down at the text from Friar: *Staring at a sink full of pinkish-brown water.*

Sam closed his eyes, the moral dilemma rushing at him like a linebacker. He needed probable cause to arrest Tess. The problem was, he didn't technically have probable cause because he had gone through her purse last night, finding the empty box of hair dye, without her permission and without a search warrant. He now needed to falsify an affidavit, stating that the contents of Tess's purse had been in plain view. He'd have to say he bumped into Tess on his way into the kitchen, causing the purse she'd been carrying to fall off her shoulder, its contents spilling out onto the floor. He *had* encountered Tess, that much was true. He and Tess had even conversed. It was just the timing that was off. His version of how things went down last night would be corroborated by the fact that he'd walked back to Kate's room and confronted her about her relationship with Cameron. How else would he have known, had he not run into Tess?

He was unsettled at how quickly he'd convinced himself to become a dirty cop. He'd never before lied about anything while in the line of duty. Now he was about to arrest Tess on a lie in order to throw her in jail. But there was no way in hell he'd let her continue carrying out whatever sick and twisted plan she had formulated. It wasn't like he was falsifying evidence—or worse, planting it.

Take a sample of the water before unplugging the sink. I'll be in touch, he texted.

"Everything okay?" Kate asked.

"No, it's not," he replied, then approached Tess and said, "I'm sorry."

"Sorry?" Kate wore a puzzled expression, her eyebrows knit.

Sam took hold of Tess by the arm. "Tess Conway, you are being placed under arrest for the murder of Winter-Dawn Harris. You have the right to remain silent—"

Kate lunged out of her seat and grabbed hold of Sam, trying to remove his hand from Tess's arm. "For chrissake, what in the hell are you doing?" she shouted at him.

"Kate, it's okay," said Tess, seemingly unruffled as she stepped away from the counter stool, allowing Sam to lead her toward the front door.

"Anything you say can and will be used against you in a court of law. You have the right to an attorney and have him or her present with you while you are being questioned."

"Kate, don't. Just let me go. I need to go."

"Have you lost your mind?" Kate was still shouting, but this time at Tess, for having spoken while being placed under arrest. "Don't say another word! Not one word. Do you hear me?" She marched behind Tess and Sam. "I'm following you down to the station. Tess, I'll be right behind you. Shit! I don't have my car. Where are your keys?"

Sam continued reading Tess her rights as if Kate weren't there: "If you cannot afford to hire a lawyer, one will be appointed to represent you before any questioning if you wish—"

"Tess, your keys!"

"Upstairs, in my room." Tess's voice was quiet, subdued.

Sam opened the car door, his hand on the top of Tess's head as he ushered her into the backseat. "You can decide at any time to exercise your rights and not answer any questions or make any statements. Do you understand each of these rights as I have explained them?"

Kate shoved her body between Sam and the open car door. Her face was only inches away from Tess's. She steadied her voice, speaking sternly: "I know you didn't do this. Promise me right now you won't say one word until you have an attorney present." Tess said nothing and Kate lost it again, yelling, "Promise me!"

Sam gently moved Kate so that he could close the car door and then he walked around to the driver's side, phone in hand, calling Tess's arrest in to his chief.

Kate pulled at his shirt, causing him to spin around. She poked him in the chest with her finger, hard. "How could you?"

"Do you think I would be doing this if I didn't have the evidence to back it up?" He reached into his back pocket and took out the receipt he'd found in Tess's purse. The one that showed the purchase of the hair dye, bought on the same day Winter-Dawn was found dead with a bad dye job. "Here, this belongs to Tess. Look at the date. In her purse you'll find an empty box of Medium Red L'Oreal temporary hair dye, matching the color and item number listed on the receipt." He knew he didn't need to tell her that both items would be marked and bagged as evidence. "Winter-Dawn's hair was dyed with a temporary color. Think about the other coincidences you brought to my attention this morning. Ron Wells is dead, Kate. Not many people know your story. Not many people know he left you and Tess for dead in an open grave in October of 1985. But your cousin knows all of it."

Tess was staring at them through the car window, a strange smile spread across her face.

C HAPTER TWENTY-ONE

KATE RACED TO TESS'S BEDROOM, planning to grab her cousin's car keys and haul ass to the police station. The odd smile on Tess's face flashed in Kate's mind, reminding her with a chill of the way Tess had acted that dreadful night so many years ago.

Kate felt herself being pulled toward the four-poster bed, as if it were willing her to explore the contents of Tess's purse haphazardly strewn across it. She knew it was only a matter of time before the police showed up at her house with a search warrant to seize Tess's personal belongings. And Tess would have to be booked and processed at the police station before she'd be allowed visitors. Kate abandoned the keys and sat on the edge of the mattress within arm's reach of the purse. Her mind reeled back and forth between Sam and Tess.

Sam was a good cop. He played by the books. Yet Kate couldn't shake the feeling that he'd used her to get to Tess. She spread the contents of the purse out on the bed and picked up the empty box of hair dye. The model's hair pictured on the front of the box without a doubt resembled Winter-Dawn's hair color.

Kate picked up the memo notebook, the one Tess used as a calendar, and flipped through its pages. She saw dates at the top of each page followed by words remind-ing Tess of an appointment or date. For as long as she'd known Tess, this had been her way of keeping her life together.

She paged through the notebook until she reached the end of December, paying closer attention to what Tess had written in the previous four weeks.

Nothing jumped out at her until she reached the sec-ond week of January and Tess's word strings no longer made sense. Some of the entries read more like a journal log than a to-do list. And down at the bottom of each page were tiny inked slashes, varying in number, as if Tess had been counting something.

1.15. Dirt. Bed. Shovel. Car. Migraine. At the bottom of the page were two tiny slash marks. January 15 was the day Red #1 had been found dead in the cemetery.

She flipped to the date that police surmised the Mis-sion County Killer had taken the second victim. *Migraine. Migraine. Migraine. Migraine . . .* The single word was written over and over, filling up the entire sheet of paper. Three inked marks were slashed across the bottom of the page. Kate flipped forward three days to when the sec-ond victim was found slumped against a headstone in the county cemetery. *Phone. Unlocked. Car. Nauseous. Ron.* Two more inked slashes appeared at the bottom of the page. What about Ron? Had Tess known Ron was dead?

Kate felt the early stages of panic setting in as she read the remaining entries, her fingers unable to separate the lined paper fast enough.

01.30. Migraine. Black. Audi. Four more slashes at the bottom of the page. January 30 was the day Winter-Dawn was found murdered and naked on the courthouse steps.

Tess had never told Kate why she'd needed to borrow her car that night. Kate knew from Sam that her own license plate had shown up on the list of vehicles driven down Chestnut Street during the time frame that Harris's body was displayed on the courthouse steps. She replayed the chat she and Tess had had over dinner, the one about Kate's conversation at Cali's Coffeehouse with Winter-Dawn.

Kate turned the page and then the next, but the remaining sheets were blank. She wasn't sure if she was disappointed or relieved that there were no entries for yesterday or today.

She reached into her suit pocket and pulled out the receipt Sam had handed her. According to the little slip of paper, Tess had gone to a drugstore on the outskirts of town at one a.m. on the thirtieth of January. Just two hours before Bowers had found Winter-Dawn dead on the courthouse steps. Usually, Kate and Tess frequented the twenty-four-hour drugstore downtown—the most convenient. Kate continued to examine the receipt. Tess paid for the box of hair dye with cash. She almost never paid for anything with cash, rarely having more than a few dollars on her. And now, according to the receipt and the quick calculation Kate made, Tess had paid for the hair dye with a fifty-dollar bill. Had she used cash to avoid leaving a paper trail? Why keep the receipt?

Kate had already started to doubt Tess's word. But never had she imagined that lack of trust would have her questioning whether or not Tess had committed murder. And that was exactly where her mind was headed. No, it was exactly where her mind already was.

She placed the drugstore receipt on the nightstand while her eyes passed over the rest of the contents on the bed. She spotted two pill bottles. Just as she had told her father on the phone last night, all of the signs were there. *Just like last time,* Kate thought. She had suspected Tess was in a bad way, but actually seeing the pill bottles confirmed her suspicions. She should have confronted her cousin as soon as she'd felt the distance growing between them. She should have tried harder to keep the lines of communication open.

Kate picked up the prescription bottles, rolling them around in her palm and noting the labels had been ripped off. Misbranding. A misdemeanor criminal offense, she thought, out of habit.

She didn't need to open the pill bottles to know she'd find some sort of sleep aid inside. But she did anyway, removing one of the tablets. She stared at the tiny pill until it looked like a blur of blue in the palm of her hand.

Ron Wells was dead. Tess was at the police station. Judy was back in the picture. Tess was popping pills. And Kate had been feeling like shit lately. The anxiety, cold sweats, paranoia, inability to sleep more than an hour at a time. She wondered how her life had gone from calm and organized to a total shit-show in only a few weeks.

Kate's attention snapped back to the blue pill in her hand. About a year ago, Kate's doctor had prescribed her Ambien, but she hadn't been able to handle the medication, her body too sensitive to it. The sleep aid had the opposite of its intended effect on her, allowing her to sleep for a short period immediately after it was ingested, but then causing insomnia, anxiety, sweating and chills, and paranoia—the same symptoms she'd been experiencing over the past few weeks. Had Tess been drugging her? Drugging Kate and drugging herself?

She sprinted out of Tess's bedroom and down the hall toward her own room. She rushed to her desk and powered on her laptop, googling *Ambien.*

Headaches, daytime drowsiness, dizziness, hallucinations, anxiety, heart palpitations, nausea, amnesia. Rare side effects of Ambien CR include sleepwalking. Do not take with alcohol, as memory blackouts can occur.

The side effects read like a list of what Kate had been experiencing over the past few weeks; her nightmares involving Ron Wells probably heightened due to the drug. And how many times had she shared a glass of wine with Tess over dinner? Her head accused Tess of what her heart couldn't believe was true. She needed more proof.

Kate grabbed her briefcase off the desk, hurried back to Tess's room, and snatched the keys from the nightstand.

Once she was in Tess's car, she pulled out her cell phone. Five missed calls. All from her father's chambers. She listened to the voice mail, her father's voice filling her ear, his tone grave.

"Kate, Detective Hart has notified me of Tess's arrest. I'd like you to call me immediately so we can figure out the best way to handle this with the press. This is going to cause a huge uproar in the courthouse and on the political front. For both of us. Call me."

She merged onto the highway and turned on the car radio, switching through the channels until she found WKRU, the local talk station. The host was discussing the current state of the public schools in Mission County and taking calls from listeners. *Good,* thought Kate. Nothing was being reported on Tess. At least not yet.

Her father was right: it was only a matter of time before her family's name was all over the news, linked to the Mission County Killer. Hell, Kate's office would be prosecuting Tess. She'd be officially taken off the case and completely screened from any further dealings between police and the DA's office. Extreme precautions would be taken to ensure Kate had no further knowledge of the case and its details. Would they expect her to testify during the trial, if it went that far? But before she could worry about any of that she needed confirmation as to whether or not Tess had been drugging her, and then she needed to visit her cousin.

CHAPTER TWENTY-TWO

KATE USED HER KNEES TO STEER WHILE she located Keira Davis's number on her phone. Keira worked as a sexual assault nurse examiner, or SANE, at General Hospital. She was used by the district attorney's SVU team as an expert witness in sexual assault cases that went to trial. She and Keira had hit it off from the moment they'd met.

"Keira, hi. This is Kate Magda. I need a favor." She explained that she needed her blood drawn and a tox screen performed. Fast. Keira told her she could have the results within fifteen minutes.

Kate waited in the lab for her friend, tapping her foot on the floor so rapidly that even her shoulders vibrated. When Keira finally appeared—her long black ponytail swinging from side to side, her tall, slender body making the purple scrubs she wore seem fashionable—Kate nearly jumped up to kiss her.

Within moments Kate was slumped in the metal chair, her arm laid out on the armrest. She didn't feel the prick of the needle as Keira inserted it into her vein. And she was oblivious to the look of worry that washed over Keira's face. All Kate could think about were the results and what it would mean if her suspicions were confirmed.

"You said it would only take fifteen minutes to process?"

"If that," Keira replied. In one fluid motion she untied the rubber band around Kate's arm and applied pressure with a gauze strip. "When is the last time you ingested a controlled substance?"

"I think yesterday morning. In my coffee. But I can't be sure."

Keira's normally smooth coffee complexion exhibited deep creases in her forehead and around the eyes. "When I test your blood and run the tox screen, what exactly am I looking for? It will help me get the results back to you faster."

Kate thought for a moment. What if Tess was giving her more than just Ambien? "Test for all controlled substances."

"You got it." Keira took the tray with the vials of blood and strode down the hall, disappearing behind swinging double doors.

Kate's phone rang, the loud trill distinct from the noise of monitors and intercom pages in the lab. "Hello?"

"Kate, it's Sam."

"I have nothing to say to you—"

"Do not hang up. It's about Tess. She's had her preliminary arraignment hearing. She waived her right to a lawyer—"

"WHAT!"

"Let me finish. She waived her right to a lawyer and pleaded guilty for purposes of the arraignment."

"Tell me you're joking."

"She also confessed to killing the other two women."

Kate's knees buckled but she caught herself before she

hit the ground. *Oh, Tess. What have you done?*

Sam continued: "She's being transported to the Hill Street Prison as we speak. We plan on interviewing her once she's admitted. You need to get her a lawyer. Regardless of whether she wants one."

"I want a copy of your affidavit. In fact, scan it and e-mail it to me. I'd like to read it. Now." She sounded like a bitch and she didn't care. She couldn't believe how quickly he had filed his affidavit of probable cause, securing Tess a pre-arraignment hearing in front of the district judge.

"What are you going to do once you read the affidavit? I don't have to tell you that you're in a tough spot, being a member of the DA's office and a relative of the defendant."

"Her name is Tess. And no, you don't have to tell me."

"Tess was denied bail. I've tried to keep things as quiet as possible but the chief is holding a press conference at ten o'clock. I've already notified your father." He paused. "Today's going to be a long one—for all of us. How about I stop over tonight with takeout, check on you to make sure you're all right?"

Kate looked at her watch. Ten o'clock was only twenty minutes from now. She paced, her heels clicking as she moved back and forth across the checkerboard linoleum squares. There was so much she wanted to say to Sam, so many questions. But something told her not to ask them. He was no longer on her side. "Send me your affidavit. Don't even dream of conducting a single interview with Tess until she has a lawyer present. And Sam?"

"Yes?"

"I don't need you checking up on me. I don't *want*

you checking up on me. Don't contact me. Don't contact my father. You've done my family enough favors."

"Kate, you're not being fair," he said. "What did you want me to do? Ignore the evidence staring me in the face?"

She couldn't answer because she knew he had done exactly what she would've done had their roles been reversed. He'd done his job. And how could she fault him for that?

She looked up to see Keira striding out the double doors and toward the stations. She broke off her conversation with Sam, offering nothing more than the push of the *END* button on her phone.

Keira handed Kate the printout. "If you want me to go over the results with you, I can."

"Can you just tell me what, if anything, showed up in my system?"

"Sure. You tested positive for zolpidem, most likely known to you as Ambien. The amount in your system was on the high side, which is unusual because it has a relatively short half-life."

"What does that mean?"

"Meaning, the time it takes the drug to lose half of its pharmacologic activity and essentially leave your body is short. Usually only a few hours. So the fact that you have more than trace amounts of it in your blood means you either ingested the pill within the last two to three hours or you have a buildup in your system. A buildup is uncommon for a drug like Ambien because, one, it's highly addictive and your doctor would prescribe it so that you had no such buildup, and two, it's dangerous if taken in higher doses or more frequently than prescribed."

Kate wasn't sure if Keira was giving her a lesson or a warning.

"If you look here," Keira went on, pointing halfway down the page, "you'll see you tested positive for the benzodiazepine Xanax, along with Adderall."

None of which I've ingested knowingly, Kate thought, completely stupefied. What the hell was Tess trying to do to her? "Adderall is used to treat ADHD, right?"

"ADHD or narcolepsy."

"How would that react with the Ambien?" Kate asked.

"Well, it depends. Because the Adderrall can cause insomnia, the Ambien might counteract that, but you'd have to be careful and really monitor your intake. Especially if you add Xanax into the mix."

"Thanks, Keira." Kate wanted to add that they should finally get together for those drinks they were always talking about, but given this new information, she didn't think the suggestion of alcohol would go over too well.

Keira softly gripped Kate's shoulder before she had a chance to turn away. "Listen, Kate. If you're in trouble, or if you need help, I'm here."

"I *was* in trouble," she responded, careful not to say too much, "but I'm okay now." And that much, at least when it came to the drugs, was true. Tess was in jail, bail denied.

CHAPTER TWENTY-THREE

AS KATE WAS CLIMBING THE STAIRS of the Hill Street Prison, Chief Detective Kevin Joseph was making his way up the steps inside the courthouse's rotunda toward the podium. Microphones jutted out from the wooden box, eager to capture the words spoken by the chief detective. Sam stood off to the right of the podium with Bowers, the two of them whispering, heads bent toward each other.

Members of the press occupied the folding chairs set out in the domed, circular arena. They waited quietly, leaning forward in anticipation. The chief was a man known for few words and even fewer press conferences. This marked his second public address in a week.

Sam and the chief had agreed ahead of time that Kate and her father would be left out of the dialogue. The press and public could make their own connections to the Magda family. He wasn't sorry that he'd arrested Tess, but he was sorry he'd hurt Kate. She did everything in her power to disassociate herself professionally with her father and his political relations, only to end up more connected than ever.

Chief Joseph cleared his throat. "Ladies and gentlemen, thank you for being here. I'm going to keep this brief. It has been a long few weeks for our detectives, especially Detective Hart, who's been working around the clock to locate and arrest the Mission County Killer."

Sam cringed at the mention of his name.

"And I know it's been a long few weeks for you, the public, as well. We're aware the community has been on edge with the Mission County Killer walking the streets of our town freely, but that ended today. At approximately eight thirty this morning Detective Hart arrested and lodged the Mission County Killer—"

The crowd erupted and questions about the killer were hurled at the chief.

"Who was it?!"

"Can you give us a name?!"

"A name!"

"Have you identified the victim?"

Chief Joseph raised his hands, silencing the crowd. "Tess Patricia Conway, a resident of Mission County, has been arrested for the murder of Winter-Dawn Harris. Detective Hart, during his investigation, discovered evidence directly linking Ms. Conway to the third victim's murder. Ms. Conway was preliminarily arraigned an hour ago and she pleaded guilty in front of District Judge McManus. While Ms. Conway was being arraigned, she openly confessed to being responsible for the first two victims' deaths."

Again, voices exploded. Sam lowered his head, hands in his pockets, while the questions reverberated off the hundred foot–high domed ceiling. He felt the hair on his arms stand up as they shouted his name, congratulating him.

This time, Chief Joseph didn't have to worry about silencing the crowd because as Cameron Cox strolled across the rotunda floor toward the podium, brushing the chief aside, the room quieted. Not one person spoke. Not even the chief.

"Excuse me, Kevin," Cameron said as he stepped into the chief's spot in the center of the podium. He wore a crisp oxford shirt tucked into slim-fitting jeans, under-dressed compared to the designer suits he usually wore around the courthouse. He took his time adjusting a few of the microphones. "I'm sorry, folks. I just want to be sure everyone can hear what I'm about to say . . . I've become aware of several courses of action taken by our county employees throughout the Mission County Killer investigation. I would be remiss not to share my findings with you."

"What the fuck is Cox doing up there?" Sam mumbled to Bowers. Why wasn't the chief telling Cameron to get lost? Instead, he'd stepped aside, allowing the public defender to command the microphones.

"Ladies and gentlemen, I'm afraid Chief Joseph left out a few key points from his announcement. You should know the Mission County Killer, Tess Patricia Conway, is the niece of President Judge Tommy Magda and the cousin and housemate of ADA Kate Magda. I guess the chief didn't find the information worthy of sharing?" Sarcasm hung at the end of Cameron's sentence.

Sam was willing to give the chief about half a second longer to put a stop to this before he would handle Cameron himself.

"Something else worth mentioning," the public defender continued, "would be how elected official DA Bowers personally assigned ADA Magda to the case just four days ago. Perhaps she was assigned when Detective Hart became suspicious of the ADA's cousin? Or better yet, when the ADA herself became aware that the heinous monster murdering innocent people was none other than her relative? Think about it, folks. Do you really believe that ADA Magda, whose attention to detail and skill in reading people has helped solidify her flawless trial record, could live under the same roof as her cousin without suspecting her as the killer?

"How long did Detective Hart, DA Bowers, and ADA Magda know Tess Conway was the murderer? Perhaps Detective Hart and ADA Magda carefully planned out when Hart would arrest Ms. Conway and on what charges, allowing Ms. Conway to walk free on a technicality, one worked out ahead of time between Hart and Magda. Or maybe just the fact that Detective Hart and ADA Magda are sleeping together is enough to cause a circus during the trial—"

Sam rushed the podium, fists clenched, the veins in his neck bulging. The chief grabbed hold of Sam, stopping him in his tracks. "Think about what you're doing," he whispered harshly. "Do you really want to be on the news for beating the shit out of that piece of scum? Do you want a lawsuit on your hands?"

"Why the hell is he up there? Why are you letting him speak?" Sam asked quietly through clenched teeth, then shoved past the chief.

Cameron grabbed the mic connected to the courthouse's sound system, unlatching it from the stand, and walked briskly off the makeshift stage to where his wife stood in the back of the room.

The press swung their bodies around in their chairs to face Cameron even though his voice boomed throughout the courthouse.

"When the Mission County Killer's identity came to light, the DA's office and detectives did everything they could to cover it up, to buy the family some time. Until it became inevitable that an arrest had to be made. And even then, they only arrested Ms. Conway for the murder of Winter-Dawn Harris, leaving the other two victims' families without closure and peace. Remember, it was Conway herself who admitted to committing the other two murders. No thanks to our law enforcement. I'm not willing to live my life in danger, my family's life," he gestured to his wife, making sure to showcase her pregnant belly, "all because Tess Conway happens to be politically connected. The corruption within these four walls is despicable.

"And I think it's fair to say that while today is a triumphant day, with Tess Conway behind bars, it is also a sad day because we were willing to allow leniency and special favors at the cost of our citizenry. And this is just the beginning." He turned to face Bowers. "I'm uncovering corrupt actions by county employees that would make your head spin. And as soon as I can straighten out the facts, understand exactly what's taking place in this county, I promise you, you'll be the first to know. And this is why you need to elect me, Cameron Cox, as your Mission County district attorney. Where justice will be served every day, regardless of your last name." He smiled, his even, perfectly white teeth flashing the crowd.

Sam was finally at Cameron's side. "Are you finished?" he asked, reaching for the microphone.

"I am," Cameron replied, a victorious look on his face.

"Good to know." Sam took the microphone with his

left hand, pulled back his other fist, and punched Cameron square in the jaw. The man went straight down, his head smacking the smooth granite as his wife dashed to his side. The reporters who weren't rushing to encircle Cameron huddled around Sam. The same reporters who only moments ago had chanted Sam's name in victory now spewed questions at him, mistrust and disdain in their eyes.

"Is it true you knew Conway was the killer weeks ago?"

"Were you aware of the relation between the judge's family and Ms. Conway?"

"As lead homicide detective, why did you allow ADA Magda on this case?"

"Are you romantically involved with ADA Magda?"

Sam just stood there, fists still balled. He hadn't felt such rage since he'd found out about his wife's affair. Cameron's political outburst was ballsy, even for a weasel like him. As Sam's head began to clear and his fists unclenched, he realized that what Cameron Cox had just done bordered on genius. Because no matter what Bowers did to combat Cox's statements, the seed had been planted that Bowers was corrupt. And a seed was all Mission County needed. All Cameron Cox needed in order to slide into Bowers's chair, hands behind his head and feet up on the desk.

Sam repeated "No comment" continuously to the press until they turned their attention to the chief, allowing Sam to slip away. He was getting ready to head downstairs to his office when he noticed someone still sitting, facing the podium. He could see the man held a square paper in his hand, slapping it off his thigh again and again. Sam moved closer, realizing the paper was a color photograph. The man's shoulders rose and he finally stood, pivoting on his heels and almost smacking into Sam.

Sam Hart and Nick Granteed stood face-to-face, mere inches from one another.

C HAPTER TWENTY-FOUR

FROM THE OUTSIDE, THE PRISON RESEMBLED a medieval fortress—a fortress that housed rapists, murderers, pedophiles, and now Tess. A stone wall surrounded the prison itself, pillars springing up along the top of the wall, capped by stone peaks similar to a spiked dog collar. Beyond the wall, slender towers rose upward, allowing the prison building to be seen from a distance. Tiny windowpanes were cut out of the stone that wrapped around the circular turrets, the bars on the windows looking like decorative grates from afar. Only close up could one see the grates were actually steel bars.

Inside, the entrance and hallways were poorly lit. An unbearable heat emanated from the building twelve months a year, regardless of the season. The heat only exacerbated the constant stench of body odor, urine, and stale air.

Kate followed behind one of the guards, a friend of her father's, bypassing the waiting room where visitors crowded, anxious to spend time with their loved ones by way of two phone receivers separated by a thick sheet of Plexiglas.

The Hill Street Prison was a coed facility that housed "defective delinquents," a term voided by the Supreme Court in the 1960s but still used by the warden.

She signed in at the next station. It was one of the only requirements still done by hand; the rest of the prison bureaucracy had years ago converted to all things electronic. Kate was familiar with the procedures, having frequented the facility whenever informants or defendants decided to rat or come clean in the hopes of garnering a decent plea deal. Even so, she could never shake the eerie feeling that overcame her when she visited.

The guard behind the counter requested identification while he reviewed the information Kate had provided in the logbook. "You have to include your attorney ID number," he said, pointing to the spot on the page that had been left blank.

"I'm not here in that capacity. I'm actually visiting my cousin. Perhaps there was some confusion with Guard Bowen," she said, referring to her father's friend who had led her to the sign-in area.

Usually, when Kate paid a visit to the jail, she was taken to the tiny rooms used for inmate visits with lawyers and law enforcement. Today, she planned on visiting Tess the same way the other family members visited the incarcerated. Through the glass.

"Hold on," said the guard. His pudgy fingers began striking his keyboard.

Kate started to run through a mock conversation with her cousin in her head, similar to how she prepared for cross-examinations of witnesses and defendants. She didn't get very far with the dialogue before the guard spoke.

"I'm sorry. It seems Ms. Conway didn't list you as a visitor. You need to be on the list in order to visit the inmate."

"Can you check again? She knew I'd be visiting. It's important that I speak with her."

He turned the monitor so that Kate could see the screen. On it, under *Allowed Visitors,* was one name and one name only—*Judy Conway.*

"There has to be a mistake." Tess would never list her mother as her only visitor.

"I'm sorry. Rules are rules, even for you guys." He pointed toward her badge, which she'd been holding open as identification.

Kate flipped her wallet closed and peered directly into the guard's eyes. "I am, in fact, here on behalf of the DA's office. And I'd like to see Tess Conway in one of the meeting rooms."

"Fine. You know the drill." He held out his hand. "I'll need your cell phone and Dictaphone, along with any other recording or audio devices you have."

"I left everything in the car," replied Kate. "Like you said, I know the drill."

She was escorted down the hall to a steel door. The guard punched in a code on the keypad and they both watched as it slid open. Kate stepped across the threshold alone and made her way down the cinder-block passageway toward a chain-link gate.

The guards sitting inside the glass-enclosed control room to Kate's right flashed smiles and waved. She couldn't help but wonder if they'd be listening while she spoke with Tess. A guard with a shaved head reached under the desk and pushed a button, activating the mesh gate. Kate's stomach fluttered at the sound of metal skimming across the tile floor.

She removed her coat, laying it across the small table,

and set her purse on top of it. She slid into the plastic chair that faced the door and was positioned directly in front of the red alarm button, not because she feared Tess, but because it was her mandated seat. It was also mandated that she not show her bare arms, and despite the sweat trickling down her neck and back, she kept her suit jacket on. She removed a legal pad and pen from her purse and waited, tapping the pen on the paper. Since she had lied to the guard about visiting Tess in a prosecutorial capacity, any information she got from Tess would be secured under false pretenses. A problem for whoever ended up prosecuting Tess's case. She wasn't sure if her sweating was from the heat wave surging inside these walls or the fact that she might no longer have a job when she walked out of the prison. But what was a job compared to her cousin's life?

She looked up to see Tess standing in the doorway, surprise frozen on her face. Tess entered the room shackle-free and wearing the standard orange jumpsuit and canvas sneakers, and dropped into the chair opposite Kate.

Tess spoke first, her defiant eyes locking with her cousin's. "I have nothing to say to you."

Kate was taken aback by the hostility in Tess's voice. "Clearly," she replied, thinking of how Judy was the sole name on Tess's visitor list. "But I have plenty to say to you."

Tess traced something invisible on the table with her index finger.

"I'd like to know why I have prescription drugs in my system."

Tess continued to trace the table.

Kate spoke louder: "How long have you been drugging me?"

Tess offered no explanation, just a simple shrug of her shoulders and a nonchalant, "Sorry."

"That's not good enough. Not this time. How long and why?"

Tess let out a long sigh. "I thought I was *helping* you sleep."

"That's bullshit. You don't help someone sleep by drugging them throughout the day. You wanted to make me think I'd gone crazy."

"No. I just wanted you to be less . . . perfect."

"Less perfect?" Kate knew what Tess was trying to do—frustrate and anger her to the point that she'd walk out. It wasn't going to work. But Kate also knew the back-and-forth about the drugs was pointless. There would be time in the future better suited for the confrontation. Kate needed to focus on Tess, her issues, and why in God's name she'd confessed to the murders.

She relaxed her shoulders and pushed her body back into the wedge of the chair, her arms resting lightly on the table. "I went into your room after Sam took you to the station. That's how I found the pills. I also read through your planner. A lot of it doesn't make sense."

The only sounds in the room were the hissing pipes as heat pumped into the small space, seeming to taunt Kate as sweat continued to pour from her body.

"I saw words like, *dirt, car,* and *shovel.* What does it all mean?"

Tess ran a hand through her hair, picking out a few strands and twirling them around her finger, a lifelong habit.

"We need to talk about what's going on. Please don't shut me out. Let me help you," Kate pressed.

Tess pushed her chair back a few inches. The legs scraped off the tile. She folded her arms across her chest, her eyes narrowed. "Why? So I can tell you every little detail and you can make a career case out of me? Stay on your perfect little path as star prosecutor? I don't owe you anything, Kate. I've spent my entire life feeling the guilt you've blanketed on me. Feeling the weight of what happened to you. Constantly hanging back, allowing you to shine in the spotlight. Always placing your problems ahead of my own. I'm done being your shadow."

"That's what you think of me?" Kate replied. "That I'm here to advance my career?" With her voice soft and low, she went on: "There is no case. You confessed. Case closed." She tugged at her bottom lip. "I'm far from perfect, Tess. I'm full of insecurities and I screw up all the time. I lied in order to see you. I violated the rules of professional responsibility and the canons I swore to uphold as an assistant district attorney. Who knows if I'll even have a job when I walk out of here. Please trust me when I tell you my meeting with you has nothing to do with my career as a prosecutor. I'm here because I'm pissed off at you. I'm scared for you. Fearful the repercussions to what you've falsely confessed will be more vast than you can imagine. But above all that, I'm here because I love you. Because I want to find out the truth."

Tess didn't uncross her arms, but the tight line of her lips softened slightly.

Kate tried to swallow, her saliva thick, while she debated whether to question Tess about the evidence Sam had found.

During a trial, when defendants took the stand, cocky and scoffing at the prosecution's attempt at questioning,

Kate searched for an in. A way to ease the witness so the layers of untruth would peel away and the jury could see them for whoever they truly were. Sometimes it worked and sometimes she failed miserably, having to rally around a different tactic. But one aspect remained constant—she always started by asking the witness about less important facts, saving the crucial testimony for when she saw the shoulders relax or hunch forward a bit.

Kate knew Tess's planner entries were important. Probably more important than the hair dye. She also knew they were Tess's private notes. Something she hadn't planned on sharing with anyone. Now Kate just had to ask the right questions.

"Forget about the planner," she said carefully. She fought the urge to fan herself with the legal pad in front of her. "What about the box of hair dye? Why did you have it?"

Tess responded with little inflection: "I don't know."

"How do you not know?"

"I've been blacking out. I can't seem to remember much, especially at night."

The drugs, thought Kate. She remembered reading that blackouts and amnesia were possible side effects of Ambien. Depending on how many pills Tess was popping, the blackouts could be plausible. "You don't remember purchasing the hair dye? But you had the receipt in your purse."

"I found the receipt and the empty box of hair dye in my purse the next morning. I don't remember being at the drugstore, purchasing the dye, or using the dye. I don't remember paying for it or how I paid for it. I was planning on getting rid of the box but Sam found it before I had the chance.

"I never put two and two together when you told me the intern at the DA's office had been murdered, with her blond hair dyed red. It wasn't until Sam arrested me that I realized what I was capable of . . . what I'd done to the intern and what I'd done to the other women."

Kate immediately shushed her, perplexed over how easily Tess had accepted that she was the Reds killer. She glanced up toward the camera lens suspended in the corner and the audio mic in the middle of the ceiling. "Please. Stop outright admitting you did this."

"But . . ."

Kate closed her eyes and touched her finger to her lips. "Let me think for a moment," she said. "Do you suppose someone else could have bought the dye and used it, and then you put the empty box in your purse?"

"Why would I put someone's empty box of hair dye in my purse?"

"I don't know. Maybe there wasn't a wastebasket handy. Have any of your friends dyed their hair recently?"

"Cindy, but she bleached it blond."

"What about the actual purchase? Does your bank statement reflect a cash withdrawal?

"I don't know but I seriously doubt it."

Kate made a note on her legal pad to stop by the drugstore, see if they were running surveillance cameras the night Tess allegedly bought the dye. She gripped the edge of the table. "I want to revisit the planner. Please don't fight me on it. As I said, I saw words like *dirt, car,* and *shovel*. What does it all mean?"

Tess drew in her breath, the muscles in her neck swelling. "I started using my notebook to record things I did or discovered that didn't make sense to me."

"During your blackouts?"

"Yes."

"And those little slashes at the bottom of each page?"

Tess looked away, her cheeks flushed. "I've been prank calling Cameron's house. I mean, I think. I know it sounds childish, but it's the only thing I can think of, considering I have numerous dialed calls to his phone number but don't remember speaking to him."

Cameron's claim that someone in the police department had traced calls to him back to Kate now made sense. Tess and Kate shared a cell phone plan because Kate received a discount for working in the DA's office. Tess's phone was in Kate's name.

"I couldn't care less about the phone calls," Kate said. "My main concern is you and figuring out what's going on. There are two days in the notebook—I need you to tell me what the words mean. The first was on January 15. You wrote, *Dirt. Bed. Shovel. Car. Migraine.* And then, on the day the second victim's body was found, you wrote, *Car. Nauseous. Ron.*"

"I began writing words down the day after things happened. So what's written for January 15 were really my recordings of what I could remember from the night of the fourteenth through the next morning."

Kate made a note on her legal pad. "Okay, so what does it all mean?"

"A few weeks ago, I woke up in my bed and noticed the sheets were filthy. My feet were caked with mud as if I'd walked barefoot through the woods. I had dirt on my hands and underneath my fingernails.

"I had been out drinking the night before and figured I'd done something stupid with the girls, and that I'd hear all about it in yoga class later that day. I thought it might end up being funny.

"I changed my sheets, showered, went downstairs, and pulled up the newspaper on my laptop. The front-page headline read, 'Girl Found Dead in Moses Cemetery.' I read the entire article. I couldn't believe how much it reminded me of what Ron did to us.

"I left the house, taking my yoga mat and a change of clothes with me so I wouldn't have to come back home before class. When I opened the back door of my car to toss my stuff in, I found a shovel in the backseat, dirt all over it. Just like how the cops found Ron's shovel in the backseat of his car."

Kate figured the police were combing her house at this very moment looking for evidence to solidify Tess's confession. "What did you do with the shovel?"

"When I went to yoga there were no funny stories to be told. The girls wanted to know why I'd left the bar without saying goodbye. No one knew where I'd gone. At the time, I didn't think I was the one who had killed that girl—"

"You weren't," Kate couldn't help but interject.

"—but something told me to get rid of the shovel. I drove to the Advocacy Center and tossed it in the dumpster."

Kate thought about how devastating that fact would look to a jury if Tess happened to withdraw her confession and head to trial. "And what about the entry pertaining to the car, Ron, and being nauseous?"

"I can't remember anything that happened that night either. I woke up at seven a.m. in the front seat of my car in the Logan Diner parking lot. I had the worst migraine. I had to pull the car over a few times, unsure I'd make it home. But I didn't want to call you. I knew you were already at work and what would I have told you? That I'd slept in my car all night?"

You'd have lied, thought Kate. Something Tess had perfected over her whole life.

As Tess continued to recall the sequence of events based on the words she'd written in her notebook, the coolness in her voice disappeared, replaced with an almost relaxed, conversational tone. A tone Kate was much more familiar with.

"I tried to make it upstairs to my bedroom. My head—I had to lie down. I stumbled my way to the couch and collapsed. When I woke up a few hours later, my migraine had lessened. I left the couch for the kitchen and a diet soda so I could take a few pills." Tess gulped, the admission out of her mouth before she could stop it. "For my headache."

She eyed Kate, daring her to voice an opinion. But Kate remained silent, her eyes focused on the legal pad in front of her and the notes she'd been scribbling.

"That's when I saw the envelope on the counter with my name on it," Tess continued, "and I knew Ron had been in the house. The letter was from him."

Kate looked up, pen down. "Ron?"

"The envelope wasn't postmarked and there was no stamp on it. Just my name on the outside of it."

"So, at the time you believed Ron had escaped from prison, broken into our house, and left you a letter?"

"I still believe it."

"What did the letter say?"

"That he had waited a long time to see me again and it was a shame I was having such a hard time remembering."

"Wait. The letter referenced your blackouts?"

"Yes."

"Tess, that letter wasn't from Ron."

"Yes it was."

Kate slid her hand across the table and gently rested it over Tess's. "I need to ask you something. Please be honest with me, okay?"

Tess shrugged.

"Is there any way you wrote that letter to yourself? Maybe during one of your blackouts?"

"Ron wrote the letter." She lowered her voice to just above a whisper. "The letter mentioned stuff only he knows. Stuff from when he lived with me and my mom in New York."

Kate knew Tess's scenario was impossible. Not only had Ron Wells failed to escape from prison, he'd taken his last breath within the four walls that had confined him for the past twenty-five years. Four days before Tess had even received the letter.

"Ron Wells did not write that letter—"

"The letter was from him! The handwriting wasn't mine. It was sloppy and hard to read." Tess fought to regain her composure.

Kate wanted to explain that Ron had died weeks ago, but Tess rambled on, barely taking a breath. "At first, I thought he was killing those women and somehow framing me. I knew you had your suspicions about him being the Mission County Killer, even though you hadn't come out and said it. So I read through your files, trying to pick up on clues that hadn't been made public. I thought if I could find Ron, lure him into a trap or something, I could make everything better again. Put him back in jail and solve the Mission County Killer case. That was until I realized *I* was murdering the women. Not him. He just knew about it . . . somehow."

Kate felt like she had landed herself in a *Twilight Zone* episode. Tess was all over the place. One minute she couldn't be bothered with anything, the next she was fanatical over hunting down the killer. And the outright confessions—so quick to admit her guilt when she had no recollection of any of it. Kate couldn't help but think her cousin could successfully plead insanity.

Tess leaned in toward Kate, her eyes glassy, making their blue even more striking. "He's up for parole next year, you know. I can't have that, Kate. I can't exist in a world where he walks free."

"Ron Wells didn't escape from prison. He died in his jail cell right around the time we think the first murder occurred. A heart attack. A full week before you received the letter."

"Died?"

"Yes. He's dead. I found out this morning." She gently added, "He didn't write the letter." The words hung in the air as tears slipped down Tess's cheeks and onto her orange jumper.

"I didn't write it," Tess whimpered. "Please believe me."

"Where's the letter? Did you keep it?"

"In my car. In the glove compartment," she hiccuped. "I didn't want you to find it."

"But why?"

Tess tried to catch her breath, but couldn't. Kate's question seemed to have distressed her even more.

Kate squeezed her cousin's hand. "We'll figure this out. I'm going to get you out of here."

Tess was now sobbing. "Just let me stay. I don't want to go back home. I deserve to be here." She wiped the snot that dripped down her nose with the back of her hand. "I'm no different from Judy. Look at me, Kate. I can't go one night without a drink. I'm begging friends for sleeping pills, lying about why I need them. I was drugging myself, drugging you. I wanted us to be able to forget—forget all of it. Then and now." Her shoulders heaved up and down with each short breath she took. "I'm sorry. I'm so sorry."

Tess stared straight down, strands of hair clinging to her wet face. "I've become Judy," she murmured. "I'm everything I hate about her. And now I'm hurting innocent people, hurting you, all because I can't handle what he did to me. What she allowed him to do."

Tess was no different from the women Kate represented in court. And Ron was no different from the defendants she prosecuted. He would never stop haunting them.

Kate rose from her chair and took a few steps toward Tess. The guards would be in the room within seconds, as soon as they saw the physical contact, but she didn't care. Tess went limp in her arms. "You're not her," Kate whispered. "You're not Judy."

She heard the click of the gate and the sound of metal sliding across the tile floor. Two guards rushed toward them, one opening the door to the room they occupied and the other standing close by in case backup was needed.

Kate released Tess and quickly turned toward the guards, her hands in the air. "I'm sorry. We're done here. I'm the one who initiated the embrace. She had nothing to do with it." She stuffed her legal pad in her briefcase, grabbed her coat, and hurried out of the room. She didn't stop until the first gate slammed shut behind her. She had been so worried about the guards punishing Tess for the long embrace that she'd practically run out on her cousin. She pivoted, once again facing the meshed metal. She could see her cousin turned away from her, head bowed, shoulders sagging. "Tess!" she shouted.

Tess turned to face her.

"I'm going to figure this out, I promise," Kate said.

Tess pressed her body against the gate. Her hands rose from her sides, fingers curling around the metal links. Her face was swollen, her nose red, her eyes bloodshot. *I'm sorry,* she mouthed.

Kate wandered out of the prison. She had more questions than answers, but she did know one thing—Tess was in a bad way. Addicted to prescription pills and alcohol, she had no alibi for the nights the victims were found dead or the nights they were taken.

Regardless of Tess's role in the case, Kate knew she wasn't a murderer. The shaved bodies, the gag cloths, the cyanide poisoning. The revenge plot was too intricate, too elaborate. The thought of Tess committing the murders while blacked out was absurd. The real killer was still out there. Now she just had to prove it.

Kate opened the glove box and retrieved the envelope with Tess's name on it. The glue on the fold remained dry: whoever had left it for her had not bothered to seal the envelope. *Intentional?* Kate wondered. She had to analyze every aspect, assume every detail had a meaning behind it.

The handwriting looked nothing like Tess's neat, loopy writing, but it wasn't sloppy. Still, the words were severely left-slanted so that the penmanship was almost illegible. The lettering was small and closely strung together. Kate squinted to read it, holding the paper close to her face.

Most of the letter was a repeat of what Tess had already told her back in the meeting room. Everything until she reached the last line: *In the end, everyone's a disappointment. Maybe she was better off six feet under?*

There would be another dead body. She was sure of it. And Kate couldn't help but imagine it might be hers. She wanted to call Sam. Drive to wherever he was and show him the letter. She would walk him through the events Tess had explained to her and force him to believe the killer was still on the loose. But she couldn't bring herself to call the man who had so blatantly betrayed her trust.

She fished for her cell phone in the car's console and began dialing her father's number. She stopped after entering the first few digits, a nagging string tightening in her chest. Her father blamed himself for ignoring Judy's sickness. He also blamed himself for not trusting Kate's instincts about Ron Wells. Sometimes Kate felt her father's guilt was fairly placed.

Now her father no longer turned a blind eye but instead involved himself in her life to the point of suffocation. She knew it was his way of making up for his mistakes—his misjudgment of Judy and Ron Wells. Without hesitation, her father would take Kate's phone call seriously. She was surprised he hadn't already demanded the police reopen the case, although at this point she wondered if his demands would look like nothing more than a political ploy to take the heat off his family.

Conflicted, she punched in the last two digits of his

phone number and waited for him to answer. With each ring, her concern increased. Something was going on with him. Had he also received a letter like this one? If she was right and the killings were not serial but rather a revenge plan against her, was her father out of harm's way? His phone turned over to voice mail. She dialed his chambers.

"Good afternoon, President Judge Magda's chambers," chirped Gertie, her father's secretary.

"Hi, Gertie, it's Kate. Is my dad around?"

"Oh! It's you," she said, and then Kate heard the sound of food being chewed. "I thought it was going to be another reporter calling." More crunching. "Your father went to meet Bear for an early lunch."

Bear was Robert Moretti, Kate's dad's old law partner and longtime friend. Bear's presence was soft and friendly until you crossed him in court or offended his family and friends. Awhile back, one of his clients referred to him as a bear in the courtroom and the nickname had stuck.

"My father's not answering his cell phone," Kate explained, "and it's important I speak with him."

"His cell is here, in chambers. I heard it ringing just a few seconds ago. He was in a hurry to meet Bear; he probably just forgot to bring it with him. You know your father."

She did know her father and *forgetful* wasn't one of his character traits.

"Well listen, love, I have to run. My lunch hour is only a lunch minute these days. I'll let your father know you called. In the meantime, you hold that head of yours high. Don't listen to any of that garbage Cameron Cox is blabbing about."

The call ended with Kate even more confused than before. Cameron Cox?

She pulled out of the prison's parking lot. She couldn't sit around waiting to hear back from her father. Maybe Sam's assessment of her, though harsh, was accurate. Maybe she *was* a rogue prosecutor—always going off on her own, breaking the rules to seek justice. *So be it,* she thought.

Unwavering, she drove in the direction of the drugstore, prepared to do whatever was necessary to find the true killer. She felt that her cousin's life—and her own—depended on it.

CHAPTER TWENTY-FIVE

SAM LED NICK GRANTEED THROUGH THE CROWD of reporters in the rotunda toward the detectives' offices in the basement of the courthouse. Why had Nick attended the press conference?

In the back of the office, next to the coffee pot, were two doors. One led to Chief Joseph's office and the other gave way to a small room which you had to pass through to get to the meeting room. That small room, painted beige and carpeted, served as Sam's office.

Sam sank into his leather desk chair and motioned for Nick to have a seat in one of the two chairs opposite. Sam balled his fist, then stretched his hand open, wiggling his fingers to make sure Cameron's face hadn't caused any damage. "Please sit," he prompted when he noticed Nick still standing.

Nick shifted his legs and dipped his fingertips into the back pocket of his jeans. The same pocket into which Sam had watched him slip the photograph. Finally, he sat on the very edge of the chair, his knees bent at a ninety-degree angle.

"You should probably get some ice on that," said Nick, staring at Sam's hand, although his mind seemed focused on something else.

"Nah, I'll be fine. How's Gina doing? You two working things out?"

"I found out who she was sleeping with—some pharmacist. I'm pretty sure I'm on my way out."

Sam ran his hands through his hair, not sure what to say. He decided to avoid the topic altogether. "When I ran into you upstairs, it seemed like you were wrestling with something. Want to talk about it?"

Nick waited a moment before he spoke, not answering Sam's question. "It must feel good to have the Mission County Killer case closed," he said. "A full-blown confession. That's unheard of, right?"

"Not unheard of, but rare."

"You must be thrilled to no longer have the killer on the loose."

Sam forced a smile.

"Did she say how she did it?" Nick asked.

"Who?"

"Tess Conway."

"We know how she did it . . . for the most part."

"I know the newspapers reported death by toxic asphyxia but, I mean, did she confess to the intricacies of the murders?"

"Her confession is part of the public record. If you're that interested, look it up. I'm sure it will be all over tomorrow's newspapers."

"Are you going to ask her how she got away with it until now?"

"Our office will question her in detail. No need to worry."

"It's my understanding that cyanide is fairly easy for the average person to purchase. Almost common," Nick said.

Sam's research showed that hair stylists and professional photographers used it. Hobby shops and electronic stores carried it, and practically anyone could order the poison online without a license.

"How weird about the red hair," Nick added, rubbing his palms along his jeans. "I wonder what the significance is behind that."

Jesus, thought Sam, *what's with the twenty questions?* "Why are you so interested?" he asked.

"I'm just curious to hear her version of the events."

"It will all unfold soon enough."

"Didn't you mention that Magda and Tess Conway live together?"

"No, I didn't."

"Could you imagine living with such a sick and twisted—"

"What are you doing here, Nick?" Sam cut in. The caretaker had him on edge.

"I heard Chief Joseph was holding a press conference. Figured it had to be about the killer. I wanted to hear the news firsthand."

"I'm going to ask you again: what were you doing at the courthouse?"

Nick's Adam's apple bobbed as if he'd swallowed a marble. He cleared his throat. "I do have a personal interest in the case, being that the first death occurred in my cemetery."

Kate's warnings about Nick Granteed echoed in Sam's head as he watched the man unbutton the cuffs of his shirt and roll up his sleeves, exposing his hairless arms. *This is ridiculous*, he thought, reminding himself that Tess had already confessed. She had confessed without any coercion, without anyone mentioning the idea of her being responsible for the first two murders.

"I've actually been meaning to call you," Sam said.

"The other day I ran surveillance tapes from the night of January 30. The camera caught all the cars traveling down Chestnut Street around the same time the most recent victim was found dead on the courthouse steps. Do you want to know what I saw?"

"I have a pretty good idea," Nick replied.

"Thought so. Do you want to tell me why you were tailing Tess Conway at three in the morning?"

Nick nearly choked. "*Tess*?"

"Enlighten me," said Sam, picking out a paper clip from the mess on his desk and unbending the wire.

"Listen, I don't know anything about Tess Conway. Or Kate. Aside from what I've read in the papers and seen on the news today."

"I don't believe you. Why were you following Kate's SUV down Chestnut Street the night Harris was found dead?"

"Do I need a lawyer?" Nick asked.

"Oh, please don't start with this lawyer talk again. If you want a lawyer, go retain one, but I'm simply trying to have a conversation, not interrogate you. If anything changes in the course of our *conversation*, you'll be the first to know. Scout's honor."

"It wasn't intentional, I swear," said Nick.

"What wasn't intentional?"

"Following Tess."

"Let me ask you another way: why would you be following Kate?"

"Please. It's not what you think. I was . . . worried about ADA Magda."

"Why would you be worried about her?"

"Well . . . ah . . . I was on my way home from the bar when I saw Magda's SUV pull out onto Danbury

Street. She was driving real fast. Something didn't seem right, so I followed her. You know, to make sure she was okay."

Sam could feel the heat rising in his cheeks at the idea of this guy following Kate. "How do you know ADA Magda drives an SUV?"

Nick offered an uneasy chuckle. "Small town. I've seen her driving in it."

"It's not that small . . . So you followed her around town? If you were so worried, why not call the police? Or me? You have my cell phone number."

"I didn't think to call you. I guess I was too focused on her."

"That's one scenario," said Sam. "Here's another one. You weren't real happy with Kate's reaction to you giving your wife a black eye."

"I didn't—"

"So you thought you'd follow her around. Scare her a little bit. Make sure she didn't follow through on her threats of slapping you with a domestic."

"No, that's not what happened—"

"When, little did you know, you were following Tess Conway, who had borrowed Kate's car that night. Did you happen to see something? Something pertaining to the murder? Is that why you're here today?"

"No."

"How long did you follow the car?"

"I'm starting to feel like this is no longer a conversation." Nick wiped the corners of his mouth, which were white with dried spit.

"Did you follow Tess to her house?" Sam's voice was stern but composed.

"Once she merged on Route 309, I turned around and went back to the cemetery."

"Let me get this straight: you were worried about who you thought was Kate and how fast she was driving so you followed her all over town, even traveling down Chestnut Street *twice,* but when she merged onto a *highway,* you went home?"

"No, I—" Nick stopped and put his head down. "I'm sorry. I shouldn't have come here."

"But you did."

"I'm not . . . I'm trying to tell you that it was not my intention to harm Kate."

Sam wanted to believe Nick. Believe that despite the caretaker's oddities, there was good at his core. But Sam sensed something was off.

Nick stood, ready to leave, and there was nothing Sam could do about it. He didn't have reasonable suspicion to detain Nick. If the guy wanted their meeting to be over, it was over.

"About the Mission County Killer," said Nick, "maybe it's the *how* and *why* you need to focus on now that you think you know the *who.*" He slipped his fingers into his back pocket again and Sam remembered the photograph he'd been holding.

"What's with the photo in your back pocket?"

Nick avoided eye contact.

"It must be pretty important for you to be carrying it around."

"Just an old family photo. Have a good day, detective." Nick stepped out of the office and closed the door behind him.

Sam sat at his desk staring at his swollen hand and

thinking about his strange conversation with Nick Grant-eed. *What a weird man.* Sam felt the familiar tingles dot the back of his neck—the tingles he usually experienced when he was close to cracking a case, not after the killer had been caught with a full confession.

He decided to finish the day working from home. He planned on reading a few case files on his couch, in front of the television. Maybe even nurse a beer or two. No press, no chief, no assholes.

He slipped on his coat, grabbed the paperwork he wanted to take with him, and opened the door to the main detectives' office. Detective David Stark waved him over to his desk.

Sam could still envision Stark strolling into his office—only a month after Sam had found out about the affair—to invite him to a housewarming party he and Kristen were throwing. Stark had shrugged in response to the string of expletives that had escaped from Sam's mouth, claiming, *You're either going to get over it or you're not. Your choice.* So much for avoiding assholes.

"The guy you just had in your office told me to give this to you," Stark said, handing Sam a photograph.

Two young girls, maybe four or five years old, stood on the front porch of a house with adults he assumed to be their parents. The children couldn't have been dressed more differently. One donned a pink tutu with a feath-ered boa draped around her neck, while the other wore madras shorts and a collared polo shirt. Reddish-blond hair on both.

Despite their wardrobe differences, the two girls looked almost identical. They were the same height and had similar physical features, but it was their crooked smiles that captivated Sam. The tingling sensation once again sprinkled across the back of Sam's neck; he was certain he was staring at Kate and Tess. He heard Nick's voice in his head: *Just an old family photo.*

Darting out of the office, picture in hand, Sam flew up the stairs to the main entrance, taking the steps two at a time. He pushed past reporters who had been waiting for him and ran past Bowers, nearly spinning the district attorney around.

"Hey," shouted Bowers, "I was just on my way to see you!"

Sam didn't stop. He was outside within seconds, dashing toward the public parking lot, his feet smashing against the gravel as he searched for Nick's car. Nothing.

He placed his hands on his knees, huffing. The cold air pierced his lungs, stabbing at him while he tried to catch his breath. He stared at the picture clutched in his hand, examining the image of the person he had assumed to be the girls' father. The man's bulbous nose didn't fit with his sharp features and long face. Steel-gray eyes seemed to jump out of the picture and Sam noticed the man's dark, greasy hair was slicked into a low ponytail. His shirt was unbuttoned, revealing a hairless chest. *Could this be Ron Wells?*

He dialed Kate's number but it went to voice mail. He hung up and dialed again. Same thing.

"Kate, it's Sam. You need to call me back right away. It's about Nick Granteed."

Within seconds of clicking off, his phone rang. He pressed it right to his ear, not even bothering to look at who it was.

"I'm glad I reached you," came the voice from the other end of the phone. Not Kate, but her father.

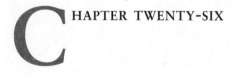

CHAPTER TWENTY-SIX

SAM TURNED THE COLLAR UP ON HIS COAT when he walked through the tunnel, lowering his head as a blast of cold air rushed at his face and Judge Magda's voice buzzed in his ear.

"I saw the breaking news regarding Cameron Cox's corruption allegations. Your cross-punch is quite impressive."

Sam chuckled nervously and braced himself.

"Kate called my cell phone earlier, but I missed her. I've since tried reaching her with no luck. Have you spoken to her?"

"No, judge," he shouted over the wind howling through the earpiece of his cell. "She won't take my calls."

"Bowers took Kate off the Mission County Killer case but I have a feeling she's still investigating."

Sam heard fear in the judge's voice and knew his concern for his daughter went beyond professional consequences. It was clear to Sam that Judge Magda, like Kate, believed the killer was still on the loose.

"I'm headed to my car now. She never came into work this morning so I'll swing by her house. See if she's home."

"Thank you. Please call me the moment you hear from her."

"Will do." Sam sensed the detective in him taking over, knowing the question had to be asked. "Uh . . . judge?"

"Yes, Sam?"

He worded his next few sentences cautiously, not wanting to upset the judge by bringing up Kate and Tess's traumatic childhood. "Kate believes her past has somehow followed her into her present. And I thought those fears would be quieted now that an arrest and confession had been made to the recent murders. I was wrong. And there's one question I have, based on something that just transpired in my office. An important one."

"If it's about Tess, I won't comment—"

"No. It's about Nick Granteed."

"The caretaker over at Moses Cemetery?"

"Yes. Do you know him?"

"I remember reading the write-up on him and his wife in the newspaper when he took the caretaker job. But I don't know him personally."

"Would it be odd if he had a picture of your daughter and niece from when they were young? Maybe five years old?"

"Very odd."

Sam figured that would be the judge's response. Then he thought about what Kate had said to him at the park, convinced the crime scenes were clues that connected her past to the killer—to Ron Wells. "You wouldn't by chance have a copy of the Ron Wells trial transcript?" he asked.

"Of course I do. After the first two murders and when you released the initials to the public, I must've read and reread it a dozen times. But it tells me nothing. I can't find any direct connection. At least not with the witnesses' testimony." Judge Magda paused for a moment. "Can you swing by my chambers and pick up the transcript? Maybe it would be a good idea for you to read through it."

Kate wasn't the only one still investigating. Sam figured the judge was waiting to see how Sam would respond to his request. If he agreed to meet the judge, then Sam was admitting to a continued investigation of the Reds case when the alleged killer was already behind bars. But as much as he believed Tess had something to do with Reds and the intern's death, Nick Granteed and Kate had cast enough doubt in his mind that he couldn't pass up the judge's offer.

Sam entered Judge Magda's office and was greeted by Gertie, smiling at him between fielding endless phone calls. A half-eaten sandwich and a fountain soda covered the papers on her desk. "Go right in," she said, gesturing toward the door that led into the judge's personal chambers.

Sam tapped the half-opened door with the back of his knuckles and stepped into what Judge Magda referred to as his personal golfdom. On the kelly green–carpeted floor were four mini indoor putting mats, strategically placed around the room. There were also half a dozen coffee mugs turned on their sides, the judge's makeshift putting holes. Sam had watched him on more than one occasion putt the golf balls into the mugs while he discussed business or settled legal disputes.

Sam was in awe of President Judge Magda. The way he seemed so at ease within his powerful position. He often wore jeans and a polo shirt under his robe—no one in the courtroom aware of his casual attire, not that he would care. Even now, despite the judge's worries, he sat on his leather couch, his loafers off, with one socked foot crossed over his knee, working the crossword puzzle while he waited for Sam.

Sam shook his hand firmly, and thanked the judge for seeing him, even though the meeting had been Magda's idea.

"Thank you for coming over. I didn't feel comfortable talking on the cell phone." The judge handed Sam a thick folder stuffed with papers and rubber bands.

Sam wondered if the judge had caught wind of the rumor that courthouse employees' phones had been tapped. Sam was still investigating the possibility of Cameron using an officer in the police department to listen in on the most private of conversations, specifically DA Bowers's.

"Do you have the photograph of the girls? The one you asked me about on the phone?"

Sam handed over the photo and sank into the leather chair next to the couch, not wanting to stand over the judge. He watched Tommy Madga's expression, a close-lipped smile that slowly turned into a grimace.

"Nick Granteed had this photograph in his possession?"

Sam nodded slowly.

"This makes no sense."

"Who are the adults in the picture?" Sam asked.

"Ron Wells and my sister Judy. This had to be taken right around Tess's birthday, if not on her birthday. They're standing on the porch of my sister's house back in New York."

Sam knew he was referring to Tess's fifth birthday. "Do you have any idea who would've taken the picture?"

"No idea. You need to find Nick Granteed. Find out why the hell he has this picture. Or better yet, who he got it from." He leaned forward, handing the photo back to Sam as if he couldn't bear to look at it any longer.

"Did Ron Wells and your sister remain married after the trial?" Sam asked.

Judge Magda chortled. "My dear sister testified on that bastard's behalf. Called my daughter a liar on the stand. As for the attempted murder, she claimed Kate had been sleepwalking. That Ron had gone out looking for her and Tess had tagged along. Can you imagine?" He shook his head with disgust. "I'm sorry. In answer to your question, yes, they remained married. Drugs and Ron Wells—the only two things my sister has ever fully committed to. I'm not sure if you're aware, but Ron Wells died before these murders even began."

"Yes, I know."

While nothing the judge was saying helped exonerate Tess, it didn't help convict her either. Something told Sam to keep investigating. He was eager to read through the trial transcript he held in his hand. The judge may have read it half a dozen times with no luck, but Sam knew the Reds case better than anyone. With Tess in jail, Sam had nothing to lose. If Tess was the killer in the three murders, she was where she needed to be. And if she wasn't, well, then at least one of the two women was safe. He performed a quick inventory in his head of what he already knew, adding to it his current conversation with the judge, when he realized he'd been looking at the case from the wrong angle. Perhaps who had testified and what they had said on the stand wasn't as important as who had been present at the trial.

"Was Ron Wells's trial high profile?"

"It was and it wasn't. Had Kate and Tess been reported missing, with police and search parties frantic to find them, I think it would've gained national coverage. But everything happened so quickly. The kids were taken out of Judy's house and found within minutes. That being said, our local press reported the hell out of it."

"Was the courtroom crowded with spectators throughout the trial?"

"It was a small courtroom. From what I remember, mostly family and local press."

"What about the day Kate testified?"

"Ah. Well, that was interesting. On the morning Kate testified, I called in a few favors at the courthouse, and with the help of the district attorney's office we filled the seats with employees and staff. The trial judge ordered anyone without a proper seat to leave. Thankfully, not one member of the press was in the courtroom to report on my daughter's testimony."

"The press could've easily requested a copy of the file from the clerk of courts."

"Yes, but the only way the testimony of a trial is transcribed is if there is an appeal. I remember Ron Wells's attorneys appealing immediately, but I don't believe the transcription occurred for quite some time. Maybe two or three weeks after the trial. By then, the press had moved on. Ron Wells's conviction was old news."

"Forget about the press," said Sam. "Even if the details of Kate's testimony stayed out of the news, nothing would prevent someone from getting his hands on the file, reading through the testimony, and essentially recreating aspects of the case twenty-five years later."

Judge Magda shot up from the couch, grabbed his putter and began tapping a golf ball toward one of the mats. "Sam, I think you've just figured out the way to prove my niece's innocence."

"I'm not following, judge."

"In Hettrich County, the procedure used to request a transcript is different from most counties. There, no one has access to the court file without a court order. Once the judge signs off on the order and the person requesting the files pays the transcription fees, the file is made available to them. The requesting party's name would appear in the caption of the court order."

"Meaning the court orders become part of the file."

"Yes. So anyone who requested the transcript, whether it was twenty-five years ago or three weeks ago, would have his or her name documented in the original file held in the clerk's office. I'd have to bet that few people would care to jump through the procedural hoops. Unless, of course, they were invested and for some reason needed to know the intricacies of the trial."

Sam was already thinking what the judge said next.

"If you wanted to review the people who made formal requests to see the file, all you'd have to do is visit the Hettrich County clerk of courts office."

Sam rose from his chair as the judge continued to putt the golf ball across the room.

The judge spoke with his head down, bent over his club. "Three weeks ago, Ron Wells dies in prison. Three weeks ago, my niece walks back into my sister's life after a fifteen-year absence. And three weeks ago, the Mission County Killer commits the first of three murders."

"Judge, are you saying that you think your sister—"

"No. What I'm saying is that I think the truth lies in Ron Wells's file."

CHAPTER TWENTY-SEVEN

THE DRUGSTORE WAS IN A SEEDY PART OF TOWN, far away from the gated developments and the hustle-and-bustle of the downtown businesses. It was a popular hangout for drug dealers, users, and the occasional prostitute. It also had a twenty-four-hour pharmacy and a drive-thru.

Kate surveyed the scene inside, noting only one cashier at the register. His name tag read, *Isaac, Asst. Manager.*

"Hi there," she said. "I seem to have a bit of a problem. Is the manager around?"

Isaac looked down at his name tag. "The manager just left for lunch. She won't be back for an hour. Is there something I can help you with?" His voice was high-pitched, cracking as he spoke, like that of a pubescent boy.

"I was in here a few nights ago. I purchased some items and when I got home, one of the items wasn't in my bag. A box of L'Oreal hair dye. I think I may have dropped it on my way out."

"Do you have a receipt?"

"I don't." Kate rubbed the back of her neck as if she was growing anxious.

"Well, there's not much I can do—"

"I have a friend who is a manager at a store like this one and he said you'd be able to scan your surveillance tapes for me, to prove I purchased the hair dye. Is that true?"

"On occasion."

"Please, if you're able to run the tapes, I'd really appreciate it."

"We really don't have the coverage for me to leave the register."

"Isn't everything digital now? I can tell you the date and time. It shouldn't take more than a few minutes. Please, I'm begging here," she said with desperation in her voice. "I really can't afford to purchase another box of dye."

Isaac sighed. "I guess I can check the tapes, but only because it's not too busy." He spoke into his walkie-talkie, asking a clerk to cover his position at the cash register.

"That would be wonderful!" Kate exclaimed. "I can't tell you how thankful I am." She gave him the date and an approximate time. When Isaac headed toward the security room, she followed.

"I'm sorry," he said, "you'll have to wait here. No one is allowed in the back room except for management."

Kate noticed the word *Restrooms* lit up in neon above an archway. "Oh, no problem. I was just going to use the restroom while I waited."

They padded through the store together until they reached the door with the stick figure of a woman.

"Meet me up front. I won't be long," he said.

If there was ever a time for Kate to perfect her flirting skills, now would be it. She reached up toward Isaac's chest, plucked off an imaginary piece of fuzz from his shirt, and flicked it toward the floor. She made sure to allow her fingers to linger just a fraction too long. She looked him in the eyes and batted her eyelashes slightly. "You had fuzz on your shirt."

Isaac blushed and stepped away. As he turned his back to her, she saw him not so subtly blow his breath into his cupped hand and sniff. Before heading into the restroom, she watched as Isaac punched in the code *1-2-3-4* on the security-room door. *Easy enough*, thought Kate.

She splashed cold water on her face and reapplied her clear, shiny lip gloss. After less than a minute, she emerged from the bathroom and peered up and down the hallway. No one. She hurriedly tapped the code on the door's keypad and slipped into the security room.

"You can't be in here!" Isaac called out, his mouth hanging open.

"I thought you said your manager wouldn't be back for an hour? I made sure no one saw me come in."

"Please, you need to leave. I could get fired."

"Don't make me leave," she said quietly. "This kind of stuff fascinates me." She pulled up a chair next to Isaac and leaned into him, placing a hand on his knee.

"*What* fascinates you? Watching a tape for your missing item?"

"No, silly. It's like we're trying to solve something, like on those crime shows."

"I don't know . . ."

She moved her hand a bit farther up his leg and lowered her voice, trying her best version of "sexy." "If anyone comes in, I'll tell them I snuck in. That it wasn't your fault."

Kate recognized the torn look in Isaac's eyes. It was the same look she'd seen on defendants' faces when they were about to make a deal, not sure if they should rat on their friends or rot in prison. *Choices*, thought Kate. She thought about the choices Sam had made and the ones she was now making, all because they both thought they were doing the right thing.

After a few more moments of Kate pleading and only seconds before she thought she'd have to whip out her badge, Isaac caved.

She inched her face closer to the screen while he fast-forwarded the digital tape until the bottom of the monitor flashed the numbers *01:00*. The receipt Tess had found in her purse showed the time of purchase as 1:09 a.m. Kate had told Isaac she couldn't remember the exact time she'd been in the store but that it was definitely between 1:00 and 1:15 in the morning.

The camera angle focused downward and to the right of the customers as they entered and exited the store. The tape was sped up so the minutes ticked by quickly. Kate stared, afraid to blink, as men, women, even children appeared on the screen. The images were very clear, easy for Kate to focus on even the minutest details. She watched in silence as one man jangled his car keys in his hand, tossing them in the air and catching them until he was out of the camera's range. Jingle, toss, catch. Jingle, toss, catch. She could practically hear the rhythm despite the lack of audio on the footage.

A man in a hoodie sauntered into the breezeway, not fully in the store but no longer standing outside. Within seconds another hooded figure came into view. Kate watched the exchange, the casual way the rolled-up dollar bills were swapped for two baggies of white powder. She wondered if Isaac was seeing what transpired on the screen. She allowed herself a quick glance in his direction, only to find he'd been staring at her. He whipped his head back toward the monitor and she did the same. When the time ticked over to 01:14, Kate sighed. Tess was nowhere on the screen, meaning Kate's hunch had been right—someone else had purchased the hair dye.

Kate wondered if one of the people she'd viewed on the screen was the real killer, when an image on the monitor caught her eye.

"Wait!" she cried out, louder than she'd meant to. "Go back." It hadn't been the person she'd recognized, but instead, what the person was doing. As she waited, her heart started hammering in her chest.

The figure came into view. It was a woman and she was exiting the drugstore, her face barely visible to the camera. "Can you pause the tape on that woman? I think I noticed the box of hair dye on the floor," Kate fibbed.

Isaac hit the *PAUSE* button and said he hadn't seen a box of hair dye. She ignored him.

At least fifteen years had gone by since Kate had last seen her, but the image was now unmistakable. The screen showed the woman's hand poised in the air, some of her hair wrapped around her finger. Had the video not been paused, it would have shown her twirling a long strand of it—just like her daughter.

"Judy Conway," said Kate. "Oh my God, it's Judy." Why hadn't she made the connection before now? She pushed her chair back and rushed toward the door. "Thank you, Isaac," she managed to say, though she felt as if balls of cotton had formed along the inside of her cheeks and tongue.

"What about the hair dye?" Isaac shouted after her.

* * *

She sat on the curb, her head between her knees, need-ing the fresh air. She stared at the wads of chewed-up gum and oil spots that stained the parking lot. *Judy.* She could have composed the letter, making Tess think it had been from Ron. She knew the secrets of Tess's childhood. She was local, checked into Cunningham Valley Hospital of her own free will, not through a court mandate. She could come and go as she pleased. And Tess had been vis-iting Judy. Had Tess told her mother about her blackouts? Kate's mind raced at lightning speed. Maybe Judy had followed her home from the parking lot and snuck into the house after Tess had fallen asleep. Tess never locked the doors, never set the alarm while she was home. Had Judy been the one to get Tess addicted to pills again? Had it all been part of Judy's master plan? It was plausible. And then Kate felt as if someone had sucker-punched her. Right in the gut, knocking the wind out of her.

She'd been so stupid for not catching what had been staring her right in the face. She wished she had a paper bag to breathe into. Cushioned between the letters *R* and *W* was a *J*—for Judy.

Kate would put nothing past her aunt. But why would Judy want to frame Tess? Why not frame Kate for the murders? After all, it was Kate, not Tess, who had testi-fied against Ron. It was Kate who'd told Ron's secret.

Kate wheezed, her new realization not making her breathing any easier. If Judy was the Mission County Killer, then her plan was to *murder* Kate, not frame her. She remembered the line from Tess's letter: *In the end, everyone's a disappointment. Maybe she was better off six feet under?*

Kate stood up, contemplating her next move. Judy's next move. She looked around. A young mother, sixteen at most, coming out of the drugstore, bags in hand and two small children clinging to her legs. Two white males in a low rider, both on their cell phones. A few other vehicles with no one inside. No Judy.

She climbed into the driver's seat of Tess's car and locked the doors. It would take more than the surveillance tape to exonerate Tess and convict Judy. There hadn't been a bag in Judy's hand onscreen. She had walked out empty-handed, twirling her hair. It proved nothing. No bag on Judy and no Tess in the frame. No one would believe Kate, especially now that Tess had confessed. She needed to visit Cunningham Valley Hospital and get her hands on their patient logs. If she could confirm that Judy was signed out of the hospital during the times that the victims had gone missing or were found by police—that would help prove her theory.

With a less than steady hand, she started the car.

CHAPTER TWENTY-EIGHT

KATE STRODE TOWARD THE DESK at Cunningham Valley Hospital projecting an air of confidence to mask the sheer terror she felt at the possibility of running into Tess's mother. She kept an eye out for Judy, certain her nemesis was lurking around every corner.

The woman behind the desk was reading a tabloid magazine, oblivious to Kate's presence. A soap opera played on the television suspended on the wall in the corner of the room opposite the counter. Kate could see the screen's reflection through the glass that separated the receptionist from the waiting room. "Excuse me," she said.

The receptionist didn't look up. "She's in the sunroom—like always."

"I'm sorry, I think you have me mistaken—" She stopped talking, realizing the woman thought she was Tess. She reached into her purse and pulled out her badge. *The end justifies the means*, she convinced herself. "My name is Kate Magda. I'm a prosecutor in the Mission County district attorney's office. If you have a few minutes, I'd like to ask you some questions." She showed the badge, leaving it out on the counter.

The woman closed her magazine and tucked it under the desk calendar. "I'm sorry, I thought you were someone else. You look so much like this young woman who comes here to visit her mother. Do you have a sister?"

"I'm an only child," Kate said, smiling. She pointed to where the woman had slid the magazine. "Seems like that actress can't catch a break in the love department." Luckily, she'd paid attention last weekend when Tess was on one of her celebrity rants.

"Oh my god! I know! She can't keep a man. Her last husband destroyed her."

"Totally." Kate shook her head in disgust.

The receptionist glanced again at Kate's badge. "You said you wanted to ask me something?" This time she smiled; there was a streak of pink lipstick on her front two teeth.

"Oh, right!" chirped Kate. "I'm working a case involving a patient here."

"You are? No one told me that. What's the case about?"

Kate figured the coworkers of the gum-smacking, tabloid-loving receptionist told her as little as possible. "Jeez, I'm sorry, I can't give you that information during an open investigation. God forbid I told you something I shouldn't and you ended up subpoenaed to testify at trial."

"Heavens no! I wouldn't want that to happen."

"Okay, here goes: if the patient checked into this facility on her own free will, is she allowed to leave the premises? Without permission?"

"Sure. As long as the patient isn't here on a judge's order. A patient can't miss a class or skip any of the components of the rehabilitation or they won't successfully

complete the program. But if there's down time, the patients are free to check in and check out."

"Great. And you have a logbook to keep track of
your patients, right?"

"Well, yes. Our patients need to use our sign-in and
sign-out sheets so we can keep track of who's here and
who's not."

The receptionist was telling her everything she wanted
to hear. Now for the tricky part. Her plan was to sound
official, matter-of-fact, and hope there wasn't a need to
fabricate the story further.

"Great. I'll need a copy of your logbooks on the following dates."

"Oh, no, I can't let you do that. We have privacy
laws."

"Well, it's in the capacity of an open case my office is
prosecuting. I was under the impression your facility was
served with a search warrant early this morning. From
Detective Hart?" *So much for not fabricating,* thought
Kate. She ticked off in her head the rule violations she
had already committed—conflict of interest, not adher-
ing to the proper investigative functions of a prosecutor,
failure to exercise sound discretion . . .

"Not that I'm aware of, but I wasn't here." The receptionist rolled her eyes and tipped her head back, seeming
to remember something. "Susan had the morning shift.
She's so flighty. Probably threw the warrant on the desk
and didn't think twice about notifying me. Maybe it's in
this stack of papers. Give me a second." She sifted through
the papers on the desk.

"Sure. In the meantime, I'll call Detective Hart to ensure he properly served your facility."

"Mm-hmm," she replied, concentrating on her task.

Kate pretended to dial Sam's office at the courthouse, noticing she had three missed calls from his cell. When the receptionist looked up, Kate smiled but made sure to seem annoyed at the detective, Susan, and everyone else involved except the two women currently dealing with the problem.

"Hello, Detective Hart?" Kate said into the phone. "Yes, this is Kate Magda. I'm at Cunningham Valley Hospital. There seems to be a problem with the warrant." She paused a few seconds. "The problem is that the hospital doesn't recall being served." She huffed into the phone and stepped away from the desk, but remained close enough for the receptionist to still hear the conversation. "So you *did* serve the hospital?" She waited a beat. "Great. Only problem is that they can't seem to find the warrant." Again she waited. "Of course I'm not happy about it. I have a million things to do back at the office and this is the second time today I've run into an issue on this case. The DA is going to have my head if I don't get the records. Can you come down here with another warrant?" Pause. "How long will you be in court?" Pause. "I need to have this to the DA within the hour. What the hell am I going to do?"

The receptionist waved her hands in front of Kate to get her attention. "I'm sure the warrant is here. Susan's an idiot. Just tell me what you need." Kate watched the woman's eyes pass over Kate's badge, which was still out on the counter.

She smiled at the receptionist, a look of exhaustion on her face from the phone conversation and the possibility of being reprimanded. "Thank you so much."

Kate requested the sign-in and sign-out sheets for the dates in question. She included the date Tess believed someone had broken into the house and left that letter. On impulse she also requested the guest logs for the past two weeks.

After a few minutes, the receptionist clipped the copied papers together and extended them across the counter. When she failed to let go of the stack, Kate followed her gaze to the television. The soap opera had ended and the news was on. A reporter stood outside the courthouse recapping this morning's press conference. Kate gripped the papers and pulled them out of the receptionist's grasp just as a picture of herself, Tess, and her father flashed on the screen and the news anchor reported on a possible corruption scandal at the courthouse. The news then cut to Sam, his name and title flashing across the bottom of the screen as he wound up and socked Cameron right in the face.

"Hey!" exclaimed the receptionist, her once-wide eyes now slits as they moved from Kate to the screen and back again.

Kate willed her body to step away from the counter before the receptionist could say anything else or reclaim the papers. Her legs gained momentum as she dashed out the front door, copies and badge in hand.

She drove eighty miles per hour down Route 309, whipping past cars, the leafless trees nothing more than a blur of brown lining both sides of the road. She even seemed to outrace the gray clouds overhead that were threatening to delay her with ice and snow. But nothing could slow her down, not even Sam's constant calls buzzing through her phone.

CHAPTER TWENTY-NINE

THROUGHOUT THE NINETY-MINUTE DRIVE to Hettrich County, Sam called Kate every few minutes, alternating between her cell and landline. He no longer cared if he seemed desperate. This went beyond their personal issues. This was now about her meddling with Reds. She could taint the case, inadvertently destroy evidence, or get herself killed. A small part of his arresting Tess immediately, in her own home, had been to protect Kate and keep her safe from the killer. Now he wasn't sure from whom he needed to keep her safe—herself included.

He had called his office while on the road, asking one of the detectives to perform a database search on Ron Wells. He needed to know whether the man had any living parents, siblings, or children. Anyone close to him who believed he'd been falsely accused and wanted revenge. What Sam found out didn't help much. Ron's parents were both deceased, he had no children, and his brother, three years his junior, had died at seventeen in a motorcycle accident.

"You have arrived at your destination," came the voice through the GPS as he pulled up to the Hettrich County clerk's office.

The brick building stood one story high and housed

only the clerk's office, which was split into three divisions: civil, criminal, and family. He strode through the door with the frosted glass that read, *Clerk of Courts' Criminal Division,* and up to the counter, opening his jacket and flashing his badge to a very old woman. Sam couldn't stop staring at her eyebrows, hairless and penciled in a dark brown. The left was arched higher than the right, making her seem in a constant state of confusion.

"Detective Sam Hart from Mission County, Pennsylvania. I need to review the *New York State v. Ronald Wells* file. I'm sorry but I don't know the file number."

The clerk spoke slowly, the slack skin around her deep-set wrinkles seeming to sag more with each word. "Our procedure here in Hettrich County—"

"With all due respect, I'm aware of your procedure. But I'm not looking to make a copy of the file. I just want to review it."

"You'd like to review the file here in the clerk's office?" Her left eyebrow rose even higher, almost disappearing into her hairline.

"Yes, please."

"No problem, detective, that's fine. And this way you won't need a court order."

The clerk excused herself and shuffled slowly across the room. She eventually disappeared behind a door and Sam wondered if she'd make it out again by quitting time. He played with his badge, clipping it and unclipping it from his waistband. He checked his cell phone for missed calls. He set the phone on the counter. Clip. Unclip. He checked his phone again, even though it hadn't rung. Clip. Unclip. The clerk emerged almost ten minutes later with an accordion file folder twice the size of the file Judge Magda had given him. She heaved it onto the counter, out of breath.

"Thank you," said Sam, pulling the file toward him. "Do you mind if I use the far end of this counter to review it?"

"No problem. Hope you find what you're looking for."

Me too, thought Sam. He flipped through the first few pages, skipping over the countless motions and other pretrial proceedings. He thumbed through the motions for appeal along with the hefty support briefs and attached exhibits. Only the actual trial transcript was left to review when he finally came across a handful of court orders. Five, to be exact. The captions listed the names *Harold Kirk, Janine Carol, Thomas Magda, Priscilla Hopkins,* and *Bruce Lentini.* He disregarded Judge Magda's request, not even bothering to read the date on the order. Hopkins's and Lentini's court orders dated back to the 1980s, but Kirk and Carol had made requests within the last two months.

Sam's disappointment in the four names and their failure to spark any sort of connection in his mind had him scowling as he continued to page through the remainder of the file. He noticed that three words in the transcript, during Judy Conway's direct examination by the defense, had been underlined in blue ink. He read the surrounding lines of text about how Ron Wells was a phenomenal husband and role-model father. According to Judy, he loved Tess like his own and would never hurt her. She said that Kate was a young child with a vivid imagination and many psychological issues that no one was willing to openly discuss. Kate had lied on the stand

and her father, Judy's brother, had put his daughter up to it. Judy said that her brother was allowing Kate, and now Tess, to live a toxic life based on lies and deception.

Sam stared at the underlined words: *Kate, psychological,* and *toxic.*

Sam had yet to figure out why the killer's method of choice had been toxic asphyxia. Was it as easy as connecting the underlined words? Would he be dealing with three victims of fatal stab wounds had the word *knife* appeared underlined instead of *toxic?*

Kate had admitted to Sam that she'd been feeling paranoid. He remembered last night and how she had come sprinting out of the tunnel, flinging herself into his arms, a frightened look on her face. Was the killer playing a head game with her? He thought of Tess and how she could've easily baited Kate, purposefully making her feel insane. Yet Tess's name did not appear on a single one of the court orders requesting the transcript.

He flipped to the next page, perplexed. The transcript was out of order, jumping from page 126 back to 63. On this particular page the prosecution was conducting the direct examination of the neighbor who had found Kate in the cemetery. The words *open grave* were underlined. He flipped again, nearly ripping the thin piece of paper— page 128, the defense's cross-examination of the arresting officers. Underlined were the words *shovel* and *dirt.*

"Excuse me," Sam said to the clerk, trying to remain cool, "I need a pen and paper." He watched her start to slowly reach toward a memo pad and a pack of pens on the desk behind the counter, then lunged forward and grabbed both himself. He went back to the beginning of the transcript and paged through each sheet. He jotted

down the underlined words. A few of the words had been
underlined twice. He made a separate column for those.
When he finished, he had a list that would make even the
most laid-back of men lose control.

Kate
psychological
toxic
open grave
shaved
shovel
dirt
73
red hair

Underlined twice was the phrase *Six feet underground*. A few pages later, the word *Again* was also underlined twice.

Someone had expected him to come here. In the same
thought, he realized the transcript had been meant for
Kate. Just like the intern's body lying on the courthouse
steps had been left for her to find. The killer had known
she'd make the connection to her past and refuse to leave
the case alone.

The underlined words could not be strung together to
form a sentence or give him any deeper meaning, except
to verify what he already knew about the killings. And
the certainty that Kate was in danger. The only thing on
the list he couldn't make any sense of wasn't a word at
all, but a number. He skimmed the pages back to where
the number 73 had been underlined. It was during the
prosecution's case-in-chief and Kate was on the stand.

The prosecutor had been questioning her about the kidnapping and what took place at the cemetery.

> *"What happened when you got out of the car?"*
> *"Ron made me walk."*
> *"What do you remember about the walk?"*
> *"I remember that I was scared and I wished I could hold hands with Tess."*
> *"When did you stop walking?"*
> *"When I got to 73."*
> *"I'm sorry?"*

Sam figured the prosecutor had anticipated Kate saying that she and Ron stopped walking when they reached the open grave. The number Kate had supplied had clearly thrown the prosecutor. Sam continued to read.

> *"Can you explain to us what you mean by 73?"*
> *"I counted the whole way from the car to the hole in the ground. Even when Ron was pushing me and hurting me, I kept counting. I got to 73 steps before he told me to stop walking. But one time I counted to 100 and my teacher gave me a gold star."*

The 73 had been underlined once.

> *"What happened when you got all the way to 73?"*
> *"Ron made me get in the hole."*
> *"Did he tell you why you had to get in the hole?"*
> *"He said I was a bad girl."*
> *"Did you do what Ron wanted you to?"*

"Yes. I mean no. I asked him not to make me go in there and then he pushed me. I fell in and hurted my knee."

"Did you hear him say anything else to you?"

"Uh-uh."

"Can you answer with a yes or no?"

"No."

Sam finished reading the page and then flipped to page 73 of the transcript. Nothing was underlined and the page seemed insignificant.

"Do you know any of these names?" he asked the county clerk as he held up the court orders.

"Let's see. This gentleman here," she said, referring to Bruce Lentini, "wrote for the *Chronicle* back in the eighties and nineties. A real button-pusher. Passed away a few years ago from cancer. Priscilla Hopkins is the daughter of Viola and Todd Hopkins. Priscilla moved to California in the nineties. Beautiful girl." She cupped a hand to the side of her mouth and whispered, "She met someone on a vacation there. A lady friend. She never came back home."

"What about Harold Kirk and Janine Carol?" Sam asked, trying to keep the woman on task.

"I don't recall a Harold Kirk. Name isn't familiar to me. I think I remember Janine Carol. Petite, young. I remember her because she was granted the court order but didn't have enough money to pay for the transcription. Usually they go hand in hand. She ended up reviewing the file like you are right now."

"Does Janine Carol live around here?"

"Not that I know of. I had never seen her before.

Come to think of it, she came in here with a gentleman."

"Do you remember what he looked like?"

"Thin and tall. Dark hair. I think he was wearing a flannel shirt."

"Thank you!" shouted Sam, already out the door, the piece of paper with the word list folded up in his jacket pocket.

Sam was back in his Crown Vic, barreling down the interstate. Thinking back to his encounters with Nick Granteed, he could not picture the man in anything but a flannel shirt, sleeves always rolled, his forearms exposed. The clock on the dashboard read 4:30, which meant most, if not all, of the detectives would be gone for the day. He tried the main line, hoping someone had stayed late. He wanted one of the detectives to check up on the caretaker.

Sam's next thought made him nearly swerve off the highway, the car jerking to the right, his body vibrating as his tires rumbled over the sleeper strips on the shoulder. He quickly corrected the wheel and glanced in his rearview mirror, embarrassed. How could he have missed what was staring him right in the face? The way Judge Magda had hinted at his sister's possible involvement in the Reds case. A Hettrich County court order issued to a Janine Carol. *Just an old family photo.* Judy Conway's testimony and how she'd defended Ron on the stand, claiming Kate's version of the events was inaccurate.

"Detective's office," answered Stark.

Sam never thought he'd be so happy to hear the man's voice. He now cared less about checking up on Nick than he did about searching the database for Janine Carol.

"Stark, it's Sam. Is Stevens still around?"

"Nope, it's just me."

Stark would have to do. "Something's come up and I need a search done on a Janine Carol." He spelled out her full name. "Extend the search to the tristate area. I need a location on her."

"That's a pretty common name. Can you narrow it down at all?"

"Not really," Sam replied, remembering how the clerk had described her as young, but when you were as old as that woman, everyone appeared young. "After you search Janine Carol, cross-reference the name with Judy Conway. It may even be Judith Conway. I'm not sure. Conway may be using Janine Carol as an alias."

"Conway as in Tess? A relation?"

"Her mother," Sam said, unable to keep the impatience out of his voice. He accelerated, weaving in and out of traffic on the three-lane highway.

"You still investigating the Reds case?"

"Thanks for helping me out on this," he said to Stark, ignoring the question and ending the call.

Sam's foot remained heavy on the gas as he drove down I-81 in silence, the gray sky morphing into a starless black. No music, no talk radio. Nothing but his thoughts. He recalled Tess's arrest and the way he had marched her out of Kate's kitchen. Her strange behavior and how the clues had added up, all pointing a guilty finger in her direction. What he'd been so convinced of just hours ago was lining up in a whole new way.

CHAPTER THIRTY

NOT WANTING TO GO HOME, knowing she wouldn't be able to concentrate while worried that Judy was creeping around outside, and surely not able to go to work, Kate went to the one place no one knew to find her: the third floor of the Cotterman Public Library.

Stained-glass windows ran from floor to ceiling, the swirl of colors brilliant with even the slightest bit of sunlight streaming through. The floor was a thick smoked glass, tinted green, and also served as the ceiling for the second level. Nothing but shadows and shapes could be seen below, the coolest division of floor levels Kate had ever seen. Lining the middle of the room were bookshelves tall enough that, if she wanted, she could pace up and down the rows undetected.

The clock on the wall read 4:30. That should give her enough time to call the Hettrich County district attorney's office before they closed and have them fax over Ron Wells's trial transcript—the last item she needed and, hopefully, the final time she'd have to bend the rules and violate the sworn oath she'd pledged to uphold.

She roamed the perimeter of the third floor, ensuring she was alone before she made the call.

"Hettrich County district attorney's office. How may I direct your call?"

"Hello, my name is Rebecca Winn and I'm with the Mission County DA's office. We're currently investigating a serial murder and we feel there may be a connection with a case your office prosecuted back in the eighties."

"You'll have to contact the clerk's office after obtaining a court order from one of the judges, but they're all gone for the day, I'm sure."

"I was hoping your office had a copy of the *State of New York v. Ronald Wells* file handy. Perhaps you could fax it to me?"

The woman sighed.

"Please," Kate begged. "My team is desperate to solve this case and we believe there is a connection to Wells. If we thought we had the time, we'd absolutely be using the proper channels. We may have caught a break. If we could just review the transcript—"

"Ronald Wells has been like a boil on my ass for the past twenty-five years. He's tied up our office with years of appeals. I swear to you I brought in cupcakes the day after I learned he'd kicked the bucket in prison."

Kate instantly liked this woman.

"Six feet under, he's still giving me a headache," the administrative assistant continued. She told Kate she'd fax her the transcripts but nothing more. All Kate had to do was fax a document to the Hettrich County DA's office requesting the transcripts and certifying the information was necessary for purposes of an ongoing investigation in the Mission County DA's office. A half lie at best.

So what if Kate had pretended she was ADA Winn, who happened to still be on leave. So what if she'd have to forge Winn's signature on the document. She needed the file. More importantly, she needed the file without her office knowing she was still investigating the Reds case.

Kate hurried down to the first-floor computer lab and quickly drafted and printed her transcript request.

"Hi there," she said to the librarian sitting behind the desk at the lab. Stacks of books surrounded her like a protective fort. Kate eyed the copy machine, figuring it had a built-in faxing mechanism. "Does your fax machine have long distance–dialing capabilities?"

"Yes, of course," the librarian replied, "but we don't let the public use our machine." She smiled kindly at Kate, creases forming around her green eyes.

"I only have one sheet and a cover page. It's a very important legal document."

The librarian lifted a few books off the desk and placed them on the cart behind her with a thud.

Kate pulled a ten-dollar bill from her pocket. "Please, the deadline for this document to be received is today at five o'clock." She placed the money on the circulation desk.

The librarian shook her head. "You can keep the money. We have unlimited local and long distance," she said, and reached for the paper with ADA Winn's forged signature on it.

Kate watched as the librarian dialed the number and the machine emitted a series of beeps and static. The confirmation sheet printed in no time and the machine fell silent.

The librarian handed her the document. Kate remained at the circulation desk and wrote out a check to the library while she waited for her own incoming fax.

The machine once again sprang to life, spitting out page after page of *State of New York v. Wells*. Kate imagined that as each page dropped onto the plastic tray, along with it came the missing clues that would link Judy to the killings.

"I assume you're Rebecca Winn?" the librarian asked, reading the cover page of the Hettrich County fax.

"She's my colleague, but the fax is for me." She slid the check over to the librarian. "I hope this will cover replacing the ream of paper and ink."

"We don't allow the public to receive faxes through our—" The librarian abruptly stopped speaking when she glanced down at the check Kate had made payable to the Cotterman Public Library.

CHAPTER THIRTY-ONE

SAM WASN'T SURPRISED TO FIND the Moses Cemetery gates closed when he rolled up to the entrance. It was close to six thirty p.m. and the sun had set almost two hours ago, meaning visiting hours for the dead were over. He punched in the code. The gate slid open and Sam traveled down the now familiar road past the first crime scene and toward the Granteeds' home, Nick's picture set on the passenger seat.

He parked behind a black Trailblazer—Gina's car. He was disappointed not to see the caretaker's maroon pick-up truck in the driveway, but maybe the caretaker was home, his car somewhere else on the property. He rapped on the door and waited. And waited. He placed his ear against the solid wood and swore he heard a muffled noise. He rang the doorbell. Nothing. He was starting toward the side of the ranch when the door finally opened.

"I'm sorry!" Gina Granteed called out, her head poking out from the door. "I was in the shower."

Sam padded back to the porch. "I'm looking for your husband."

"He's not home. He won't be back until late tonight. Do you want to come inside?" She tightened the belt on her knee-length bathrobe, crossing her arms under her chest.

"No thank you. It was really Nick I was hoping to speak with. How are the two of you doing, by the way?"

"If you mean has he hit me recently, the answer is no. If you're referring to the affair he told you I'm having, well, I don't have much to say. Nick's a very different person than the one I fell in love with. Some days I don't even recognize him at all." She looked out beyond where Sam stood as if trying to search the grounds for the Nick she'd married.

Was Gina trying to tell Sam something? He waited until her eyes focused back on him before holding up the picture. "Do you recognize these people?" He watched Gina closely, gauging her reaction. Her face remained blank.

"I'm sorry. I don't." And then she asked, "Should I?"

"Your husband stopped in to see me today. He left me this picture and hinted at it being family." Had he said too much?

"That's most definitely not his family. Nick has three older brothers and his father is still living. His mother died while giving birth to Nick. Hold on, I think I have a picture right here." She stuck her head inside the doorway and then out again. She held a picture of four men standing around an elderly fifth man in a wheelchair. Gina sat in the old man's lap, her head tipped back and laughing. No one in the picture resembled Ron Wells.

"What about extended family? Cousins, aunts, uncles."

"Nick and I have been in each other's lives for a long time and I'm telling you, I've never seen the people in this picture before."

"What about your family?" Sam asked.

"What about them?" She eyed the detective warily.

"Are you an only child?"

"I have a sister in Connecticut. She's a plastic surgeon. I'm hoping she's the ticket to my very own fountain of youth." She laughed but it sounded hollow and forced.

"And your mother and father?"

"Upstate New York. Both doctors as well. My father is an ENT and my mother's a pediatrician."

"I guess you decided to break the mold?" Whatever Gina did professionally, she wasn't a doctor.

"It's in their DNA, not mine. I'm adopted."

"Tell me, Gina, do you know anyone by the name of Janine Carol?"

"No, I don't." She looked Sam directly in the eye when she spoke, but he could've sworn he saw her flinch at the mention of the name. He remembered the clerk's description of Janine Carol—young and petite. Gina fit the general description.

"What's your maiden name?"

"Lee," she replied, smiling. "May I see that picture again?"

He handed it to her. She flipped it over and then back again, staring at the faces, her brow crinkled.

"See, this is what I mean. Now, why on earth would he go to your office, show you this picture, and tell you it was a family photo? He's off his rocker. Totally lost it."

Something told Sam to stop the conversation with Gina. If she caught on to Sam's suspicions and then confronted her husband, she'd probably be dealing with more than a black eye. Sam needed to find Nick. Fast. Nick was connected. Nick knew Janine Carol. Sam was sure of it.

Nick had been trying to tell Sam something back in the office but it was still too cryptic for him to understand.

"Listen, I'm sure it's nothing. In fact, when Nick gets home, don't mention I stopped by, okay? When did you say you expect him home?"

"He told me he'd be home late and not to make dinner. He's probably at some bar drinking and wasting more of our savings."

"I'll swing by Pockets. That's usually where he drinks, right?" Sam stepped off the porch, heading back to his car.

"Yes. Uh . . . Detective Hart?"

He turned, eager to hear what she had to say.

"I'm having company over tonight." She looked down at her robe, uncomfortable.

Looks like Gina Granteed is preparing for a night in with the pharmacist, thought Sam. Perhaps the guy was already inside; Sam remembered the muffled noise he had heard while waiting for her to answer the door.

"Maybe it would be easier for me to call you when Nick pulls up. Let you know he's home. That way you won't have to make a trip over here again for nothing."

"That would be great. Thanks for your time, Mrs. Granteed."

"Please, call me Gina."

Sam used the car's computer system to run the license plate on the Trailblazer. Within seconds, he found that the vehicle was registered jointly to Nick Granteed and Gina Granteed. The system also allowed him to then search the named individuals for prior offenses and outstanding warrants, along with any aliases. Like Gina had said, she had an alias listed as *Gina Lee* and there were even a few documents where she'd signed her name *Gina Lee Granteed.*

Satisfied, Sam drove off, glancing back in his rear-view. He saw Gina still standing in the doorway, looking at the framed picture she had showed him of Nick's family. *Why the hell does anyone get married?* he wondered as he once again passed by the road that led to the Mission County Killer's first victim's staging. Not even a football field away from the Granteeds' home. And that's when it hit him, the underlined 73 finally making sense.

What Sam hadn't seen as he drove out of Moses Cemetery was Nick Granteed's maroon pickup, empty and hidden among the individual mausoleums on the hill. Nor did he see the four-door sedan parked directly behind Nick's truck, the driver's-side window cracked open, plumes of smoke seeping through as Judy Conway puffed away on a cigarette.

CHAPTER THIRTY-TWO

KATE SPREAD OUT THE PAGES OF THE TRANSCRIPT, creating small piles of each witness's testimony. She reached into her briefcase, pulling out the copies she had obtained from Cunningham Valley Hospital along with the letter Tess had received from a dead Ron Wells.

With her cell phone set to silent mode, she pored through the materials. First, she combed over the hospital logs, scanning the sheets until she reached January and found Judy's name. She was disappointed to see that Judy's signature in no way resembled the script in the letter that had been left for Tess. Had Judy made someone else write the letter as she dictated?

Whenever Kate saw Judy's name in the logs, she jotted down the date and time Judy had signed in and out. She stared at the dates, befuddled. Although several matched up with the killings, the timing was off. Judy seemed to consistently leave the facility in the late afternoon but was always signed back in by dinner. Kate's face flushed with frustration. She flipped to January 30. Nothing. She flipped over to the thirty-first. Again, Judy's name wasn't listed. *Impossible*, she thought, recalling the clear image of her aunt on the drugstore surveillance footage. Judy must have been sneaking out at night, not recording her absences. Or someone was signing her back in while Judy was still out. Kate had been hoping for the logs to corroborate her theory, not confuse her further, but her aunt seemed to be a master manipulator.

She printed Judy's name at the top of her legal pad in big block letters—she wasn't about to give up on her theory. Judy was involved. She'd bet her life on it.

The visitor logs looked similar to the patient logs except the headings included the guests' names along with who they were visiting. Kate learned Tess had visited her mother four times over the last two weeks, the final visit occurring two days ago. The same night Winter-Dawn had gone missing and was later found on the courthouse steps. Tess's visit before the thirtieth also coincided with the second victim's disappearance. Was Judy summoning Tess to the hospital on certain days in order to frame her? *Too many questions*, thought Kate.

She continued to scan the list until her eyes fixed on a familiar surname. On January 30, only thirty minutes after Tess had left her mother, another person had come to visit Judy. Under *GUEST* was the printed name *Nick Granteed*.

She thought back to the first time she'd met Nick Granteed and the instant uneasiness she'd felt in his presence. The way he had looked at her as if he'd known her or had seen her before. She had wanted nothing to do with him, her anxiousness rising as she, Nick, and Sam sat in the Granteeds' kitchen, listening to some bullshit story about how he'd hit his wife in self-defense. And now he was visiting Judy? Could they have known one another from AA meetings? She remembered Sam's theory that Nick was a closet drunk. *No way,* she thought. *It's too coincidental.* She jotted the name NICK GRANTEED in the same big block lettering she'd used for Judy, placing the caretaker's name directly under her aunt's.

She leaned back in her chair, rocking on its back legs, and massaged her neck with her fingers, kneading the knotted muscles. Perhaps luring the killer would be more effective than burying herself in paperwork, she thought. She placed the logs in her briefcase, trying not to feel defeated, and turned to the transcripts.

Kate read through the testimony of the prosecution's expert psychiatrist. Next, she read the testimony of the crime unit investigator who had found trace evidence in Ron's car and at the scene of the crime, and then the arresting officer's testimony. Kate hesitated when she came to the next pile. The top of the page read:

Prosecution: Your Honor, the State now calls Kate Magda to the stand.
Judge Kimble: Proceed.

Kate pushed the papers back and closed her eyes. By the time the trial had rolled around, her family, including Tess, had already made the move to Pennsylvania. Her father had joined Bear at his firm, while her mother became a full-time stay-at-home mom.

The drive was four *Cosby* shows—her dad's way of telling her how long the trip would take from her new house in Pennsylvania to the New York courthouse. She remembered her father had driven her back and forth countless times in the days leading up to the trial, always stopping for ice cream on the way home.

On the morning of the trial, the whole family, Tess included, had packed into her father's black Mercedes four-door sedan, the sun gleaming off its body while the diesel engine rumbled and knocked as they traveled down Interstate 81.

She pictured what she'd been wearing—a white cotton eyelet sundress with white strapped sandals. The headband, meant to keep her hair off her face, had served more as a plaything; she constantly bent and flicked the banded material with her fingers.

She'd been in the witness room, eating a package of crackers, when the arresting officer had poked his head in the door and said, "You're up, kid."

The officer led Kate through the swinging doors and into the courtroom. The smell of disinfectant filled her nostrils as she shuffled her feet across the red carpet flecked with gold. The three rows of wood benches on either side of the aisle, made available to the public, were packed with people, but Kate only looked straight ahead, which is what her father had told her to do.

She passed her father, who sat at the very end of the bench closest to the prosecution table and reached out, giving her hand a squeeze as she went by. He was the only family she had in the room besides Aunt Judy, whom her parents had told her not to speak to. As soon as Kate had been called to the stand, her mother had left the courthouse, hand-in-hand with Tess, on their way to the park.

Kate climbed the stairs to the witness stand, the police officer still by her side. He took two thick legal books and placed them on the padded seat. Her legs dangled off the chair, not long enough to reach the floor.

"Hi, Kate," said one of the female prosecutors, once she had been situated. "Even though we all know your name," she motioned to the other attorneys, her father, and the judge, "the jury doesn't and they want to get to know you. Can you lean into the microphone and tell these folks your name and how old you are?"

"My name is Kate Magda. I don't have a middle name. I'm six years old. I live at 232 Birch Lane and I have a new puppy named Goldie. She's yellow."

A few jurors laughed and smiled at her.

"Thank you, Kate. Now, remember what we talked about a few days ago? Only try to answer the question I ask you. Just answer my questions the best you can— okay?"

Kate nodded and then quickly remembered that this had been one of the rules the prosecutor had taught her the other day. *No head shakes.* Everything Kate was thinking had to be said out loud.

"Oops! I mean, yes," she said, pleased with herself for having remembered the rule.

"Do you remember when your cousin Tess turned five years old?"

"Mm-hmm," she said, swinging her legs back and forth.

"Did Tess have a birthday party?"

"Yes."

"Do you remember going to Tess's house?"

"Yes. I was at Aunt Judy's for Tess's birthday party. My mommy and daddy said I could sleep over because it was a special day for Tess."

Her dad and the judge had promised Kate that no one could hurt her while she spoke into the microphone. She imagined a big bubble around where she sat, see-through but impossible to burst. That's why she wasn't too afraid of Ron or anyone else in the room. Still, she made sure not to look in his direction, instead focusing on her dad.

"And do you remember who was at Tess's birthday party?"

"Mm-hmm. Me, Tess, Aunt Judy, and Ron."

"Do you see Ron in the courtroom today?"

She lowered her eyes, fingering the eyelet lace on her sundress. "No."

"Are you sure? Why don't you take a look around the room?"

"I don't want to."

The judge leaned toward her. "Psst," he whispered, his hands around his mouth so only Kate could see and hear him. "Remember what your dad and I told you about sitting up here? No one can hurt you, honey. All you have to do is point to Ron and then you never have to look at him again."

She raised her eyes from her lap and glanced toward where the prosecution had shown her Ron would be sitting. She pointed in his direction and quickly averted her eyes, looking once again at her father. He sat up tall, making it easy for her to lock eyes with him, but now she saw he had tears in his eyes and his mouth was puckered. She bent forward in her chair. "Daddy, don't be sad. We're getting ice cream after this. Remember?"

He nodded his head up and down, removing his glasses and wiping his eyes. He tried to smile through the tears. She heard sniffles from a few of the jury members.

"Your Honor, may the record reflect the witness has identified the defendant," stated the prosecutor.

"Reflected, counselor."

"Thank you. Kate, can you tell us what you remember about Tess's birthday?"

Kate recalled the dance party she and Tess had and how her cousin couldn't wait to open her presents. The prosecution asked her what kinds of presents Tess had opened. If Kate had had a piece of birthday cake. Did Judy have a piece of cake? Finally, the woman began to question her about Ron.

"How do you know Ron?"

"I just do," Kate had said, not understanding the question.

"Did you visit Ron a lot?"

"Sometimes."

"And you stated earlier that Ron was at Tess's birthday party, correct?"

Kate did not answer.

"Kate, was Ron at Tess's birthday party?"

"Yes." Kate had smiled, happy she finally understood the question. Based on the prosecutor's return smile, Kate thought she had answered it the right way.

"Did Ron like to play games with you and Tess?"

"Yes."

"Do you remember the games?"

"He played dolls with us and hide-and-seek."

"Do you remember if he played any games with you on Tess's birthday?"

"No."

"You don't?"

"Nope."

"Do you remember when Tess blew out the candles to her birthday cake?"

"Yes."

"Did you help her blow them out?"

"No."

"Did Ron help her blow them out?"

"Uh-uh."

The prosecutor had paused, slightly flustered. The line of questioning wasn't going smoothly and Kate was answering differently than she had during the witness prep. While the attorney took a minute to regroup, Kate played with her headband and tried to kick off one of her sandals.

The prosecution jumped ahead to when Kate had entered the bathroom and had seen Ron giving Tess a bath.

"Do you take baths, Kate?"

"Yes."

"And who is in the bathroom with you when you're taking your bath?"

"My mommy and daddy. But not together."

"So your daddy bathes you sometimes?"

"My daddy gives me baths all the time."

"And does he make you wash with soap?"

"Yes, and a washcloth, 'cause it's the only way you can get clean."

"Tell us how you 'get clean' when you take a bath with your dad."

"Well, first my dad fills up the tub. Sometimes with bubbles. And he lets me put my hand in the water to make sure it's not too hot. I have to hold on when I climb in because I'm little. Daddy squirts my bubble-gum soap on the pink washcloth. It has a picture of Minnie Mouse on it."

"What has a picture of Minnie Mouse?"

"The washcloth. I have a robe with Minnie Mouse on

it too. And when I put the hood up, I turn into Minnie. Right, Daddy?"

He nodded, his eyes still puffy and red.

"Have you ever taken a bath where your dad didn't use a washcloth to get you clean?"

Kate shook her head.

"You have to answer out loud," said the prosecutor.

"Oops," said Kate. "No."

"And are you ever allowed to take a bath by yourself? With no one in the bathroom?"

"No."

"And does your dad ever climb into the tub with you while you're taking a bath?"

Kate giggled. "No, he'd get all wet."

"What does your dad wear when he bathes you?"

"Lots of stuff."

"Does he ever take off his clothes to bathe you?"

"No, but sometimes he pushes up his sleeves."

"When you walked into the bathroom and saw Tess in the tub, was she alone?"

"No."

"Was someone in the tub with Tess?"

"Yes."

"Do you remember who?"

"Ron."

"What was Ron wearing?"

"Nothing."

"Do you remember what Ron was doing?"

"He was kissing Tess."

"And was he helping Tess 'get clean'?"

"I don't think so." She looked down and rubbed her pink nails with her pointer finger. Her nanny had painted them for her yesterday while her mom was doing laundry. The prosecutor moved closer to the witness stand.

"Okay. Well, did Ron have a washcloth?"

"No."

"What was Ron using to help Tess get clean?"

"His hand."

A voice interrupted Kate's thoughts, bringing her back to the present. She jumped in her seat, a grunt of surprise escaping from her mouth.

"I'm sorry. I didn't mean to scare you," said the librarian. It was the same woman from the circulation desk. She carried her coat in her hands and her hat was already on her head. The woman eyed the papers scattered everywhere. "I hate to disrupt your work, but the library is closing in five minutes." She glanced at her watch. "The speaker system is broken up here so I guess you didn't hear the ten-minute warning."

Kate couldn't believe the clock read almost eight. She'd been sitting here for four hours, reading through the logs and transcripts. She needed to get home and let Bundy out.

"You're the last patron here, so if you could flip the light switch on your way down, that would be most helpful."

"Sure thing," Kate replied, already standing and packing up her belongings.

She stuffed the transcript into her briefcase and headed for the door. She glanced down at the glass floor and saw a shadow moving below her. *Probably the librarian checking the floor one last time*, she thought. She strode back to the carrel where she'd been working. The figure moved below her as if it was her own silhouette.

She clipped the long strap that had been tucked inside her briefcase around its handles, creating a shoulder strap, and slipped it diagonally across her chest. She moved toward the door. The dark blob matched her steps. Her gut told her not to leave the room. Not yet.

She turned and stalked toward the stacks, measuring each step, her head lowered, watching the shadow move with her as she passed up and down the aisles of books. She halted in the dead center between two bookshelves and pivoted, waiting a few seconds before retracing her last steps. Sure enough, the figure did the same on the floor below. Panic overcame her.

She dialed the circulation desk with her cell. The automated message on the machine told her the library was currently closed. She thought about screaming, but doubted the librarian would hear her down on the first floor. Maybe if she stayed up here long enough, the librarian would come searching for her? She looked at the floor and knew if she stayed, the shadow would come upstairs and find her before the librarian even had a clue. The idea of waiting for the shadow to make its way upstairs gave her an idea.

She set the papers she'd been carrying on the bookshelf beside her and grabbed four textbooks off it. She placed two of the books on the floor in front of her, stacked close to her body, and hopped onto them, one heel on each, so as not to create two separate images to whoever was watching her from the second floor. Because the glass was smoked, it was hard to make out actual shapes. If she could pile up a few more books to create a shadow big enough to be a person, maybe she could trick whoever was below into thinking she was still on the third floor. She placed another set of books in front of the two she was standing on, creating a square. She swung her briefcase around to her front so that it might look like she had an extended stomach and hoped her new bump was blocked by the second set of textbooks.

She viewed her escape path. The doorway, which led to the stairwell, was approximately fifteen feet from where she stood. If she climbed up onto the stacks and shimmied along the top, she'd be about ten feet from the door but only three feet from one of the carrels. Her plan was to leap from the bookshelf down onto the desk and then jump from the desk to the doorway, out of the shadow's line of sight.

She removed her briefcase from her shoulder and hurled it across the room and through the doorway. It hit the floor of the stairwell, the thud echoing off the walls.

Holding her breath, she willed herself to peer over the books she stood on. The figure was still below her, not yet making its way upstairs. She exhaled, relieved. Without her briefcase, she could move around more freely. She pulled on the bookshelf, testing its strength, and when it didn't budge she hauled herself up onto the third shelf and began to climb, making sure she stayed above the textbooks she'd placed on the floor. She felt like Spider-Man climbing up the side of a building, except unlike Spider-Man her muscles twitched and her body shook.

When she reached the last shelf she swung her legs up onto the flat metal hood of the bookshelf, so that she couldn't be seen below. She wanted to lean over the edge, to ensure the figure was still below the stack of textbooks, but she didn't dare.

She crouched, keeping her body low to the shelf in case she lost her balance, and slowly crawled her way to the end of it.

Who could be following her? She'd been careful when driving to the library, taking a different route than usual, winding up and down side streets to make sure no one was tailing her car. And she had parked in the large parking garage across the street. Seven levels of yellow painted lines, hundreds of cars.

She slipped off her heels, holding them in her hand as she judged the distance between the bookshelf and the carrel one last time before leaping onto the desk. It rocked when she landed, tipping back and forth like a seesaw, and her arms shot out in an attempt to hold herself steady. She slanted her body forward, wrapping her fingers around the edge of the doorframe, and jumped off the desk, swinging herself through the doorway. She came down on her ankle, twisting it; pain shot across her foot and lower calf. She didn't stop to nurse it. No longer standing on the tinted glass, she couldn't see where the shadow lurked. She grabbed her briefcase and raced for the steps, afraid to take the elevator.

The stairwell was lit with LED emergency lighting, its glow bouncing blue shadows off the stark white walls. Was it waiting for her in the stairwell, anticipating her next move before she even did? She didn't stop running until she reached the circulation desk; the librarian was waiting for her, seemingly annoyed and tapping her foot.

"Please . . . there's . . . someone . . . following . . . me," Kate panted, still shoeless. She was afraid to put down her things in case she needed to run out of the building.

"Ma'am, there's no one left here."

"You're wrong. Please. Call the police. There's someone on the second floor."

The librarian tugged on Kate's coat, pulling her inside the semicircular desk. Tucked underneath the counter and eye level for anyone sitting there were a series of monitors. "Look. There's no one here."

Kate watched wide-eyed as each screen flashed different angles of the three floors; none showed another human being or even movement. There was a shot of the stairwell too: empty. Kate wondered if the librarian had seen her madly descending the steps. If she had, she wasn't letting on.

The librarian clicked on a walkie-talkie. Static sounded and Kate shushed her. "What are you doing?" she asked.

"I'm radioing our security guard. He's outside having a smoke. He'll walk you to your car."

"What about you?"

"I'm fine." The woman waved her hand along the monitors. "There's no one here, dear."

"Please, let's walk out together."

"I would love to. I've been ready for the last fifteen minutes but *someone* left the third-floor light on. I need to go turn it off. Wait outside with Marvin, I'll be out in a minute."

It was like the librarian had some sort of death wish. Kate stood outside the library with Marvin while he puffed away on a cigarette. She was about to explain to him that the librarian was most likely in danger when she emerged from the building, turning around to bolt the double doors.

The three walked to the librarian's green Toyota parked in front of the library. When she was safe inside her vehicle, Marvin and Kate crossed the street to the lot where Kate had left her car.

"Bad ankle?" asked Marvin, watching Kate hobble along in her heels.

She told him how she'd twisted her ankle on her way out of the library but that she felt fine.

They rode the elevator to the sixth floor where Kate had parked. Only a few cars were left and she was happy to have an escort. She unlocked the doors and threw her bags inside. "Can you wait here a minute while I check something?" she asked Marvin.

He stood there while she peeked in the backseat, opened the trunk, and then squatted to examine underneath the car. No one. Nothing.

"Thank you, Marvin. Have a good night." She slid behind the wheel.

"You too, ma'am." He stayed there until Kate started the car and drove off, waving at her until she disappeared down the exit ramp.

Kate didn't want to go home but it was getting late and the town's shops would soon be closed. She realized her hands were still shaking, her chest still thumping against her rib cage. Maybe she would swing by her house, pick up Bundy, and head to her father's for the night. Knowing he would hear the inevitable strain in her voice, and be less than thrilled when she told him where and what she'd been doing today, she opted for a text message. At a red light she quickly texted her father: *Was at library. On way home to pick up dog. Then headed to your house. Love you.* She hoped he would rest easy until she reached his house, at which time maybe she'd be less jumpy and in a better frame of mind to fill him in on what she'd found out.

Almost immediately, her cell phone rang. She groaned at her father's persistence, then glanced down at the screen and saw a local number she didn't recognize.

C HAPTER THIRTY-THREE

S AM SLAMMED ON HIS BREAKS, his tires skidding before they came to a halt. Parked on the side of the road, he hurried toward the front entrance of the county cemetery, flashlight in hand. The county cemetery after nightfall was anything but pleasant. Unlike the privately owned Moses Cemetery, this one had no gate, making loitering and headstone vandalism a problem. Tonight, the lack of security was a plus for Sam, who desperately needed immediate access.

Two crumbling brick pillars with lights on top, their yellow glow encased in cobwebs, marked the front of the cemetery, which is where he began counting his steps. *One, two, three . . .*

Kate had been convinced the October 1985 engraving on the headstone where Red #2 was found had been a connection, but Sam had thought it nothing more than a coincidence. He felt the killer was too calculated, too clever to use the deceased's date of birth on the headstone as a connector to Kate, and nothing in the transcript pertaining to that date had been underlined. Sam was certain the staging of the second body had something to do with the seventy-three steps Kate had testified to as a child.

He was familiar with the location of the second crime

scene—a straight shot from the cemetery's entrance if you walked the grounds, rather than following the curve of the gravel road. The burned-out lampposts that sporadically lined the unpaved road cast no illumination on the land. He imagined the sheer terror that must have washed over the kids' faces when after a night of drinking they stumbled upon Red #2's body; the effects of their buzz immediately erased. *Eleven, twelve, thirteen* . . .

He held the flashlight at eye level, allowing it to scan over the headstones and frozen ground full of divots and shallow-rooted trees. He could see his breath as he mumbled the number of steps he'd taken, and wished he'd remembered his gloves.

As he approached seventy-three steps, he was still more than one hundred feet from where Red #2 was found. He cursed, kicking the trunk of the nearby tree, and then cursed again as the pain shot up his foot.

He reached into his pocket for the transcript papers, not yet ready to give up on his theory. Staring once more at the underlined words, he knew the number was somehow connected. He thought about Tess and Judy Conway. Unless they were 6'3" like him, their strides would be shorter.

Adrenaline pumped through his body and the hairs on his neck tingled as he retraced his course, searching the grounds with each step he made. The phrase *leave no stone unturned* popped into his head and the irony wasn't lost on him.

After about a dozen steps, Sam's flashlight shimmered off one of the stones, catching his eye. The stone was shiny, a black-speckled marble unlike the other headstones, but that wasn't what he'd seen. On the ground, in front of the stone, lay a dozen roses, the January cold leaving them a colorless black, their stems a lifeless brown. Wrapped around one of the roses was a gold chain. Using a pen, Sam lifted the chain from the ground. A gold locket, identical to the ones he'd seen Kate and Tess wearing around their necks, swung like a pendulum.

Sam had assumed the second crime scene—the place where Red #2's body had been found—was significant to the killer. That it had "meant" something. He'd been wrong. He now stood at the true scene, the distance approximately sixty-two steps from the cemetery's entrance . . . seventy-three steps by Judy or Tess.

His phone rang, its normally low-sounding tone piercing through the still night, stirring the night creatures, and scaring the shit out him.

"Hello, Sam?" It was Stark, finally calling him back on the Janine Carol search. Something that should have taken an hour, tops, yet Stark had managed to allow three hours to pass.

"What the hell took you so long?" asked Sam, hoping the slight crack in his voice wasn't audible.

"Must be a full moon out tonight. I'm still in the office dealing with a bunch of crazies."

Sam looked upward. No moon. No stars. "Please tell me you have something on Janine Carol."

"Well, I do and I don't."

Sam groaned for what seemed like the hundredth time today. A branch cracked behind him. He whipped his head around, flashing his light in all directions. Nothing. *Probably just a squirrel*, he thought, as he headed back toward his car, listening to Stark's voice in his ear.

"I couldn't find a direct hit on a Janine Carol in the

tristate area. She doesn't exist on paper."

"Hopefully you have a *but* coming," replied Sam.

"Sure do. In the middle of dealing with the Mission County crazies and researching for you, a fax came through at the office—the autopsy report you'd requested on Ronald Wells. I read through it." Stark had a knack for nosing around in other people's business. "Natural causes, as suspected. The last page of the report lists next of kin. Ronald Wells had a daughter."

"A daughter? No way. Detective Stevens ran a search on Wells and it came back that he had no children."

"Well, the search was incorrect because Wells listed a daughter. I thought you'd find it interesting that Wells's daughter is named Janine Carol Lee. That's a definite connection to your Janine Carol."

Sam dashed the rest of the way to his car. Peeling out, he tore down the street, not giving a damn if he broke every traffic law in the books. It would take him at least fifteen minutes before he reached the Moses Cemetery. A message flashed on his phone: a text from Judge Magda that Kate was headed to his house. Far away from Gina Granteed, whose finale seemed to be attempting to accomplish what her father never could.

Sam called Stark back and explained that Reds was anything but a closed case.

"What do you need me to do?" Stark asked.

As much as Sam hated to admit it, Stark was a good detective and strong as hell. If anyone tried to harm Kate or her family, Stark would have them on the ground and disarmed within seconds. "Alert the local police. I'm heading to Moses Cemetery now. Gina Granteed, a.k.a. Janine Carol Lee, is our killer. It's very possible she's not working alone. Send a patrol car over to Kate's house. Let them know what to look for. In the meantime, you head over to Judge Magda's residence. Make sure they're all right. Stay parked in their driveway until you hear otherwise from me."

"I'm on it."

"I have a feeling Gina is headed for Kate and she may know we're on to her," Sam added, realizing he'd said too much to Gina during their earlier conversation about Nick.

CHAPTER THIRTY-FOUR

"PLEASE! PLEASE HELP ME!" Gina's shrill and panicked voice sounded through the phone Kate held to her ear.

"Who is this?"

"Please. Nick's crazy. He's trying to kill me. Help me!"

"Gina? . . . Gina, where are you?"

"My lungs. I can't breathe."

For a split second Kate closed her eyes, her car never leaving the inside of the road's yellow lines. She was back in the grave. Ron hovered over her as the dirt rose around her body, and she was unable to breathe.

"The dirt. He kept piling it on top of me!" Gina continued to shout frantically. "In my mouth, my nose. Please! Please help me!"

Kate fought to stay in the present. She flashed back to Ron as he raised the shovel, spearing the earth again and again as he covered Kate and Tess with loose dirt. She watched as it rose higher and higher around their bodies, and she was beginning to suffocate. The dirt filled her nose and then her mouth and she tried to scream for help. The dirt rose above her head and fell into her eyes, which burned even when she squeezed them shut.

"Where are you?" Kate asked, her voice hoarse.

"The cemetery!" Gina replied.

Kate was only seconds from the Moses Cemetery. She needed to get to Gina. She needed to help her. The cops would take too long.

"Listen to me, Gina. I'm almost at the cemetery's gate. What's the code?"

Silence. She heard nothing but heavy breathing on the other end of the line.

Kate turned onto the cemetery's road, her tires squealing as she took the corner way too fast. "Gina! Please, I'm here. Help me open the gate." She tried to remain calm, tried to fight the feeling that she was back in the grave, grappling for a breath.

"I think he's dead! I used the shovel."

"Who's dead? Nick? Please give me the code." Kate thought about getting out of the car and climbing the gate. But it would take too long. Especially without knowing Gina's exact location. "Where in the cemetery are you?" Before Gina could answer, Kate lost it: "Goddamnit, give me the code!"

Gina was now sobbing, her voice raspy from screaming. "1-3-3-1," she managed to choke out.

Kate jabbed her finger into the keypad. She nearly scraped up her car, barely waiting for the gate to fully open before she was tearing past it, barreling down the paved road, phone still to her ear. "Gina, can you hear me? I'm inside the cemetery. Tell me where you are." Was Nick really dead? Her body shook as she waited—prayed—for Gina to speak.

"I'm at the crime scene." Gina was out of breath and Kate wasn't sure if she had been running or if she was still in the grave. Kate remembered she and Sam walking to the crime scene from the road. About forty yards.

She drove the road as far as it went before slamming on the brakes and throwing the car into park. She spotted a pair of Tess's boots in the backseat and reached around to grab them.

"I'm getting off the phone now," she told Gina. "I need to call 911. Don't move. Don't do anything. I will be there soon."

She didn't wait for Gina to respond. She ended the call and immediately dialed 911.

"Please state your emergency," spoke the operator.

"I need your help. My name is Kate Magda and I am at Moses Cemetery. The code to the gate is 1-3-3-1. This is an emergency!"

"Ma'am, can you please tell me what's wrong?"

Kate ended the call, shoving the phone into her pocket. She needed to reach Gina. The police would be here in no time. At least, that's what Kate told herself as she took off running toward the killer's first crime scene.

The storm, threatening to break throughout the day, finally unleashed. Pellets of hail and freezing rain shot from the sky like a warning, attempting to slow Kate down as she sprinted toward Gina.

C HAPTER THIRTY-FIVE

"GINA!" KATE WAS NOW SHOUTING at the top of her lungs as she squinted, spotting Gina, her petite body crouched next to an unmoving figure. Both were only inches away from the open grave. Kate rushed up and grabbed Gina from behind, moving her away from the hole and the body sprawled out on the ground.

"Is he dead?" Gina sobbed, burying her face in Kate's neck and gripping her so tightly, Kate felt pain.

Kate released herself from Gina's grasp and held her at arm's length, her hands on the woman's shoulders. "I don't know," she answered, dry-mouthed.

"He tried to bury me. There was so much dirt. So much . . . I don't know how I climbed out. Something took over my body . . . I used the shovel on him . . . I had to . . ."

Kate's eyes had begun to adjust to the dark night. She could see Gina's hair was disheveled. Her bangs stuck to her forehead, matted and wet from the freezing rain. Dirt was smeared all over her face and caked in the corners of her mouth. Mascara-stained tears continued to slide down her cheeks, camouflaged by her already blackened face. Her shirt was ripped near the collar, exposing the top of her bra. She hung her head slightly as blood trickled from her nose, spattering on the front of her shirt. She wore no coat and her jeans were muddy and frayed from her calves down to her shoeless feet. Gina used the back of her hand to wipe her nose.

"Please, tell me he's dead," Gina cried, a crazed look on her face.

Kate forced herself to once again peer at Nick Granteed. She took a few steps toward him, noticing how he looked like a disjointed dummy. "He's not going to hurt you anymore, Gina." Kate thought of the many women she had said that line to, Tess included. She wondered if there was any truth in the words today. It seemed, regardless of the distance formed, that the scars might remain.

Kate watched as Gina bent down, poking at her husband's body, waiting for him to spring back to life. Grunting, Gina rolled Nick over so that both women could see his face, bloody and swollen. Gina placed a hand on his chest and her ear by his mouth.

Kate gently set her hand on top of Gina's. "He's gone," she whispered. She looked down at Gina's hand, brown from the earth that her husband had tried to bury her with. She bent closer, frowning as she examined Gina's fingers. She had very little dirt underneath her nails—too little for someone who had just climbed out of a grave. Kate remembered what her own fingers had looked like, flesh torn open from unsuccessful attempts at clawing her way out. Some of her nails had been ripped off and the ones that remained were caked with dirt. Gina's looked nothing like that; they looked only dirty, as if she'd been gardening without gloves.

Kate stared down into the black hole. Very little loose dirt lay at the bottom. Hadn't Gina said Nick had tried to bury her alive? She shakily rose from her crouched position and took a few steps back, away from Gina and Nick. She watched as Gina appeared to ascend from her husband's body and turn toward her.

"Where are you going?" Gina asked.

Kate couldn't take her eyes off the woman. Her back hit the thick bark of a tree. She reached into her jacket pocket for her phone, wondering where the police were and wishing she had called Sam. An owl's shrill cry rose above the sound of the wind and freezing rain, seeming to taunt and ridicule Kate for her stupidity.

"I wouldn't do that if I were you," Gina said, nodding at her phone.

Kate watched, frozen with fear, as Gina reached into her back pocket, removed a white rag, and took a step forward.

"Something wrong?" Gina's harsh voice whispered, her breath hot and sickeningly sweet.

Kate tried to swallow the bile creeping up her throat as the rag covered her nose and mouth. Her eyes opened wide as she attempted to let out a shriek. Not because the cyanide burned her lungs, not because she felt as if her heart was about to explode from inside her chest, but because as she stared into Gina's eyes, she saw nothing but a twisted rage—a look she had witnessed only one other time in her life: the night Ron Wells took her from her bed and buried her alive.

Kate was out cold before her body hit the ground.

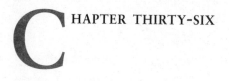

CHAPTER THIRTY-SIX

KATE'S EYES REMAINED CLOSED, her eyelids too heavy to open. Her mind felt hazy, filled with the white snow that sometimes crackled on her television screen when the cable was out. She wasn't sure if she was alive. Perhaps she was somewhere between life and death.

She struggled to quiet the static in her head, eventually hearing the sound of the freezing rain as it coated tree branches, power lines, and the headstones. She remembered she was in the cemetery. Her eyelids became less heavy and she was finally able to open them. The ice pelted her face; she felt the wet ground, a half-frozen mud paste, under her fingers and toes and she knew she was still among the living. Barely.

She lay at the bottom of the open grave in nothing but her bra and panties. How long had she been unconscious? Where were the police? Surely they should've been here by now. She gulped in the night air, traces of the poison from the rag still burning her nose and throat. As the air filled her chest, a pain so great pierced her ribs that she felt light-headed. Her hand shot to her rib cage, swaddling her bruised, maybe broken, bones.

Unable to stand, she tried to sit up, using her elbows and stomach muscles to pull herself into position. Dizzy, she inched her body backward, pain searing through her limbs with every move, until she was butted up against the dirt wall. Her teeth chattered, her body's attempt to generate heat as she pulled her legs toward her chest, coughing and sputtering mucous and blood. The position was one she knew well, one she had experienced over two decades ago but had never forgotten. Soon there was nothing left to do but look up. When she did, she saw Gina hovering over the grave, her eyes dancing as she returned Kate's stare.

"You're awake." Gina displayed a toothy grin. She wore a puffy winter coat with a furry hood and Kate wondered if she'd been passed out long enough for Gina to have gone back to the house to get it. Gina looked like a rabid animal, the blood from her nose now dried and caked on her upper lip and chin.

"For a moment, I thought I'd used too much of the toxins," Gina sneered. "Tell me, Kate, does it burn?"

Kate closed her eyes once again She feared that if she managed to survive and find a way out of the grave, Gina's face as it looked right now would forever haunt her dreams.

She'd had a nagging feeling back at the library, so close to remembering something important. She knew there was something that linked Ron's trial to the Reds case. As she sat bruised, broken, and close to dead, she realized the answer hadn't been in her testimony but in what had happened after she'd stepped off the stand.

The prosecutor had helped her climb down from the witness box, Kate's small hand tucked inside the woman's. Her father had met them back inside the witness room, embracing Kate as soon as his little girl walked through the doors.

"I'm so proud of you," he had gushed. "You're the bravest girl I've ever met."

"Thanks, Daddy. I have to go to the bathroom."

Her father had glanced at the clock and then back at Kate, most likely wondering where his wife had wandered off to and why she had yet to return with Tess.

"I can take her," offered the prosecutor.

"Thank you. I'll wait right here," her father replied.

Once again, Kate took hold of the prosecutor's hand as they headed toward the public restrooms. When they entered the bathroom, Kate saw a young girl, a few years older than her, propped up on the sink and crying while a woman tried to calm her down.

"This was a mistake. We shouldn't have come," said the woman sternly.

"I want to see my daddy," the girl moaned. Tears streamed down her cheeks as the woman tried to wipe them away, unable to keep up with the steady flow.

"What do you want me to do about it? There were no seats!"

Kate stared at the girl, saddened by her hysteria. "What's wrong with her?" she asked the prosecutor.

The prosecutor replied in a hushed tone: "I don't know, but I'm sure she'll be fine. Why don't you hurry up and use the bathroom so we can get back to the witness room?"

Kate walked toward one of the stalls, turning around as she closed the door. The girl stared at her as the pink metal door swung shut.

Kate lined the seat with toilet paper like her mother had taught her, still listening to the little girl outside the door.

"C'mon, Janine," said the woman, a harsher tone in her voice. "Blow your nose and let's go. I've had enough."

Kate now opened her eyes again, contemplating the forgotten memory—a memory she had never connected to the trial.

"Try to keep your eyes open," Gina hissed, glaring at her over the side of the grave. "You're starting to piss me off."

"You were there that day. At the trial," Kate said, her voice raspy. "You were—" She wheezed, her diaphragm bruised and not cooperating with her mouth. She tried again: "You were the girl in the bathroom. Janine—"

"Bet you wish you would've figured that one out before now," Gina sniggered. "Did you really think you'd get away with what you did to him? The lies you told about my father?"

"They weren't lies," sputtered Kate, wincing.

Gina ignored her, pacing back and forth along the edge of the grave but with an eye on Kate. "Because of your lies, my father went to prison and I ended up in foster care. Eight years old with no one to want me. You destroyed my family."

Ron had been married to Judy, the two of them living together until he went away to jail. Kate had never heard of Ron having a kid, another marriage, another anything. Surely Tess would have told Kate about a stepsister had Ron brought her around. The lawyer in Kate wanted to question Gina; the survivor in her warned her to keep her mouth shut.

"I had to wait ten years to see my father again. Ten years before I was old enough to visit him on my own. From the day I turned eighteen to the day he died, I saw him every week in prison. Sometimes we'd talk about you and Tess. Toward the end, you were all we talked about. He'd tell me the things you had testified to, the story you had concocted on the stand. He hated you. Hated your guts."

The feeling was mutual.

"And the more I visited, the more pissed off I got. Knowing he didn't deserve to be there—in that hellhole. All because of the lies you and your cousin spread!"

"He tried to kill me!" Kate rasped, unable to contain herself.

"You deserved it!" Gina roared. She began to hit herself in the head with an open hand, muttering words Kate couldn't quite understand. Whatever sanity Gina had left seemed to dissolve with each smack. Kate said nothing and hoped that if she continued, she'd somehow knock herself out.

When Gina spoke next, there was a strange calm in her voice. And a calm Gina frightened Kate more than an agitated Gina.

"I told myself I wouldn't allow you to frustrate me. I wouldn't allow your lies to seep into my brain. My dad and I would hypothesize about all the different ways to kill you. To destroy you and your family the way you did mine. We always had a plan." She smiled wistfully.

"It was important for me to get to know you. See what made you tick. So I talked Nick into a transfer. Here," she said, a look of disgust on her face as she spanned the graveyard with her eyes. "I mean, just what I wanted to do, right? Move to a fucking cemetery. But the transfer was worth it. It meant I was a step closer to you. To Tess. A step closer to putting our plan into action.

"It wasn't hard finding out more about you. After following you and Tess around for some time, I found out she was the weak link. A total half-wit who doesn't know when to shut up. She was my connection. So I joined the yoga class she attended. It was almost too easy. She was always talking about you, bitching about how you're so perfect, how annoying it was to be your little sidekick. I made sure to go out for drinks whenever she invited me. It was the perfect way to get what I needed from her. It's a shame you never tagged along—oh, that's right. You were too busy fucking Attorney Cox."

Kate didn't outwardly react. Inside, she was scared out of her mind. If Gina knew about Cameron, that meant she'd been following Kate over the past year, well before Nick signed on as the Moses Cemetery caretaker.

"Yes, I've been doing my research for quite some time now. I know everything about you," Gina said, her lips drawn back, teeth bared like an animal. "*Everything*. I know the way you take your coffee, that you wash your clothes in fragrance-free detergent, and that when you win a trial you treat yourself to pad thai. You have a thing for combing through people's used shit at garage sales, even though you have more money than you know what to do with. And your obsession with that stupid dog of yours, taking it everywhere, letting it ride in the front seat of your car. It's fucking weird."

Bundy was surely whimpering in the window right this moment, upset that Kate hadn't come home. Tears slipped down Kate's cheeks.

"It's amazing what you can find out over drinks with your 'girlfriend,'" Gina continued. "You can pretty much ask Tess anything and she'll spill her guts. The pills were an added bonus. How was I to know she'd get addicted to that shit? It made getting answers from her even easier since she was high all the time and seemed to have no recollection of anything. Your alarm code, a key cut so I could get in your front door, a little sneaky-peaky at the journal you keep in your top desk drawer. Actually, befriending Tess was less painful than I anticipated. She's nothing like you. She knows how to let loose. I can see why my father liked her."

This time Kate did react, practically gagging on her spit. "You're sick!" she shouted, finding her strength. "You're sick, just like Ron. You won't get away with this!"

"But it seems I already *am* getting away with it." Gina batted her eyes and smiled down at Kate like a mean girl bullying her way out of a school recess confrontation. "I would have liked to take my time, really fuck with the both of you. But when I received the phone call that my father had died in prison, I had no other choice but to act. By then I had enough information on you and Tess to put my plan into motion. I have to tell you, it was so great making you think you'd lost your mind. Although I'm still pissed that Bowers found the juror's body and not you. Seeing your face when you came upon that dead bitch, left on the steps for you like a little present—that would have been so much fun to watch. Almost as much fun as I plan on having when I finally kill you. And framing Tess, well, that was almost too easy. Until you had to be the slut that you are and bring the detective home to your house.

"Your little boyfriend wasn't supposed to arrest Tess until you were dead. See, it was the perfect plan. After

killing the other women, Tess kills you in her final act
of jealousy. But Detective Hart couldn't separate the job
from you. Total bummer, if you ask me. So he arrests Tess.
Too soon. Thankfully, I'm quick on my feet. I had a backup
plan. I really couldn't stand him anyway." Gina waved
her hand toward Nick's body. "Now it will look like Nick
and Tess were in on it together—when she was arrested,
he needed to finish what they'd started. Brilliant, right?
Especially after he went to the courthouse today with
that fucking picture."

Kate had no idea what she was talking about. "Your
plan won't work!" she yelled up at the woman.

"Oh, but it will. You responded to my frantic phone
call and when you got here, Nick unleashed on you. He
came after you just like he'd been coming after me. After
all, you did give him reason to dislike you. It's not nice
to go around claiming people abuse their spouses. Your
clothes are ripped up and strewn all over the ground.
Fibers from them and even a bit of your blood will be
found underneath Nick's fingernails. Pieces of his flesh
will be found beneath your fingernails from when you
scratched at his face and neck, trying to break free from
him. And while he was fixated on you taking your last
breath, I managed to escape. Lucky me." Gina clapped
her hands together.

"You're delusional!"

"Shut the fuck up, Kate! You'd think you'd be begging for your life right now instead of pissing me off even
more with your whiny little voice spouting nonsense."

Gina disappeared from Kate's view and quickly reappeared with a shovel in her hand. As she began to spear
the mound of loose dirt, a figure suddenly appeared be-

hind her. *The police,* Kate thought, as tiny butterflies of hope fluttered in her chest. She squinted, shielding her eyes from the freezing rain and shovelfuls of icy mud, as she tried to look past Gina.

"Please help me! She's trying to kill me!" Kate shouted.

As Gina turned, two hands shot out, grabbing the shovel. Gina's hand latched on to her attacker's arm, pulling them both into the open grave. Kate gasped when their bodies hit the grave's floor, her already shallow breath caught in her throat. While Gina appeared to be temporarily immobilized, Judy stood, brushing dirt off the backside of her jeans with her left hand. In her right hand, she shakily held a gun, her finger on the trigger.

CHAPTER THIRTY-SEVEN

SAM PUNCHED IN THE CODE at the cemetery's gate. His windshield wipers were no match for the ice that coated the glass, making visibility next to nothing. He thought he heard sirens in the distance as his tires skated over the ice and he sped toward the Granteeds' house, traveling in the opposite direction of the first Reds crime scene.

Gina's black Trailblazer was parked in the same spot as before and Nick's truck was still nowhere to be seen. He wondered if he would be interrupting Gina's bedroom tryst with the unknown pharmacist as he eyed an old Toyota Camry, silver, parked behind the blazer.

Sam pounded the front door with the side of his fist, his senses heightened. The Mission County Killer had been right here all along, the first crime scene literally in the murderer's backyard. No answer. He rapped again, seconds away from breaking into the house. But when he turned the knob, the door opened easily. He shouted Gina's name and withdrew his gun from his shoulder holster. Hurriedly clearing the kitchen, living room, and the first bedroom, he saved the master bedroom for last. The door was closed. He could see a light flickering beneath the crack in the door. He cautiously entered the room. Nothing. The bedsheets were rumpled and the television had been left on, the sound muted. No Gina. No pharmacist. Where the hell was she?

He walked back into the hallway, gun still drawn but held low and pointed toward the floor. He noticed another door cracked open and headed toward it, passing the framed photographs that overwhelmed the walls. He tapped the door open with his gun. There were steps leading downstairs. A basement.

"Gina!" he shouted. "If you're down there, you need to show yourself. Now. Hands up. Nice and easy."

Nothing but the sound of hail striking the house.

Sam flicked the light switch on the wall, but no light came on. "Christ," he muttered, reaching in his back pocket for his key chain, which held a small LED flashlight. He tiptoed down the steps to the basement, which was freezing. He rounded a corner, surprised not to see any storage boxes or the usual items found in a basement. He shined his flashlight off the walls and saw another door at the far end of the room.

Turning the knob, he was surprised to find this door locked. It was a hollow door, easy enough to break the seal with a mere shoulder shove. The smell of vinegar snaked into his nostrils as the door flew open, exposing what appeared to be a small darkroom. No windows. No air ducts. Nothing but a small vent placed high on the wall. Two safelights hung from the ceiling. He tugged on the chain dangling next to one of them, dimly illuminating the room in amber-colored light. A folding table ran the length of the far wall. Cabinets hung overhead. He opened each one, exposing jugs of chemicals, paper, and other items Sam assumed were used in print photography.

The Mission County Killer's victims had suffered

toxic asphyxia. Cyanide. Sam went back to the cabinets that contained the opaque jugs. The first label read *Acetic Acid,* and underneath the label, written in black marker, were the words *Stop Bath,* though the slanted script was hard to read. The jug next to that one had a red-and-white label on it. *Liquid Orthazite*—some sort of antifog agent. A bag of powder with the Kodak seal on it. A wetting agent. He read the label on the last jug: *Intensifier.* Its main ingredient was potassium cyanide.

Knowing who committed a crime was one thing. Proving it was something else entirely. Sam turned on his heel, ready to head back upstairs and call in his findings, when he focused for the first time on the wall directly across from the table and cabinets. There was some sort of drying rack set up along with strings that hung horizontally over more table trays. Sam assumed all of this was ordinary for a darkroom. Far from ordinary were the pictures themselves. Every picture was of Kate. Her eyes, lips, her crooked smile exposing her perfectly lined teeth. Unlike the images hanging on every inch of the wall upstairs, these photos were alive. There was passion behind the lens that had snapped the shots and it scared the hell out of him. He pulled his phone out from his pocket, surprised but thankful to have service. He quickly dialed Stark's number.

"Stark here."

"Did you get to the judge's house yet?"

"Just pulled up."

"Did the patrol unit find anything at Kate's?"

"They reported a few lights on inside the house and some beast barking and howling whenever they got close to a door or window. Nothing looked tampered with or broken. No signs of anyone lurking around the house. I'm walking to the judge's door right now to let him know I'll be parked outside."

"Thanks, man. Stay there until you hear from me," said Sam.

"Roger that."

Kate was still coherent enough to realize she was experiencing symptoms of hypothermia. She felt her heart rate slow, despite the imminent danger she faced. Her mind felt increasingly sluggish, more so than before, as she looked around for something, anything, to protect herself with. In the same thought, she had an overwhelming desire to bury herself in the dirt like an animal attempting hibernation. When she tried to claw at the soil, she found she could barely lift her hands.

"Stop!" Judy shouted.

Kate dropped her hands back down to her sides, but Judy had been ordering Gina, not her.

"Sit down next to Kate," Judy commanded, directing the gun at Gina.

"Fine. Fine. I'll play along." Gina laughed. "You best act quickly, though, because little Kate is on her way out." She sat down next to Kate, then leaned over to her. "Are you having fun yet? She hates you as much as I do." Her breath was hot and Kate was surprised she could feel anything at all.

Kate knew it was over. She knew there was no point in clawing at the dirt walls, searching for a makeshift weapon. No point in screaming for help or praying the police would show up. One way or another, she was going to die. Judy had come to finish what Gina had

started. She should've known they'd been working together. Probably the only two people in the world who
had ever loved Ron Wells.

"You should have left my daughter out of this," Judy
spat at Gina.

"Spare me," Gina countered. "I think it's a little late
for you to be campaigning for Mother of the Year." She
gave an exaggerated yawn. "You're boring me, Judy."

"Did you honestly think I'd let you frame Tess? Have
her rotting in a jail for your sins while you walked free?"

Without warning, Gina lunged at Judy and the
semi-automatic pistol. Kate simply closed her eyes—too
tired and weak to focus clearly. She knew she was losing
consciousness. Then she heard the sound of a gunshot—a
distant echo despite the close proximity of the weapon.
She couldn't fight anymore. Her eyelashes were frozen
shut, she was unable to move her limbs, and the slow
beat of her heart drummed quietly inside her head. And
for the first time in Kate's life, she said a prayer for Judy
Conway. She desperately prayed Judy's life had been
spared because she wasn't sure she would survive the alternative. In fact, she knew she wouldn't. None of them
would.

Sam heard footsteps and voices above him. He jogged
out of the darkroom and back up the basement stairs,
realizing the voices were police officers. He hollered to
them, identifying himself and letting them know that the
basement had been cleared.

Red and blue lights flashed through the windows and
the open front door of the Granteeds' home. Two officers
stood in the entryway.

"We cleared everything up here," said one of the officers. "We were about to head downstairs when we heard you call out to us. Have you found the woman?"

"What woman?" asked Sam.

"911 reported that a woman called. Gave the name Kate Magda. Said she was in trouble. We were tracking the phone she used to call 911 when our system lost her. We've already called for backup and an ambulance is on its way."

Sam had heard nothing past Kate's name. And then the officers, Sam included, heard the distinct sound of a gun firing in the distance.

Sam was immediatley out of the house and speeding down the road, his car sliding all over the place, toward the first crime scene, with the officers in their cruiser close behind. He slammed on his breaks when he saw Kate's car on the side of the road. He took off on foot knowing he couldn't get any closer to the crime scene by car. *God no, please. Why did she come here?*

"Kate!" he shouted as he ran stumbling toward the open grave. He saw a woman struggling to pull herself out of the deep hole, her back toward him. A body that appeared to be Nick Granteed lay alongside her, unmoving. Without seeing her face, Sam knew the woman was Gina. He rushed at her. She didn't fight him as he grabbed her, roughly cuffing her arms behind her back.

"What the hell have you done?" he yelled, spinning her around to face him. One look in her eyes and he was almost certain that he'd find Kate dead in the six-foot hole in front of him.

The other two officers were now on the scene as well. One of them took Gina away from Sam. He stared down the hole at the two bodies—Kate and another woman. He quickly placed her: she was the woman in the picture with Ron Wells and the two girls. Judy Conway. Kate and Judy's bodies lay crumpled against one another. Sam thought he could see blood pooled alongside them.

"Please! I need help!" he shouted at the officers and the paramedics who had just arrived. Pointing at Kate, he bellowed, "She is one of ours! We need to get her out. Now!" Sam began lowering himself into the grave. The team quickly assembled around him.

Feeling only a faint pulse in Kate's neck, he wrapped his arms around her frigid semi-naked body, lifting her up toward the other men. He ignored Judy's body, hoisting himself out of the hole, and ran toward the ambulance.

"Is she going to make it?" he asked, his voice cracking. Officers and EMTs shoved him out of the way while they laid Kate's body on a gurney, carefully lifting her into the back of the ambulance. Sam felt helpless, watching as the paramedics hooked her up to the portable machines and covered her body with wool blankets. So he climbed inside the ambulance. "I'll ride with her," he told them. "C'mon, let's go!"

"We only have one ambulance. We need to get the other woman in here too."

Sam held Kate's hand as he stared out the open doors. He saw a white rag on the ground covered in ice. A cell phone, broken in pieces, next to an oak tree. He saw Kate's clothes torn and scattered near where Nick Granteed lay sprawled out on the ground next to a mound of dirt, presumably dead. He saw Gina, head bent over in the backseat of a cruiser. He watched as two officers lifted Judy's body out of the grave and into the arms of a paramedic. The old crime scene was now a fresh crime scene and he'd arrived a little too late.

Judy was placed on a second gurney and wheeled into the back of the ambulance. Sam stood between both women, refusing to release his grip on Kate's icy hand as the paramedics worked around him.

"Hey, buddy, you all right?" one of the technicians asked him.

"Just tell me she's alive," he pleaded, pointing at Kate.

"She's alive. They're both alive. But barely."

CHAPTER THIRTY-EIGHT

IT WAS FOUR DAYS BEFORE KATE WAS ALLOWED any visitors beyond immediate family. Her private hospital room was lined with get-well cards and bouquets of flowers. The scent reminded her of a funeral home, but she said nothing, overwhelmed by everyone's generosity and good wishes. Still, she couldn't help but feel disappointed that none of the cards or flowers had been from Sam.

With severe hypothermia, three broken ribs, a dislocated shoulder, and a sprained ankle, she was lucky to be alive. When she was finally moved from the ICU to a private room, she had begged and then ordered her father, who had not left her side in days, to go home, get some sleep, and shower. She hoped a visitor would drop by in his absence to answer her endless questions.

After hours of relentlessly asking her father to fill her in, she remained clueless. He refused to tell her anything, not even allowing the officers to take her statement. Where was Tess? Had Nick Granteed survived Gina's fury? More importantly, was Gina alive? And Judy?

Now that she was doing better and out of ICU, her restrictions on visitors had been lifted and her father had gone home to shower and return with lunch.

When the door opened and she saw Sam standing

there, she wasn't sure if she should scream, cry, or beg him to kiss her.

"Hey you," he said, trying to come off casual.

She had two options. She could either be unforgiving or she could cut him some slack. She looked at his empty hands. "What, no flowers?" she quipped.

"Let's be honest," he said, still standing only half inside her room, "you're not the best with anything green. Don't think the wilting flowers in vases throughout your house went unnoticed."

She had to agree with him. She had the opposite of a green thumb and no matter how great her intentions or the effort she put forth, she managed to kill every flower and plant that came her way.

"I brought you something else instead," Sam said.

Kate pushed the button on the side of her bed so that she was sitting upright. She strained her neck to see what he had for her.

Sam stuck his head back outside her door and made a few kissing noises. Bundy came barreling into the room, leash dragging, and rushed to Kate's side, showering her with sloppy kisses. Kate laughed and began cooing at the dog, talking in the baby voice she reserved only for him.

After a few minutes she looked to Sam, who was smiling widely. "How on earth did you get him in here?" she asked.

"Easy. I flashed my badge and told the orderlies that he's a therapy dog. No one said a word."

"Thank you," she said, and they both knew she meant much more than just for surprising her with a visit from Bundy. Her father had told her only that Sam had been the first one on the scene, lifting her out of the grave and staying with her from the time she'd been put in the back of the ambulance until she'd been deemed "out of the woods" by her doctors.

When an awkward silence ensued, Kate shifted the conversation in a professional direction: "No one has taken my statement."

"About that . . . We pretty much have everything figured out." Sam ran his hand through his hair. "Obviously, we need your statement to corroborate what we do have, but take comfort in knowing we have solid, direct evidence against Gina. She can hire the best defense attorney in the country and she isn't getting herself out of this one."

"That means she survived?"

"Yes."

"And Judy?"

"A gunshot wound to the stomach. Near fatal. She'd been hemorrhaging when we found the two of you. She went into hydrostatic shock. It was touch and go for the first twenty-four hours, but she survived."

Kate shuddered, not quite sure how she felt about having Judy so close to her in the hospital.

"I'm certain I passed out when Gina pulled the trigger. I wasn't sure who had been shot."

"You passed out from hypothermia. Your body was shutting down one organ at a time."

"How does Judy fit in with all of this?" Kate asked, choosing to ignore the severity of the situation she'd put herself in. She was grateful to Judy, but she was also convinced the woman could have tried to stop Gina a lot sooner than she had.

"Based on Judy's statement, Nick Granteed paid her

a visit at Cunningham Valley. Voiced his concerns about Gina. Thought maybe Judy could talk some sense into her since they both had something in common—Ron Wells."

Kate's mind flashed to Nick's body lying on the cold cemetery ground, unmoving. "Nick—is he dead?"

Sam didn't hesitate in answering. "Yes, cyanide poisoning. Once that rag covered his face, he didn't have a shot in hell."

"But I survived—"

"Different rag. We ended up finding two rags at the crime scene. One doused in the liquid poison, the other mostly saturated from the ice storm. Even though the ground was frozen and the ice would have normally hardened the rags, they remained supple in the spots where the poison had been poured. The rag used on you was practically frozen from the weather conditions; the rag we believe she used on Nick wasn't the least bit hardened. Gina's hands also had traces of the poison on them along with a rash—common when skin is exposed. We don't think she anticipated the events playing out exactly as they did. Or as quickly."

Now Sam backtracked: "When Nick went to see Judy at Cunningham Valley she swore Ron didn't have a daughter from a previous relationship and demanded Nick leave the rehab center. Nick ended up going back to see her, but this time with a picture of Ron and Gina from when Gina was young, along with her birth certificate listing Ron as her biological father. Had it not been for that, Judy would have written Nick off as crazy."

"That aspect's been bothering me, actually. The relationship between Gina and Ron. I couldn't figure out how Gina went undetected all these years by Tess and

Judy. Especially since she was such a big part of Ron's life."

"Gina wasn't a part of Ron's life. At all. She was already in foster care when Ron was arrested. Hadn't seen him in close to two years. Well before Judy and Ron's quickie nuptials."

"But Gina was at the trial," Kate said. "I saw her in the bathroom, with a woman I assume was her mother. It was after I had testified on behalf of the prosecution."

Kate understood Sam's look of surprise.

"I didn't figure it out until I was near dead. I would have told you had I remembered it sooner. Hell, I wouldn't be in the hospital if I'd remembered it sooner," she said sheepishly. "Gina had been crying in the bathroom about not being able to see her dad during the trial. Something about not enough seats. And the woman referred to Gina as Janine."

"Gina's real name is Janine Carol Lee," Sam explained. He thought back to his meeting in Judge Magda's chambers when they had been frantically searching for answers. He remembered the judge telling him how on the day Kate had testified he'd made certain ahead of time that the courtroom was filled with staff from the DA's office so that the press were denied access to the courtroom. Had Magda not pulled his weight and dictated fate, perhaps everyone would have remembered a nine-year-old girl present in the courtroom, distraught over the idea of her father standing trial. Perhaps the connection would have been immediately made to Gina Granteed.

"How did you figure out Gina was in foster care before the trial?" Kate asked. "Is Gina cooperating?"

"Not really. One of Ron Wells's old attorneys saw the news about Gina in the paper. Ron's name was mentioned in the article. The guy calls down to our local police station and lets them know what went down during the trial. Says he'll testify to his statement if Gina decides to stand trial.

"According to this guy, Ron tells his attorneys that he has a daughter. He thinks she should be present at the trial and maybe even testify on his behalf. Tells the attorneys he and Gina are very close."

Kate snorted and rolled her eyes; she was beginning to feel like herself again.

"At some point before the trial, Ron comes clean about his true relationship with Gina and his defense team immediately takes her name off their witness list. They knew it would look like shit to have the jury hear that Ron had refused to acknowledge Gina for the past year or so, that he'd been deemed unfit by Children and Youth Services, and that he'd eventually relinquished his parental rights. Which is why my search on Wells erroneously listed no offspring."

Sam paced the length of the small room. "Now, thanks to you, we have another piece of the puzzle. We know that Ron couldn't let it go. Must've thought it was a deal breaker not to have his daughter in the gallery supporting her 'father' while he stood trial. Bet he was real pissed off when she ended up not showing.

"Anyway, for the next year, Gina gets shuffled around through Children and Youth Services. This couple, both doctors, after trying every fertility treatment imaginable, becomes pregnant, but they're told the pregnancy was a miracle—a one-and-done. Fast-forward nine years and their biological daughter, who happens to be the same age as Gina, begins hanging out with Gina at the local park. They become friendly. When the doctors realize Gina is a foster-to-adopt, they take her in. They end up officially adopting her a few months later.

"Gina hadn't seen or heard from Ron in years, but when she turned eighteen she attempted to visit him in prison. He refused her visit. Her adoptive parents had no idea that she had been desperately trying to establish a relationship with Ron. They're in a bit of shock right now, but cooperating fully with the investigation. Gina was halfway off her rocker her entire life; when she got word that Ron was dead, she totally lost it."

"She told me while I was in the grave that she and Ron would come up with different ways to kill me. Different ways to make me pay for what I'd done to him."

"Not true. We have the logs from the prison. Despite Ron listing Gina as kin, he didn't have her on his calling list and refused all but one of her visits over the past ten or so years. If I were a betting man, I'd say he accepted the one visit to tell her personally to leave him the hell alone. I guess we'll never truly know."

"So you're saying Gina came up with this whole father/daughter relationship in her head?"

"Yes. Then she took it one step further and began believing her own fantasies—the trips to the prison, the phone calls between her and Ron, the close bond they shared, the plan to kill you. These were all a reality to her. I've been talking to Doc Gibble about it and he tells me Gina's disorder is similar to erotomania, but in this case the fantasies weren't romantic. She believed that she had a strong relationship with her biological father. In reality, he wanted nothing to do with her."

Kate wasn't sure if she bought the whole delusional disorder business. It sounded to her like Gina was setting herself up for a decent insanity defense. She wasn't ready to feel the least bit sorry for the woman who had killed three innocent people, framed Tess, and stalked and tried to kill Kate.

"Without Ron helping her, how did Gina know so much about my testimony?" Kate asked.

"Easy: she read the transcript. It wasn't sealed."

"When did you figure this out?"

"The day you went to meet Gina in the cemetery."

Ah, thought Kate, remembering the missed calls from Sam and her father. All of which she had ignored. Sam had continued to investigate the Reds case even after Tess had confessed to the crime. Maybe if she'd stopped acting pissed off at him for doing his job and arresting Tess, she would have known that he still had his suspicions about the murders. They could have figured everything out together. Instead, while he was hammering out the details of the case, on the verge of discovering that Gina was the real killer, Kate had been running around town trying to nail Judy.

"Has Judy been arrested?" she asked.

"No. She's been cleared."

"You're not charging her? What about obstruction of justice? Failure to report a known felony?" Kate knew she was stretching, but Judy could have ended this nightmare weeks ago. "She chose not to come forward and innocent people died."

"She should have come to us, you're right. But nothing states she *had* to come forward. She didn't have any direct proof that Gina was the Mission County Killer, which is why she began to follow Gina, hoping to confirm her suspicions. Sounds like someone else I know."

"Totally different. It doesn't matter if she had proof. Nick came to her, voiced his concerns, and they both stood by while people were murdered."

"Technically, according to her statement, Nick made Judy aware of everything after the three victims had been killed."

Kate knew Judy's statement wasn't true. She had proof that Judy had been following Gina before Winter-Dawn was murdered: she'd seen Judy on the drugstore surveillance footage. Kate felt the anger bubbling inside her and she fought to suppress it.

"She saved your life," said Sam, quietly.

Kate's voice softened. "Honestly, Sam, I'm not sure it mattered to her that I was near death. She killed Gina to avenge Tess, not to protect me. The guilt of her knowing Tess had been framed by Gina was too much for her to bear." She sighed. "But that's enough for me—I can accept that for now. Because it's the first time Judy has ever put her daughter first and Tess deserves that—now more than ever, Tess needs to know her mother acted out of love for her. Judy isn't innocent in all of this, but I am thankful for what she did in the end to help Tess."

Sam nodded and took a moment before adding, "Her story matches what forensics found at the crime scene. Had she not showed up when she did, regardless of her motive, you wouldn't be here discussing this with me."

Kate knew there was more to this story. She couldn't help but think her father had something to do with the lack of charges being filed against Judy. Saving his sister once again by using his connections in the police department and elsewhere. She wondered if he'd expect Kate to corroborate her story with Judy's since, after all, Gina was still alive.

Both she and Sam began to speak at the same time, tripping on each other's words.

"I'm sorry," Kate said, "you go first."

"No. You go."

"I was going to ask about Tess. How is she? My father won't really tell me anything."

"Tess was released from prison three days ago and has checked herself into Cunningham Valley for drug addiction treatment."

Kate imagined Tess unpacking her things and settling into the rehab facility that Judy had so recently left. The irony wasn't lost on her. "And you? I mean, you falsely arrested Tess—"

"The arrest was valid," Sam said defensively. "I had evidence of an empty box of temporary hair dye, corroborated by Dr. Friar's examination of the intern's dyed-red hair. Plus, I received evidence earlier that morning that confirmed a single piece of animal hair had been found inside the throat of the second victim. I was told the animal hair matched that of a dog's, specifically a mastiff." He glanced at Bundy. "I had more than enough evidence to arrest her."

"The search was unlawful and you know it."

"Furthermore," said Sam, fired up over Kate's accusation, "Tess confessed to killing the intern."

Kate felt her belly rise and fall. She'd managed to piss him off and she hadn't intended it.

"What I was going to tell you before you decided to cross-examine me on my affidavit of probable cause," Sam continued, a slight edge still apparent in his voice, "was that your father made a statement to the press on the day of Tess's release.

"He told the public that Tess's arrest and her confession were part of a plan orchestrated by the detective and DA's office. We knew the killer was trying to frame Tess, but we weren't certain who the killer actually was, so we used Tess as bait. She agreed to play along. Your father said it had been my idea to have her lodged and make her false confession appear legitimate, releasing the details to the public even though, in reality, she had nothing to do with the killings. He told them we did it for her safety while our offices continued to investigate the case."

While Sam seemed impressed by her father's ability to take the negative publicity surrounding her family and Sam and spin it into a positive, Kate said nothing.

She had one final question for him, one she had been avoiding: "Do I still have a job?" Dread washed over her as she waited for the answer. There was a brief moment of silence.

"DA Bowers isn't happy with you. Especially with how you self-investigated the Reds case after he took you off. And he knows about the stunt you pulled at Cunningham Valley. Someone from the facility called him. Said you had duped her into obtaining private records and she would testify in front of a grand jury in order to have you arrested. Bowers didn't have the heart to tell her that the Mission County district attorney's office doesn't utilize grand juries in making arrests."

Kate laughed despite the bad news, picturing the re-

ceptionist at the hospital surrounded by tabloid maga-
zines, hoping for her fifteen minutes of fame.

"And he knows that you went to see Tess in prison.
Lied and said you were there in your capacity as an
ADA." Kate cringed as Sam quickly added, "Bowers has
been having a rough go of it. He's dealing with a lot personally and I think the stress is getting to him. Maybe
if we can get him to see past his own problems, he'll be
easier on you."

She knew Sam was willing to try anything to make
her feel better about the possibility of not having a job
when she walked out of the hospital. She couldn't
blame Bowers. She'd fire her ass too. She had broken
the rules. She'd compromised the integrity of the DA's
office; she'd violated the ethics code and the oath she'd
sworn to uphold. Not only should she be fired, but she
could also be disbarred. She also realized Sam was still
talking.

". . . we're on the brink of cracking open a corruption
case tied to the upcoming district attorney race."

"Cameron—"

"None other," Sam cut her off with a look of disgust.
He ran his hand through his hair and walked over to the
bed, patting Bundy's head. "I know Bowers briefed you.
Not sure where you stand on the research assignment,
but our office is very close to arresting Cox."

"I've done the research and, unfortunately, arresting
Cameron isn't going to solve Bowers's problems. I found
quite a few rules that Cameron has violated. I also found
a few laws. It would disqualify him from running in the
election and then some. And if your office could find out
if Cameron was, for certain, tapping phones, he could

be slapped with a felony—a maximum penalty of seven years, along with a hefty fine."

Sam let out a whistle, a smile on his face.

"I wouldn't celebrate just yet," said Kate. "Cameron could also come after Bowers for the actions he took in a case Bowers handled. One my father presided over." She didn't want to say too much, unsure if Sam knew the full situation. "It's a tit-for-tat, really. While Bowers's actions are nowhere near as serious as Cameron's, I think it would ruin Bowers politically or at least deny him another four years in the district attorney's office."

"You're saying Bowers should just bow out? Allow Cameron to pull this shit with no repercussions? We have someone on the inside watching Cameron's every move and we're pretty sure Officer Victoria Wood was the one putting taps on phones and passing along digital tape to him . . . Doesn't surprise me since Cameron seems to have a way with those who wear the occasional skirt."

Kate wasn't sure if Sam was taking a jab at her or not, but she let it go. She had always known a way to sink Cameron's campaign but had not been willing to put her reputation on the line to do so. But a new idea had come to her. She thought she might know of a way to protect her good reputation, and maybe even get back in Bowers's good graces.

A light tap on the door interrupted their conversation.

"Now, how on earth did you get that dog in this hospital room?" Keira Davis asked, eyebrows raised and grinning. "That was one hell of a scare you gave us. How are you feeling?"

"I'm okay. A little sore is all."

"A little sore? Girl, let's be honest, you're *a lot* sore."

She handed Kate a sticky note. "Here is my extension at the hospital. It rings the main desk on the fifth floor and if I don't answer, someone else will."

"Thank you," said Kate.

"I'll be back to check on you before I leave for the day. We need to get you healed and out of here so we can go for those drinks we're always talking about."

"I couldn't agree more," Kate replied, knowing this time she and Keira would finally get their act together.

CHAPTER THIRTY-NINE

FOUR WEEKS LATER, KATE WAS HOME from the hospital and mostly healed. Had Bowers not mandated she take a six-week leave of absence, she would have been on her way to work. Instead, she was driving her car, with Bundy in the passenger seat, to the local diner where she knew Cameron Cox ate breakfast every morning, alone. A Tori Amos cover of a Zeppelin song blasted through the speakers while she reflected on the last few weeks.

The first ten days after Gina was arrested had been a complete media frenzy, but things had since quieted down. Bowers had said nothing to the press about Kate's violations. When the receptionist from Cunningham Valley ran to the media outlets with a story about an ADA who had lied about a warrant in order to obtain privileged information, Bowers blamed it on a miscommunication within his office. Kate had been shocked at Bowers's loyalty, but hugely grateful for it. These were the times when she wondered whether the kind treatment he showed her was because she was an employee of the courts, or because her father was the president judge of the county. The lines were certainly blurred, but she'd gone through too much in the past few months to care what others thought. All that mattered to her now was that she'd still be a member of the DA's office by the end of her six-week leave. She belonged there, working for the commonwealth and for the innocent victims of crimes.

She thought about Tess and how much was still unsettled between them. Tess wasn't accepting any visitors at Cunningham Valley, with the exception of Dr. Friar, and Kate had respected her wishes. *In due time,* she hoped, sliding the chain of her locket around her neck.

Gina had been sent to a local prison that had a psychiatric ward. She would remain there until the court determined whether or not she was competent to stand trial. The police recovered everything, from the potassium cyanide to the black marker Gina had used to write the initials *RJW* on the small cloths stuffed inside the victims' tracheas. Her adoptive parents released a formal apology to the victims' families, asking for forgiveness for Gina, a woman suffering from severe mental illness.

Last Friday, the pharmacist Gina had been sleeping with, and who had supplied her with the pills used to drug Tess, took a plea of nolo contendere. Judge Roberts sentenced him to six months of incarceration followed by three years of probation, along with the loss of his pharmacy license.

Gunnar Moses had held a proper burial for his caretaker, Nick Granteed, and since Gina was locked away, Kate had gone to pay her respects to a man she had misjudged. A man who had suffered—torn between his love for his wife and his good conscience.

She pulled into the diner's parking lot and cut the engine after cracking the windows for the dog. She locked the car doors but didn't bother looking over her shoulder, knowing her shadow would be the only thing she'd see. Kate felt really good, an even better version of her old self, and she needed that confidence to get through the next few minutes of her life without gagging.

Sure enough, Cameron sat in a booth alone, eating his egg whites and turkey bacon. His tea, not coffee, steamed in the thick mug next to his plate. His face was relaxed while he read the local newspaper on his iPad. He almost reminded Kate of the man she'd known before she had found out what a liar he was.

She slid onto the padded bench opposite him and waited for his acknowledgment. When he looked up at her, but said nothing, she didn't waste time getting to the point: "We need to talk."

"I don't think we do," Cameron replied, although his usual icy tone toward her was absent.

"I'll get right to it, then. I know what you're doing to Bowers. Blackmailing him, using illegally obtained information to destroy his campaign. And you're about to find yourself in a bad situation."

"I disagree."

"Right, I know. You disagree because you think you have dirt on Bowers that would preclude him from arresting you."

"I don't think I have dirt. I *know* I do. If Bowers comes after me for anything—and please don't take my statement as an admission that I've done what you're alluding to—the retaliation will destroy our sitting district attorney. Bowers needs to bow out of the election. There's no way around it."

"I guess this is where I happen to disagree with you," Kate said evenly. She reached into her purse and removed a copy of a picture that had been taken with her phone. She slid it across the table.

Cameron looked at the picture of himself and Kate. They were seated at a round table, lit votives decorating the white tablecloth. Roman's had been their favorite place, quiet and private and on the outskirts of town. There was no worry in the small Italian restaurant that their relationship would be discovered. On the table, next to the votive candles and the slice of tiramisu with two forks, was a velvet box, its contents—two-karat blue topaz and cushion-cut diamond earrings—already in Kate's pierced ears. Cameron was embracing her in a passionate kiss for the camera while she fingered the new jewelry. It was the only picture Kate had of them, taken on her thirty-fourth birthday, the night he told her he loved her for the first time. Three weeks later, she found out he had no plans of leaving his wife.

Cameron pushed his plate to the side and leaned forward. "This picture has no bearing on the race. You're wasting your time."

"I have to disagree again. Your whole campaign so far has been based on family and honor. You claim publicly that your moral compass is sharper than anyone else's and with that compass you will succeed as our new district attorney. Every chance you get you're showboating your wife and her pregnancy. And then, because you can't seem to help yourself, you interrupted a press conference last month. I'm sure you remember it well. During it you alleged a relationship between Detective Hart and myself, insinuating it led to foul play in the DA's office and with the arrest of my cousin. What would the public think if they knew you were sleeping with me, buying me lavish gifts, while your wife was home carrying your child and being shoved to the side? Come on, Cameron, you may be pigheaded but you're not stupid. Even if you couldn't care less if your wife finds out about us, the public can never know about our relationship. The consequences to you are too great."

"You would never make this picture public. I know you and it wouldn't look good for your career. Sleeping with not only a married man, but a public defender who oftentimes sits across from you in court, representing the defendants you're trying to put behind bars. The implications are endless."

"If you knew me better, you'd know that Bowers forced me to take a leave of absence while things quieted down around the courthouse, agreeing weeks ago that I would drop off my formal resignation once I was back on my feet and feeling well again." She reached into her purse, this time removing a manila envelope addressed to Bowers and marked *Confidential*. "My days as a prosecutor are over, and unlike you, I have nothing left to lose."

The smug expression on Cameron's face was now completely erased and Kate knew she had him.

"By the end of today you're going to bow out of the race," she said with utter calm. "You will hold a press conference in which you tell the public that due to unforeseen circumstances, you are no longer running for district attorney. You will use the exact phrase, *It's funny what we do for family*. I don't care how you use the phrase or in what context, but you must use those exact words." She hoped Bowers would recognize that he'd used those same words when referring to his son.

Kate went on: "The office knows about your friend Officer Victoria Wood, and how the two of you are illegally tapping the phones of public officials in order to obtain information. I suggest you end all illegal communications. Furthermore, you're to notify the cop that was involved in Bowers's son's case—the one you most likely threatened or paid to lie about Bowers—that his services are no longer needed. And you will forget about reporting my father to the judicial conduct board for allegedly conducting ex parte communications with Bowers. It's laughable and you know it.

"If you don't do everything I'm telling you to do, I will make sure you're arrested, and all bets are off regarding this picture leaking to every media and news outlet in Mission County."

Cameron opened his mouth to respond but Kate held up her hands, silencing him. "In return, I will make sure no one ever sees this picture, your wife is none the wiser, and Bowers doesn't press charges against you. You continue on with your private practice and your part-time public defender gig and everyone wins in the end."

She slipped the paper and manila envelope back into her purse and edged out of the booth, giving Cameron no chance to say anything in return.

Outside, she watched him through the window as he shook his head and picked up his phone. She was certain he was contacting his campaign manager to work out the details of a press conference to be held in the very near future.

Had Kate stuck around a few minutes longer, she would have seen Cameron end his call and make another. Not to the judicial conduct board but to Federal Agent Chase. What Cameron knew about Judge Magda went way beyond mere ethics violations and way beyond ex parte communications with DA Bowers. He'd already planted the seed weeks ago that would destroy Judge Magda and his family.

"What's your status?" he asked the agent.

"I told you before, I can't give you any more information."

"Without me, you wouldn't have a case against Magda. I'm just making sure you're following through." Cameron grinned to himself, knowing full well the FBI was following through.

"Let's get something clear: this operation is bigger than you. We appreciate the heads-up. Now, let us do our job."

Cameron ended the call. If the feds claimed they had something bigger on their hands, well, that was nothing but good news for him. He returned to his newspaper, the confident smile returning to his face.

Kate dropped off the manila envelope marked *DA Bowers* at the courthouse mailroom. The envelope, which did not contain a formal resignation but a personal apology, would be delivered to the DA within the hour. While she waited for word that Cameron had followed her advice, she spent the day with Bundy, pampering him with a trip to the pet store, a bath at the groomer's, and a stop at the local dog park.

Her phone rang on her way home. She held her breath as Bowers's voice filtered through the earpiece.

"Kate, it's Lee Bowers. I, uh, well, have you seen the news?"

"No sir, I haven't."

"Cameron's dropped out of the race, but I have a feeling you knew he was going to."

Kate didn't reply. Her heart pounded to the rhythm of the ticking second hand on her wristwatch.

"Your six-week leave is over in two more weeks. I suggest you do something relaxing with your time, maybe take a trip, somewhere with palm trees, because when your two weeks are up, you'll be so busy you won't see the light of day."

"Sir, does this mean—"

"I got your letter. The apology. I read it. Reread it. Nicest letter I've ever received. You write beautifully. No one thinks to do things like that anymore. Write letters. No one takes the time to . . . well, never mind, it doesn't matter."

Kate pictured him swatting his hand in front of his face, annoyed at himself for his constant bursts of unnecessary dialogue.

"I understand why you did what you did," Bowers said. "I may not like it and I certainly don't agree with it, but I understand. I'd like to have you back once your six weeks are up. The office is busier than ever. Felony cases out the wazoo. *Wazoo.* That's such a strange word, isn't it?"

Kate imagined the fly swat once again and this time she smiled.

"As I was saying," Bowers continued, "I'd like you back in the trenches. That is, of course, on two conditions: When the media reports on your return and tries to question you, you mention not one word to them about anything that went on with the Reds case, especially with

Tess Conway. And two, you never pull a stunt like that on me again. You adhere to the prosecutorial code. Period. If I give you a directive, you follow it, despite what you may think of my decision or what you personally deem is right."

"I can't thank you enough."

"There's no need to thank me. You're a part of this office, part of a prosecutorial family, if you will. And as the sitting district attorney, I'm kind of like the patriarch. You following me? I guess what I'm trying to say is—it's funny what we do for family."

Kate couldn't stop smiling.

"Will I see you at the country club tonight?" Bowers asked.

Tonight was the Mission County Hospital's annual black-tie gala. Over five hundred people would be at the fundraiser, including Kate, since her stepmother was chairing the event.

"See you there."

CHAPTER FORTY

SAM AND KATE INCHED FORWARD in the line of cars making their way to the front entrance of the country club.

"I can't believe you stopped for fast food," she said. "The food here is always amazing."

"I needed sustenance for the two hours of socializing I'll have to do before dinner." Sam crumpled up the food wrappers and tossed them in the backseat. He waited for Kate to scold him, but she said nothing, only sighing.

Sam had visited her every day in the hospital, bringing her homemade meals and crime novels. And when she was finally well enough to go home, he had picked her up from the hospital, making sure the pad thai and bottle of wine were waiting for her at the house.

"Maybe the band will play the Stones tonight," he said. "We can revisit the magic of our first official date." He wiggled in his seat, arms above his head and biting his lower lip, making fun of her dance moves.

"That wasn't even close to our first date and that is not how I dance."

"I respectfully disagree on both counts."

They finally pulled up to the entrance. Kate was already waving to the people she recognized as she hopped out of the car. She turned back to Sam. "Are you sure you don't want to valet it?"

"I'm sure. I'll meet you inside." He watched as she headed toward the door, the beads on her black gown shimmering in the headlights.

The parking lot was massive, and almost at full capacity. He parked in the last row, last spot, next to a white windowless van. He figured he could use the walk and fresh air. Mingling with people, most of whom he didn't know, and chatting about mindless topics, felt stilted. A waste of time. But he'd promised Kate he'd play nice.

As he bumped and nudged his way through the mob of people crowding the entrance, he rethought his refusal to valet, worried it would take him the entire cocktail hour just to reach Kate. He made a hard right, away from the crowd and through the club's locker room, knowing there was another exit that would land him within feet of the ballroom—and hopefully Kate.

He heard voices coming from one of the rows of lockers and was surprised to see it was Judge Magda talking to two guys who Sam didn't recognize. He was about to approach the judge when he realized he'd walked in on a tense conversation—one that wasn't meant to be overheard. He couldn't get to the other exit without being seen, so he hung back, out of sight.

"...I'm certain the feds have tapped my phones," Judge Magda was saying. "There's a constant static on my landline. I cancelled the service yesterday. Let those fuckers figure out another way to listen in on my conversations."

Sam wanted to interrupt the judge and tell him it was probably Cameron, not the feds, who had tapped his phones—just like Cameron had done to DA Bowers—

but then he remembered the white unmarked van he'd parked next to in the lot.

Still out of sight, Sam watched the men through the large mirror that lined the front of the locker room.

"We need to talk about the cash," said one of the other two men. He had a thick head of silvery-white hair and continuously ran his hand through it.

Tommy Magda seemed caught off guard by this. "What cash?"

"The boxes of cash. Explaining the cash is going to be a problem if we're subpoenaed." The man loosened his bow tie. Sam could see that he had sweat marks under his arms.

"I don't know anything about boxes of cash," said Magda.

The silver-haired man looked like he was about to say something but he was interrupted.

"Tommy, why don't you head back to the party?" said the third guy. He was shorter than the other guy, and calmer. "Go dance with that beautiful wife of yours."

Sam knew from the man's tone that he wasn't giving Judge Magda an option. Magda didn't put up a fight and didn't question either man any further. Sam quickly retreated to the corner of the lockers and turned his back, not wanting the judge to recognize him as he passed.

When he was certain Judge Magda was gone, Sam slipped back out the door through which he'd come, leaving the other two men to their conversation. He headed outside, fighting the surge of people trying to enter the building. He hopped into his car, wishing he'd ordered an extra cheeseburger at the drive-thru. Switching between watching the van and checking his rearview mirror, he waited.

Just as he'd suspected, the silver-haired man soon made his way through the parking lot, anxiously glancing around and seeming to do everything in his power not to break into a jog.

Sam crouched down in his seat as the man knocked on the back of the van. He was inside the vehicle and out within minutes. Sam watched him move back toward the club, noticing that he appeared calmer now, not bothering to look anywhere but straight ahead.

The feds, thought Sam, had, in fact, found another way to listen in on the judge's conversations.

Sam found Kate seated in the ballroom, head tipped back and laughing. Probably at one of her father's jokes. She looked happy and at ease. Kate, her father, and her stepmother reminded Sam of the picture that comes in a new frame—a look he'd never seen in his own family photos. He took his seat next to her, relieved that the formal dinner had yet to start, and apologized for being late.

"You missed the entire cocktail hour," Kate said, a concerned look on her face. "I called your phone. I was worried."

"I'm sorry, I was on the phone with the chief," he lied. Now wasn't the time to tell her what he'd overheard.

"A homicide?"

"No, nothing like that." He brushed his lips against hers, feeling fortunate that she rarely questioned him when it came to his work.

"Well, I'm glad you're back. I wanted to introduce you to someone. Stay right here." She disappeared from the table and quickly reappeared.

"Sam, I'd like you to meet Bear. My father's old law partner and practically my second dad."

"Nice to meet you," said Sam, a forced smile on his face as he extended his hand to the silver-haired man.

Kate smiled her way through dinner despite the obvious tension between her father, Bear, and even Sam.

Dessert was served during yet another lull in what would normally be a boisterous conversation at the table. She watched her father spoon his tiramisu—moving it around on his plate without actually eating it.

The band eased into a slow tune and she convinced Sam to dance, figuring she could at least get to the bottom of his odd behavior.

"Have you met Bear before?" she asked as they made their way to the dance floor.

"Never. Should I have?"

"You've just been acting strange around him. And my father too, for that matter. Tense. Uncomfortable."

Sam slid his hand around Kate's waist as they fell into a slow sway. "Have you noticed anything strange going on with your dad lately?" he asked.

"My father? Not really," she said, though she wasn't being entirely honest. She had. He was growing increasingly paranoid, often refusing to make calls on his cell phone or demanding that she turn hers off when they were having a face-to-face conversation. He seemed scatterbrained and quieter than usual. She had chalked it up to the recent spate of events, but now she wasn't so sure.

"We should talk," Sam said. "Not here. I want to run something by your father first, but then I promise I'll fill you in. And it isn't much. Just give me a day or two, okay?"

Kate leaned slightly away from him as they continued to step in rhythm to the song. "Sam, you're scaring me. Is my father in trouble? Is he sick?" She couldn't imagine what Sam knew that she didn't. But by the somber look on his face, one thing was clear: it wasn't good.

She tried to will away the nausea creeping up in her belly and the countless questions running through her mind. She would trust Sam. She would give him the time he had requested. But she felt another storm brewing. Whether it was the Ron Wellses of the world or her family's personal demons, she could never quite quell the devil's thunderous baritone that seemed to follow her down life's path.

"Forty-eight hours and then you'll tell me what's going on. Deal?"

"Deal," Sam replied.

Kate looked him in the eye. "Consider this a free pass. I'll give you the time you're asking for because I know there has to be a good reason for all of it. But this is my family. This is the only parent I have left. I have a right to know what's going on."

"Maybe you should talk to him," Sam said gently.

"Maybe I should," Kate muttered resignedly. She closed her eyes as she rested her head on Sam's shoulder. She took in his masculine scent, the way his shoulders felt strong in her arms, and the way their bodies seemed to sway in perfect rhythm. She thought about her job waiting for her and Bowers's kind act of forgiveness. The plane tickets she and Sam had purchased for a quick get-away, at Bowers's advice. She thought about what she was thankful for—the good she had in her life. And she quickly brushed away the tear that had managed to slip down her cheek as the band's rendition of Clapton's "Wonderful Tonight" came to an end.

She could sense this big new storm blowing in, though she could not yet determine its direction.